A QUESTION OF FOUL PLAY

There were no visible marks on the body until it was lifted carefully out of its snowy grave for transfer to the waiting ambulance. Then Doc Mallard had spotted an area of matted blood on the back, left-hand side of the scalp, and there had been some excitement when the SOCOs had found some flakes of rusted paint-coated metal, two caught up in a tear in the back of the overcoat and another on the ground beneath.

'Presumably snagged in the cloth on impact,' said Draco. 'If so, forensic will find out. Hit and run?'

'Looks like it. Though if so . . .' Thanet was thoughtful.

'What?'

'I was only thinking . . .'

Draco shifted impatiently. 'Come on, man, spit it out.'

'Well, the injury is to the back of the head, and the tear is on the back of the overcoat . . .'

'So?'

'The implication is that he was struck from behind. If he was knocked into the ditch by the impact, you'd expect him to be on his face or his side, not neatly laid out on his back.'

'What are you suggesting? That whoever knocked him down then stopped his car, got out, and dragged the body into the ditch?'

Thanet shrugged. 'It's a possibility, isn't it, sir?'

Agatha Christie

Death on the Nile
A Holiday for Murder
The Mousetrap and Other Plays
The Mysterious Affair at Styles
Poirot Investigates
Postern of Fate
The Secret Adversary
The Seven Dials Mystery
Sleeping Murder

Dorothy Simpson

Last Seen Alive
The Night She Died
Puppet for a Corpse
Six Feet Under
Close Her Eyes
Element of Doubt
Dead on Arrival
Suspicious Death
Dead by Morning

Elizabeth George

A Great Deliverance
Payment in Blood
Well-Schooled in Murder

Colin Dexter

Last Bus to Woodstock
The Riddle of the Third Mile
The Silent World of Nicholas Quinn
Service of All the Dead
The Dead of Jericho
The Secret of Annexe 3
Last Seen Wearing

Michael Dibdin

Ratking

Liza Cody

Stalker
Head Case
Under Contract

S. T. Haymon

Death of a God
coming soon: Ritual Murder

Ruth Rendell

A Dark-Adapted Eye
(writing as Barbara Vine)
A Fatal Inversion
(writing as Barbara Vine)

Marian Babson

Death in Fashion
Reel Murder
Murder, Murder, Little Star
Murder on a Mystery Tour
Murder Sails at Midnight
The Stalking Lamb
Murder at the Cat Show

Dorothy Cannell

The Widows Club
Down the Garden Path
Mum's the Word

Antonia Fraser

Jemima Shore's First Case
Your Royal Hostage
Oxford Blood
A Splash of Red
coming soon:
Cool Repentance
Quiet as a Nun

Margery Allingham

Police at the Funeral
Flowers for the Judge
Tether's End
Pearls Before Swine
Traitor's Purse

DEAD BY MORNING

Dorothy Simpson

BANTAM BOOKS
NEW YORK · TORONTO · LONDON · SYDNEY · AUCKLAND

*This edition contains the complete text
of the original hardcover edition.*
NOT ONE WORD HAS BEEN OMITTED.

DEAD BY MORNING
*A Bantam Book / published by arrangement with
Charles Scribner's Sons*

PRINTING HISTORY
*Scribner's edition published August 1989
Bantam edition / September 1990*

ISBN 0-553-28606-4

Published simultaneously in the United States and Canada

Bantam Books are published by Bantam Books, a division of Bantam Doubleday Dell Publishing
Group, Inc. Its trademark, consisting of the words "Bantam Books" and the portrayal of a
rooster, is Registered in U.S. Patent and Trademark Office and in other countries. Marca
Registrada. Bantam Books, 666 Fifth Avenue, New York, New York 10103

PRINTED IN THE UNITED STATES OF AMERICA

RAD   0 9 8 7 6 5 4 3 2 1

To Jenny and Ian

Thanet lifted the edge of the curtain aside and peered out into the dark street. 'It's nearly half-past twelve. Where can she be? She's never been as late as this before. And—yes—it's beginning to snow, look!'

Joan joined him at the window. 'So it is. The temperature must have risen.'

Earlier on it had been freezing hard.

She returned to her seat by the fire. 'Darling, do come and sit down, you're driving me mad prowling about like that.'

'How you can sit there so calmly I just do not know. She's always home by half-past eleven. Anything can have happened.' Thanet, who had seen far more than his share of broken bodies during his years in the police force, blanked off hideous images of Bridget mutilated, injured, suffering appalling pain or even now dying, perhaps. He plumped down beside Joan on the settee and, leaning forward, put his elbows on his knees and his head in his hands.

Joan put her hand on his shoulder. '"Anything" includes perfectly ordinary things like being delayed at work, Tim's car not starting, being held up because they witnessed an accident...'

Their daughter Bridget was now nearly seventeen. She had managed to scrape one or two respectable grades in her GCSEs last summer and, always keen to have a career in cookery, was taking a year off to gain some practical work experience in the kitchens of a local restaurant before starting a year's Cordon Bleu course in September. Tim was one of the waiters, and gave her a lift home each night that their stint of duty coincided.

Thanet's shoulder twitched impatiently. 'Yes, I know... But in that case, why hasn't she given us a ring?' Perhaps Tim wasn't as trustworthy as he had appeared. A married man with two children, he had seemed a decent enough young man, but what if his offer of lifts for Bridget had had an ulterior motive, what if...?

Thanet jumped up and crossed to peer out of the window once more. 'It's coming down more heavily now.'

The snow was already beginning to lie, mantling the ground with a thin gauzy veil of white. Huge soft wet flakes swirled around the fuzzy orange globe of the street lamp on the pavement outside their house and hurled themselves silently against the windowpane like moths attracted to the light, melting from the contact with the warm glass as they slid down. Thanet peered hopefully down the street. Nothing.

'We should have refused Tim's offer, insisted on fetching her ourselves.'

'That would have looked really churlish, as he actually has to pass our house on his way. Anyway, it's ridiculous turning out late every night if we don't have to.'

'Better than having to sit here and wonder where she is and what's happened to her.'

Joan laughed. 'It looks as though you're in for a really bad time.'

'What do you mean?'

'Don't look so alarmed! I simply mean that this is only the beginning. We've been unusually lucky up to now but no doubt this is only the first of many, many nights over many, many years when we're going to lie awake waiting for the sound of her return, wondering where she is, if she's all right...'

'How can you make so light of it?'

'I'm not making light of it. It's just that... well, I'm a little more resigned to it, I suppose. I can remember how my own parents used to fuss when I was late home after going out with you.'

'Do you? Did they? I never knew that.' Thanet took her hand, momentarily distracted.

'They certainly did. But I wasn't going to tell you, naturally. It would have made me sound like a little girl, to be fussed over.'

He grinned. 'The ultimate insult.'

'Exactly. And that's precisely how Bridget will take it if she gets home and finds us sitting here like a reception committee.' Joan stood up, decisively. 'So come on, let's go to bed.'

'But . . . '

'Luke! Come on.'

Grudgingly, he allowed himself to be persuaded upstairs. 'But I'm not going to let it go, mind. If she's going to be late like this she really must let us know.'

'All *right*. I'll speak to her about it. Tactfully.'

Thanet caught her eye and grinned. 'Not too tactfully.'

She smiled back. 'Agreed.'

They had just got into bed when outside in the street a car door slammed. A few moments later they heard the front door close. Quickly, Joan switched off the bedside light. When Bridget had crept past their door on the way to her room, Joan said, 'That wasn't all that was worrying you tonight, though, was it?'

Thanet turned to face her in the darkness. There was no point in denying it. 'No,' he admitted.

'Draco again.'

''Fraid so.'

'Why didn't you say?'

'I should think you're sick and tired of hearing about him.'

'Nonsense. It enlivens my days no end.'

He could hear the laughter in her voice.

'Seriously, though,' she said. 'What's he been up to this time?'

'That's the trouble, we're not sure. There're all sorts of rumours flying around. Some new campaign he's planning... But one thing's certain, it's sure to make life even more uncomfortable for the rest of us.'

Just over a year ago Superintendent Parker had retired and Goronwy Draco had taken over at divisional headquarters in Sturrenden, the small country town in Kent where Thanet lived and worked. The new Superintendent was a fiery, dynamic little Welshman who was firmly of the opinion that a new broom should sweep clean as quickly as possible. Suffering under the new regime of regular morning meetings and tighter control, Thanet had grudgingly to admit that under Draco's ever-watchful eye divisional headquarters at Sturrenden had become a much more stimulating place to work. Enlivened by newly decorated offices and higher standards of cleanliness and efficiency, the place now crackled with a new energy and there had been a gratifying increase in crimes solved and villains safely ensconced behind bars. Draco may not be popular, but he certainly got results.

Thanet sighed. 'I expect we'll survive.'

As soon as he opened his eyes next morning he was aware of the difference in the quality of light. There must have been more snow overnight. He hoped that the fall had not been heavy. Snow was very picturesque but it brought problems. However hard the local authority tried, it never seemed to make adequate preparation for bad weather. A mere skim of snow brought its crop of traffic jams and minor accidents; anything over six inches, severe disruption. And of course, there was the cold. Thanet hated the cold and the tip of his nose told him that the temperature in the bedroom was at a far from acceptable level. February was definitely bottom of his personal popularity chart of favourite months. He allowed himself the indulgence of a few more moments in the warm cave that was the bed, then braced himself and slid out, careful not to allow a gush of cold air to disturb Joan, who was still sleeping peacefully. He padded across to the window. Might as well know the worst.

Despite his dislike of the inconvenience snow brought in its wake he could not escape the inevitable sense of wonder at its transforming beauty. Beneath its mantle of pristine white, his familiar world preened itself in the first rosy light of a clear winter dawn. He peered at the roof of the garage, trying to gauge the depth of the fall: not more than a few inches, by the look of it. Good. It shouldn't take too long to clear the drive, with Ben's help. And the gritting lorries had been out last night, so the roads shouldn't be too bad.

Three-quarters of an hour later, fortified by the porridge that Joan had insisted on making, he and Ben had almost reached the front gate. Up and down the road warmly clad figures shovelled and swept drives and pavements. In the road cars seemed to be making slow but steady progress.

Joan appeared at the front door. 'Luke? Telephone.'

'Finish it off, will you, Ben?'

Ben, thirteen, gave a reluctant nod.

'Sergeant Pater,' said Joan, handing over the receiver.

The Station Officer. Something out of the ordinary, then, to necessitate an early morning call, in view of the fact that Thanet was due at headquarters in half an hour or so.

'Thanet here.'

'Morning, sir. Just had the report of a body in a ditch at the side of the road, out at Sutton-in-the-Weald. Found by a man walking his dog.'

As in his last case, Thanet thought. If you were a dog owner you certainly seemed to run a greater risk of stumbling over a corpse than most.

'You've reported it to the Super?'

'Yes, sir. He says he's going out there himself.' Pater's tone was carefully non-committal.

'Ah.' Thanet's heart sank. This was new. What was Draco up to now? He remembered wondering, when Draco first arrived, just how long the new Superintendent would be content to sit behind a desk. All that restless energy needed numerous outlets. Thanet hoped that active participation at ground level wasn't going to be one of them. It would be impossibly inhibiting to have Draco breathing down his neck.

'Apparently there's been quite a bit of snow out there, fifteen inches or so, with some pretty deep drifts in places, so it's going to make transport a bit tricky. The Super's put through a request to the Council to clear the road as soon as possible and he's asked for a couple of Land Rovers to be laid on for you. He wants you to meet him here and he'll go out with you.'

'I see. What time?'

'Eight-thirty.'

'Right. I'll be there. Have you contacted Sergeant Lineham?'

'I'll do that next, sir. I'll arrange for the SOCOs and the CCTV sergeant to come in the other Land Rover, and pick up Doc Mallard on the way. I thought I'd let you know first.'

So that Thanet wouldn't be late for Draco, no doubt.

'Thanks.'

Grateful that he had already had breakfast and that the driveway was clear, Thanet put on thick socks, wellington boots, sheepskin jacket, gloves and woolly hat in anticipation of hours of standing around in the snow. 'I feel like the Abominable Snowman,' he said as he kissed Joan goodbye.

She grinned. 'You look like him. Here.' She handed him a Thermos.

'Thanks, love. Oh, hang on. Better take some shoes, in case. I can't go tramping in and out of houses in these.'

'Sure you wouldn't like me to pack a suitcase for you?'

'All very well for you, in your nice, centrally heated office.'

Joan worked as a Probation Officer in Sturrenden.

'Courtroom, actually.'

'Courtroom, office, what's the difference, it'll be *warm*.'

'Stop grumbling,' she said, pushing him out of the front door. 'Go on, you don't want to keep Draco waiting, do you?'

Thanet rolled his eyes. 'Heaven forbid.'

As he got into the car he realised that he had been so put out by the prospect of Draco's presence that he had forgotten to ask whether the body was that of a man or a woman.

It was another couple of hours before he found out.

The journey out to Sutton-in-the-Weald had been

irritatingly protracted. The first few miles hadn't been too bad but then the snow had begun to deepen and a little further on they had caught up with the snow plough sent out at Draco's request. After that they had resigned themselves to travelling behind it the rest of the way, at a snail's pace. Fortunately a local farmer with a snow-clearing attachment on the front of his tractor had eventually turned up coming the other way and after a certain amount of manoeuvring they had been able to proceed more quickly.

There then followed a long wait for the second Land Rover bringing Doc Mallard and the Scenes-of-Crime officers. Meanwhile, there had been little to do. The body lay in a roadside ditch backed by a high stone wall, only a few yards from the lion-topped pillars at the entrance of the driveway to Longford Hall Country House Hotel. From the road nothing could be seen but the upper surface of a sleeve in distinctively bold black-and-white checked tweed, lying along the edge of the ditch as it had been uncovered by the dog. Although the arm was patently stiff with rigor mortis, PC Yeoman, the local policeman who had been first on the scene, had understandably cleared the snow from the man's face, to make quite sure that he was dead. The rigid features, pallor of the skin and open, staring eyes had told their own tale and thereafter he had left well alone, winning Thanet's approval by erecting a temporary barrier of sticks stuck into the snow and linked by string.

Despite his years in the force Thanet had rarely been able to overcome a dread of his first sight of a corpse, but today, uncomfortably preoccupied by Draco's presence, he had approached the body with no more than a twinge of trepidation and, gazing down at the dead face set deep in its ruff of snow, he felt no more than his usual pang of sorrow at a life cut short. Blurred as the man's features were by snow, it was difficult to estimate his age with any accuracy, but Thanet guessed that he had been somewhere between forty and sixty. Time, no doubt, would tell.

No further attempt had yet been made to clear the snow from the rest of the body. Thanet wanted photographs

taken first. Not that he thought this very important.
Covered with snow as it was, the body had obviously been
placed or had fallen into the ditch before or around the
time the snow started. Still, one never knew. It paid to
be scrupulously careful and, with Draco taking in every
move, Thanet had every intention of playing it by the
book.

In any case, the marks in the snow told their own story:
a scuffled, disturbed area betrayed the dog's excited investigation of this interesting and unusual find and there were
two sets of approaching and departing footprints, belong-
ing to Mr Clayton, the dog's owner, and PC Yeoman.
Thanet, Draco and Lineham had been careful to enquire
which were Yeoman's tracks, and to step into his footmarks
when they approached for their brief inspection of the
body.

As yet the snow had kept most people indoors and there
had been little traffic up and down the road. Half an hour
ago a tractor had begun clearing the hotel drive and any
minute now Thanet expected someone to arrive and de-
mand an explanation of the activity just outside the
gates.

'Where the devil are they?'

Draco, who along with Lineham and Thanet had been
stamping up and down the road in an attempt to keep
warm, was finding it difficult to contain his impatience.
'They should have been here half an hour ago.'

'Perhaps Doc Mallard was out on a call.'

Draco snorted, two dragon-like puffs of condensation
emerging from his nostrils. Short, square and dark and
sporting an astrakhan hat and a heavy, fur-lined overcoat,
he looked like a Russian statesman awaiting the arrival of
foreign dignitaries. The backdrop of snow served to height-
en the illusion.

'Like some coffee, sir? I've got some in the Land Rover.'

'Thank you. Excellent idea. Should have thought of it
myself.'

'My wife's, actually.'

Thanet fetched his Thermos from the Land Rover and
he, Draco and Lineham took it in turns to sip the steaming
liquid. Lineham had been very quiet so far, subdued no

doubt by Draco's presence. Thanet had to suppress a grin at the memory of Lineham's face when he had seen Draco climb into the Land Rover. The sergeant evidently hadn't been warned.

A vehicle could be heard coming down the hotel drive and a moment later a Range Rover pulled up between the stone pillars. A man and a woman jumped out.

'What's going on here?'

It was, unmistakably, the voice of authority, cultured and self-assured. Its owner, clad in country uniform of cords, thick sweater, Barbour and green wellies, was in his late forties, tall and well built with slightly receding dark hair and slate-grey eyes which quickly summed up the situation and unerringly selected Draco as the person to approach. 'What's happened?'

Draco handed the Thermos cup to Thanet and, drawing himself up to his full height, announced, 'Superintendent Draco, from divisional police headquarters at Sturrenden...'

But the man wasn't listening. He had caught sight of the arm in its boldly checked sleeve and his expression changed. 'My God, that's...'

He spun around, putting out his hand to prevent the woman behind him from coming any closer.

'What is it, Giles? What's the matter?'

Clear, ringing tones, another Barbour and more green wellies. A beautiful woman, this, a little younger than her husband, in her early forties, Thanet guessed. She, too, was dark, her long hair swept back into a thick French plait, accentuating the classic bone structure of her face. She would look much the same, he thought, twenty years from now.

'I think you ought to get back into the car, darling,' said her husband.

She shook off his restraining arm impatiently. 'What do you mean, what are you talking about?'

The movement gave her a clear view of the man for the first time and she gasped. 'My God, that's Leo's coat.'

Draco stepped forward. 'Leo?'

'My brother.' Her gaze was riveted to the arm, her eyes

appalled. She clutched at her husband, who put an arm around her. 'Is he ... ?'

'Dead?' said Draco. 'I'm afraid so. If it is your brother, I'm sorry that you had to learn of it like this.'

'But why are you just standing around drinking coffee, for God's sake! Why aren't you trying to get him out? You can't just leave him there!' She grabbed the stick marker nearest to her, tugged it out of the snow and, tossing it impatiently aside, started towards the ditch.

The three policemen darted forward to stop her, but it was her husband who grabbed at her coat and tugged her back. 'No, Delia. Can't you see? If it is Leo, there's nothing anybody can do now.'

'But it's awful. It's ... inhuman, just leaving him buried in the snow like that!' She turned on Draco, her eyes blazing. 'How dare you!' Her contemptuous gaze swept around the little group of policemen and returned to Draco. 'The Chief Constable is a personal friend of ours. I shall report you to him. Immediately!'

Thanet studiously refrained from looking at Lineham.

She turned to her husband. 'Come on, Giles. We'll go back to the house and get something done about this absurd situation.'

And with another furious glance at Draco she swung herself up into the car and sat gazing stonily through the windscreen as her husband manoeuvred the Range Rover around and drove off.

'A lady who's used to getting her own way, I presume,' said Draco, apparently unruffled. 'You're going to have your hands full with her, Thanet.'

Just what Thanet had been thinking. Though the prospect intrigued rather than dismayed him. He raised an eyebrow at PC Yeoman. 'Who are they?'

'Mr and Mrs Hamilton, sir. Owners of Longford Hall. She runs the hotel, he runs the estate.'

'There are the others now, sir,' said Lineham.

'About time, too,' growled Draco.

Doc Mallard's half-moon spectacles glinted through the windscreen as the Land Rover drew up.

'Where the devil have you been?' snapped Draco as

Trace, the SOCO sergeant, got out, followed by his team.

Mallard accepted Thanet's steadying hand. 'My fault, I'm afraid, Superintendent. Blame it on a doctor's irregular lifestyle. I was out at a confinement. Woman was on her way to hospital, but the ambulance got stuck in the snow. Luckily I just got there in time.' He beamed. 'Bouncing baby boy, mother and child both right as rain, I'm glad to say. Nothing like bringing life into the world to cheer you up, you know.'

'I'm sure.' Draco turned to Trace. 'Well, let's get on with it now you are here. If we have to stand around out here much longer we'll all turn into blocks of ice.'

2

By the end of another hour Thanet felt as though Draco's prophecy were coming true; his feet were numb, he felt chilled to the bone and he had long since regretted using up his precious flask of coffee so early. Perhaps, soon, they would be able to go up to the hotel and have a hot drink.

There had been much to do. Screens had been erected, photographs of the relatively untouched area of snow had been taken, Doc Mallard had officially pronounced the man dead and then there had been a long wait while the Scenes-of-Crime officers had patiently scooped the snow away from the body, pausing to take samples or more photographs when necessary. Eventually the corpse was completely exposed, proving to be that of a man of around fifty with thinning brown curly hair, dressed in well-cut cavalry twill trousers, Aquascutum sports jacket and the black-and-white checked tweed overcoat. A wallet in his breast pocket contained twenty pounds in notes, various receipts and other scraps of paper and, more importantly, a driving licence and several credit cards in the name of Leo Martindale. It was always a help to establish identification at the outset of a case.

There were no visible marks on the body until it was lifted carefully out of its snowy grave for transfer to the waiting ambulance. Then Doc Mallard had spotted an area of matted blood on the back, left-hand side of the scalp, and there had been some excitement when the SOCOs had found some flakes of rusted paint-coated metal, two caught up in a tear in the back of the overcoat and another on the ground beneath.

'Presumably snagged in the cloth on impact,' said Draco as they gathered around to peer at the samples in their plastic envelope. 'If so, forensic will find out. Hit and run?'

'Looks like it. Though if so . . . ' Thanet was thoughtful.

'What?'

'I was only thinking . . . '

Draco shifted impatiently. 'Come on, man, spit it out.'

'Well, the injury is to the back of the head, and the tear is on the back of the overcoat . . . '

'So?'

'The implication is that he was struck from behind. I'm just trying to visualise what happened. If he was knocked into the ditch by the impact, you'd expect him to be on his face or his side, or crumpled into a heap, not neatly laid out on his back.'

'What are you suggesting? That whoever knocked him down then stopped his car, got out and dragged the body into the ditch?'

Thanet shrugged. 'It's a possibility, isn't it, sir?'

'One among many, I suppose. But it is surely equally possible that he could have been thrown into that position by the collision?'

Thanet disagreed. But it would not have been politic to say so. Draco did not appreciate opposition. 'I expect we could do some experiments, sir.'

'Quite. And then, it's also possible that he wasn't killed outright by the impact. He could have remained conscious—or regained consciousness—and crawled or staggered to the ditch in order to get off the road, and lain down in it in the most comfortable position, which just happened to be on his back.'

This was much more likely. 'True.'

'Or,' said Lineham, contributing to the discussion for the first time, 'he could have been deliberately run down.'

This earned him a scowl from Draco. Murder investigations were both time-consuming and expensive. 'Anyway, if these metal flakes are from a car we shouldn't have any problems in tracing it.'

Thanet nodded. They all knew that it was a relatively straightforward matter these days to trace a vehicle from paint samples. Forensic science has reduced it to a fine art.

They all peered again at the largest sample. 'Looks like a mid-grey. And definitely going rusty,' said Lineham.

'I'll get forensic to hurry it up,' said Draco.

'Thank you, sir.' There were, apparently, advantages in having the boss along.

'You'd better do a house-to-house, get the men to check all local vehicles. Radio in for reinforcements. I'm going back to headquarters now.'

Another bonus. Thanet suddenly felt a lot more cheerful. Even his toes didn't seem quite so cold.

One of the ambulancemen approached. 'We're ready to leave now, sir.'

Draco glanced at Thanet. 'Might save time if you got Hamilton down from the hotel first, see if he can make a formal identification.'

Thanet had every intention of doing so. 'Right, sir.' And to the ambulanceman, 'If you could just wait a little longer . . .'

'Good. Good.' Draco gave a little bounce on the balls of his feet, preparatory to departure. The thought of his snug office must be enticing. 'I'll take one of the Land Rovers and get it sent back, in case you need it to get off the beaten track. Can I give you a lift, Mallard?'

'Thank you. Be glad to get back to civilisation.' Mallard picked up his bag, brushed snow off the bottom.

'Just one thing, Doc,' said Thanet.

Mallard twinkled at Thanet over his half-moons. 'Thought you wouldn't let me get away without asking. Time of death, right?'

Thanet nodded.

'Well I'm afraid you're going to be disappointed. In these particular circumstances it's virtually impossible to hazard a guess.'

'All the same . . .' pressed Thanet.

'Really, Luke . . . Well, I suppose the best I can do is to say that it must have been some time last night. Say, any time between six o'clock and . . . ' Mallard shrugged. 'What time did the snow start, do you know?'

'Around half-past twelve, in Sturrenden. Could have been earlier here, of course.'

'Well, you'll have to check. But it's obvious that most of the snow fell after the body went into the ditch. Say between six o'clock and four A.M., then, to be on the safe side. Not much help I'm afraid. Sorry, but I have to allow for the fact that it might not have been the accident that killed him. He could have died of hypothermia.'

Draco was shifting from one foot to another in his eagerness to be off. 'Right, then, Thanet. Keep me informed— in fact, you'd better report in at about five. Interesting to get back to grass roots for a while.'

'Let's hope he's had enough of grass roots,' said Lineham, gazing after the departing Land Rover. 'What now?'

'Better call in for those reinforcements. Tell them to come up to the hotel.' Thanet beckoned to PC Yeoman who had kept well away from Draco and was now patiently waiting near the entrance to the hotel drive. 'I hope you're not frozen stiff.'

'No sir, I'm fine.' Yeoman didn't look it. His narrow face was pinched with cold, his nose red-tipped, eyes watering.

'You did well here, before we arrived.'

'Thank you, sir.' A faint flush warmed the pallor of his cheeks.

'I gather Mrs Hamilton's brother, if that's who the dead man is, was a stranger to you.'

'I knew she had a brother but I've never set eyes on him before. I've only been here two years and he left the village ages ago, everyone assumed he was dead.'

'Black sheep of the family, was he?' Thanet scented an interesting story.

'I believe so, yes. Pretty unpopular generally, from what I can gather.'

'Why was that, do you know?'

Yeoman shook his head. 'Not specifically, no. It's just the impression I've got.'

'Part of your job will be to find out, listen to the gossip. There's bound to be a lot of talk in the village after this. Meanwhile, nip up and fetch Mr Hamilton, would you?

We'd like him to identify the body. Afterwards, if the SOCOs have finished you can come up to the hotel with us and have a hot drink.'

'Thank you, sir.' Yeoman set off up the hotel drive at a brisk pace, slipping and sliding on the snow.

Thanet glanced around. 'You finished here, Trace?'

'Almost, sir.'

'Right. Get those paint samples to forensic as soon as you can, won't you?'

'Yes, sir.'

Twenty minutes later the Range Rover returned. Hamilton jumped out and the ambulancemen slid the stretcher out and uncovered the dead man's face. Tight-lipped, Hamilton nodded. 'That is my brother-in-law.'

'Leo Martindale,' said Thanet.

Hamilton looked startled. 'How did you...? Oh, I suppose he had identification on him.' He sighed and shook his head. 'The last of the line.' He grimaced. 'Sad, isn't it? There have been Martindales at Longford Hall for over two hundred years.'

'He was unmarried, then?'

'So he told us.'

'You had any reason to doubt him?'

Hamilton looked uncomfortable. 'Oh no. No. It's just that... Well, I suppose you're bound to hear. He wasn't exactly the most reliable of men.'

'I see. We'll need to talk to you and your wife, of course, so perhaps we could now go up to the house.'

'Of course.' Hamilton glanced at the Land Rover into which the SOCOs were loading their equipment. 'You seem to be without transport at the moment, Inspector. I assume that will shortly be remedied but meanwhile may I offer you a lift?'

Thanet would have liked to take his first look at the Hall in his own time, but it would have seemed churlish to refuse and he didn't want to antagonise the man. Besides, the thought of getting out of the cold more quickly was enticing. 'Thank you.'

They climbed into the Range Rover and set off up the drive, which was fenced on both sides and wound across open parkland. Before the great storm in October 1987 this would no doubt have been graced by stands of mature oak and beech, but now it was virtually bare, only the odd solitary survivor lifting its branches into the winter sky. Here and there broken and splintered trees still lay about in disarray, testament to the devastation suffered by the whole of this south-east corner of England on that one night. It was said that it would take three generations for the landscape to recover. Hamilton was evidently doing his bit to ensure that it would. An extensive programme of replanting was obviously under way, in the shape of groups of young saplings protected from the depredations of rabbits and livestock by square enclosures of wood and close-meshed wire netting.

'I suppose you lost a lot of trees in the storm?' said Thanet.

Hamilton sighed. 'Like everyone else, yes. Around eighty per cent, actually, and, as you see, we still haven't got around to clearing away all the casualties. It's a mammoth task and is costing a fortune so we're doing it bit by bit. We've tended to concentrate on replanting.'

The house had just come into view and Thanet was aware of Lineham behind him leaning forward to take a better look. If they'd been alone he knew exactly what the sergeant would have said. 'They can't be short of a penny!'

And it would have been true, of course. Longford Hall was not exactly a stately home, but it was certainly the house of an English Country Gentleman; built, he would guess, at the end of the seventeenth or early in the eighteenth century, the rich rose-red of its brickwork enhanced by the mantle of snow which now surrounded it. Its proportions were perfect: the rows of white-painted sash windows, the flat-topped steeply pitched roof with dormer windows, the stone balustrade running around the roof ridge all combining with the graceful flight of steps leading up to the front door to create a perfect harmony of shape and form often striven for but rarely achieved.

'What a beautiful house,' Thanet murmured.

Hamilton lifted an eyebrow, as if surprised that a policeman should appreciate architectural genius. 'It is, isn't it. Built by Hugh May in 1675.'

And now a Country House Hotel. Thanet wondered

how it must feel to have to turn the house that has been
your family home for generations into a haven for rich
tourists and tired businessmen. He knew that a number of
these Country House Hotels now existed but he had never
been inside one before. Should be interesting.

They had arrived. Hamilton pulled up in front of the
steps, which were being brushed clear of snow by a tall,
thin man wearing a padded anorak and a navy blue
woollen cap below which his ears stuck out like those of a
garden gnome. He gave them a curious glance as they
passed, breaking the rhythm of his movements and
straightening up to pull out a handkerchief and blow his
nose.

'Who was that?' said Thanet in an undertone when they
had gone by.

'Byfleet, our handyman-cum-chauffeur.' Hamilton pushed
open the front door with a proprietorial air and, after
stamping the snow off their boots, they followed him into a
broad inner lobby that bore no resemblance to the entrance to any hotel Thanet had ever been in before. If he
hadn't known it was one he would have thought that he
had stepped into a private house. Ranged along the right-
hand wall was an orderly litter of gumboots, croquet
hoops, umbrellas, walking sticks; exactly as if at any
moment members of the family might come out and equip
themselves for whichever outdoor activity they had in
mind. To the left, a long wooden rail screwed to the wall
sported a row of hooks from which hung an assortment of
well-worn Barbours, Burberries and tweed caps and hats.

There was no time for more than a quick glance around.
Hamilton kicked off his boots and the three policemen
followed suit. Hamilton slipped on a pair of shoes he had
left beside the door and Thanet, shooting an apologetic
glance at Lineham, unwrapped the parcel containing his
shoes, which he had removed from the Land Rover before
Draco left, and put them on, glad of his foresight. He
wouldn't have fancied conducting an investigation in a
place like this in the indignity of stocking feet. Lineham
was no doubt wishing he'd done the same.

Hamilton flung open the inner door and led the way
into a spacious hall from which a graceful staircase curled

up to the first floor. Thanet blinked, overwhelmed by the assault on his senses. The scent of potpourri and burning applewood hung on the warm air, Persian rugs glowed on the stone-flagged floor, antique furniture adorned with elaborate flower arrangements gleamed with centuries of polishing and everywhere was a profusion of fine paintings, decorative objects and porcelain ornaments. In the distance someone was playing the piano. It was like stepping back in time to a more leisured and gracious way of life.

'Just a moment,' murmured Hamilton, and he left them to speak to a young woman seated at a leather-topped desk in the left-hand corner of the room. The hotel receptionist, presumably, the first discreet indication that Longford Hall was a commercial undertaking. As if drawn by a magnet the three policemen moved in the direction of the log fire burning in the huge stone fireplace in the right-hand wall. Two women, one young, one middle-aged, were sitting on the long chintz-covered settee in front of it.

'Say,' drawled the older woman, 'you poor men look frozen to the eyeballs. Come right over in front of the fire, and warm yourselves up.'

American, by the sound of it. A guest, presumably.

Thanet smiled. 'You're certainly in the best place, on a day like this.' The warmth of the fire on the backs of his legs was sheer bliss.

The girl pouted. She was in her late teens, small and dark, with the beautifully white even teeth Thanet for some reason always associated with Americans. 'Just our bad luck, you mean. We'd planned a trip to Canterbury today. How long d'you think it'll be before the roads are clear?'

Thanet shrugged. 'Sorry, I don't know. Could be this afternoon, could be—'

Hamilton approached. 'If you'd like to come this way, Inspector, I've arranged for some coffee to be brought. You could do with a hot drink, I expect.'

The two women exchanged glances. 'Inspector!' said the younger one, scenting diversion. 'Does that mean . . . ?'

Hamilton turned on all his charm, gave her a melting

smile. 'I'm sorry. There's been an accident . . .' And, like a sheepdog herding a small flock of wayward sheep, he urged the policemen towards a door to the right of the stairs. 'If you'd like to sit down . . .'

It was a small sitting-room, elegant in blue and gold.

'When you've had coffee I'll fetch my wife.'

'Is she very upset?'

'Depends what you mean by "upset". Shocked, yes, grief-stricken—well I don't think she would pretend to that. After all, until this week she's thought her brother dead for many years now, so you could say she's had time to get used to the idea.'

There was a knock at the door and a girl in housemaid's uniform of long black dress, frilly white apron and cap entered with a tray of coffee. Gratefully they all accepted the proffered porcelain cups of steaming liquid. Thanet waited until she had gone, then said, 'When, exactly, did she learn he wasn't dead after all?' His fingers and toes were aching now as they thawed and it took considerable self-control not to betray the fact. He didn't want to do anything to distract Hamilton's attention from the conversation.

'Day before yesterday.' The muscles of Hamilton's face tightened, betraying the tension their unexpected visitor had caused. He and his wife had obviously not been exactly overjoyed at her brother's resurrection.

An interesting thought crossed Thanet's mind. What if Leo had been the rightful heir to the Longford Hall estate . . . ? Here was a motive for murder if ever there were one. Questions crowded into his mind. He flicked a glance at Lineham. *Take over*. He wanted to think.

'He just turned up out of the blue, without warning?' said Lineham.

Hamilton seemed surprised by the change of questioner. 'Yes.'

'After—how long?'

'Twenty, twenty-five years. I lost count long ago.'

Why come back now, after all these years? Thanet wondered.

'Why come back now, after all this time?' said Lineham.

Hamilton shrugged. 'He'd been living abroad for some

time, apparently, only returned to England a week ago. Went to the barber's and saw an article on Country House Hotels in one of the Sunday supplement magazines. Longford Hall was featured in it.'

Hamilton's tone had subtly changed. Suddenly he had become guarded.

'I saw that article,' said Lineham. 'Chilston Park was in it too.'

This was another well-known Country House Hotel in Kent, notable in that it was owned by the Millers, publishers of the famous *Antiques Price Guide*.

'That's right.' Hamilton was obviously relieved to be distracted from the direction the conversation was taking.

But Thanet wasn't going to let him get away with it so lightly. By now he was sure he was right. Leo *had* been the heir. Another glance at Lineham. *I'll take over again.* They had been working together for so long that this unspoken communication had become second nature to them.

'How long has the Hall been a hotel, Mr Hamilton?'

'Two years.'

'What made Mrs Hamilton decide to make the change?' He was rewarded by the answer he expected.

'Her father died four years ago and there was no way she could have kept it on without making it pay its way.'

'Was Mr Martindale aware that his father was dead?'

This was delicate ground. Hamilton's tone was carefully casual as he shook his head. 'Apparently not. As I say, he'd been living abroad for a number of years, in the South of France, although we didn't know that at the time. Everything possible was done to try and trace him, without success. Apparently the villa in which he was . . . staying, was very secluded, up in the hills. His hostess was French and they had very little contact with the local community.'

For 'hostess' read 'mistress', Thanet guessed.

'So it must have been a considerable shock to Mr Martindale, to learn that his old home was no longer a private house.'

'I suppose so. Though he didn't seem at all put out by the fact.'

'Really?' Now if true, that *was* interesting. Had Leo

hoped to cash in on all the hard work his sister must have put in to make this place into the going concern it presumably was?

'And of course to learn of his father's death,' said Thanet.

'Yes.'

An uncomfortable monosyllable. Hamilton must know what was coming next.

'The estate was left to your wife, not her brother?'

'No.'

Even more terse.

'So,' said Thanet delicately, 'there must have been a certain problem of inheritance.' He awaited Hamilton's reaction with interest.

But he was disappointed. Hamilton must have prepared himself for this moment for he simply smiled, a bland, meaningless stretching of the lips, and said, 'Not at all, Inspector. Sorry to disappoint you, but I'm sure we could all have come to some amicable arrangement. To put it baldly, it's a good-sized cake, there was plenty for everybody.'

It depended, Thanet thought, on how large a slice Leo Martindale would have wanted to cut for himself. 'How large, exactly?'

'Two thousand acres.' Hamilton smiled, the lazy, replete smile of the predator who has caught and eaten his prey. 'And the house, of course.'

Not to mention its contents, thought Thanet. They alone, from what he had seen of them, would be worth a pretty penny. He wondered how Hamilton's wife had reacted to all this.

As if on cue the door opened and a sleek dark head appeared. 'Ah,' said Delia Hamilton, 'there you are, darling. Sorry to interrupt, but there's a minor crisis. The butcher's just rung to say his van is stuck in the snow. D'you mind if Byfleet borrows the Range Rover for half an hour to go and collect the meat?'

3

At Thanet's request Delia Hamilton returned after giving permission for Byfleet to borrow the Range Rover. She sat down beside her husband with an embarrassed laugh. 'I suppose you think I'm very unfeeling, Inspector, to be worrying about such trivial matters after what's happened. But the fact remains that I'm still responsible for the running of this place and we do have guests. Not many at the moment, fortunately, but still...'

She had changed from her outdoor clothes into an elegant tweed skirt, pearls and a smoky-green cashmere jumper the colour of her eyes. Her dark hair was now folded back into a smooth pleat. Immaculately groomed, she looked every inch the country lady, an image no doubt carefully calculated to impress her guests. Of grief there was no sign.

'How many, exactly?' said Thanet, ignoring the spurious apology.

'Only eight. It's usually pretty quiet at this time of the year.'

'And they are...?'

'Four Americans—a married couple and a mother and daughter—then there's a family of three and a single man, all British.'

Should make the task of interviewing easier, thought Thanet. If it had been a bank holiday weekend, now... 'We understand from your husband that your brother arrived unexpectedly the day before yesterday, that until then you had thought he was dead.'

'Which is why I can't pretend to be devastated now. Leo was dead to me for so many years that it was his being alive I found difficult to take in.' The embarrassed laugh again. 'I suppose you think I'm pretty hardhearted, but there's no point in being hypocritical about it, is there?'

Thanet made no comment. There had been, he noted, no further word of a complaint to the Chief Constable. Perhaps it had been made and dismissed?

'Could you give us some idea of his movements since he arrived?'

She put up a hand to brush back an invisible strand of hair. 'I'll do my best, though we didn't spend that much time together. I still had the hotel to run and Leo seemed quite content to wander around by himself, renewing old acquaintances, no doubt, and revisiting his old haunts.'

'If you could just give us some idea...'

She glanced at her husband. 'Well, let me see... He arrived unexpectedly, early on Monday evening, shortly before dinner.' She grimaced. 'Shortly before we had dinner, I mean. We always dine at a ridiculously early hour so that I am free to be around while our guests have drinks and their dinner later on.'

'By "we" you mean...?'

A glance at Hamilton. 'My husband and I.'

'There are no other members of the family living here at present?'

'There's Tessa, our daughter, and our son Adam is here at the moment, too. But he didn't arrive until last night. He's away at boarding school but it's his half-term and he spent the first few days of it with a friend. And Tessa was out as usual, she'd been up to town for the day and didn't get back till late.'

'By "town" you mean London?'

'Of course. Look, is all this relevant? I can't see why it matters what we did the night before last, it's last night that matters, surely.'

'I'm just trying to get the picture, so bear with me, please. Mr Martindale gave you no warning of his arrival, you say?'

She shook her head. 'No. Just turned up out of the blue.'

'It must have been a shock for you, if you had been so certain he was dead.'

'It certainly was ... A nice one, of course.'

'Of course,' echoed Thanet, hoping the sarcasm was not noticeable in his tone. 'Anyway, I imagine Mr Martindale would have been shown up to his room, when he arrived.'

'Briefly, yes. All the rooms are always kept in a state of readiness, so there was no problem there.'

'And then you had dinner. That would have been at ... ?'

'Six-thirty, as usual. It was something of a celebration, of course, we opened a bottle of champagne. Return of the prodigal and all that.'

Thanet couldn't imagine that Leo had really been welcomed with open arms, but they had presumably gone through the motions. 'And afterwards?'

'We always have drinks with any of the guests who choose to join us in the drawing-room at seven-thirty. They like that, it fosters the private house image we try to cultivate.'

'Did your brother join you that evening?'

'Yes, he did. The idea seemed to amuse him.'

'And afterwards?'

She shrugged. 'It was business as usual.' She glanced at Hamilton. 'I believe you did some paperwork in your office, didn't you, darling, and I stayed around, generally keeping an eye on things. Leo went off to the pub in the village. He got back about nine, then disappeared to his room.'

'And yesterday?'

Delia Hamilton put a hand up to her head and said irritably, 'I saw him around from time to time, but I didn't exactly keep a diary of his movements, why should I? And I did have work to do, you know, this place doesn't exactly run itself.' Mention of her domestic duties made her glance at her watch. 'Look, can't we hurry things up a bit, we'll be here all day at this rate.'

Hamilton stirred. 'And I have things to attend to, as well. Do you really need me here any longer? I can't see that there's much I can contribute. I'm out on the estate most of the day.'

'I appreciate that, sir, but I'd be grateful if you could stay just a little longer. You might be able to clarify or corroborate what happened last night.'

Hamilton settled back in his chair, frowning. 'Very well, but let's get a move on, shall we?'

Thanet had no intention of being hurried. 'If we could go back to yesterday morning, then...'

Delia Hamilton frowned and sighed. 'If we must. I'm sure our housekeeper could help you more than I.'

'That would be...?'

'Mona Byfleet. She's married to our handyman-cum-chauffeur.'

'You saw him outside, if you remember, Inspector,' said Hamilton.

'Ah, yes. Perhaps I could talk to Mrs Byfleet later. But meanwhile...'

Delia Hamilton sat up straighter, as if to flex the muscles of her memory, then said rapidly, 'Leo had a lie-in, I believe, and breakfast in bed. I saw him mid-morning and he said he was going to wander about, revisit his old haunts, as I said. At lunch he told me he'd been for a long walk on the estate. He said he was going down to the village in the afternoon and I assume he did. Then in the evening we had dinner together...'

Some memory was making her uncomfortable, Thanet could tell, by the whitening of her knuckles as her clasped hands tightened, the way she adjusted her position in her chair.

'You, your husband and your brother?'

'That's right,' she said impatiently. 'Really, Inspector, you do like to dot your i's don't you?'

'You said your daughter was here?'

'She'd gone off to visit friends again.'

'In London?'

'No, locally.'

'What did you talk about at dinner, Mrs Hamilton?'

She met his gaze squarely but Thanet saw the toe of her shoe tilt as her toes bunched up in tension. Feet, he found, were always an excellent indicator of state of mind.

'This and that.' Her chin lifted and her tone was cool. The message was plain. *I don't see that it's any of your business.*

Thanet ignored it. 'Such as?'

She shrugged. 'Just general chat about what we'd been doing while he was away, what he'd been doing. We had a lot of catching up to do.'

Thanet decided not to probe any further for the moment. Later, if necessary, he promised himself. At the moment he just wanted to get the general picture. 'I see. And later, after dinner?'

'I didn't see him again after dinner.'

'And you, Mr Hamilton. Did you?'

'See him again?' Hamilton shook his head. 'No, I didn't.'

'Didn't you think that strange?'

This time they both shook their heads, spoke together.

'Not at all, no . . .'

'Not in the least. Why should we?' This was Delia Hamilton. 'This isn't a council house, Inspector, we're not exactly tripping over each other all the time. And there are a number of ways in and out, you could go all day without seeing someone else who is living in the house if your activities didn't happen to coincide.'

'Did he say what he intended to do, after dinner?'

More headshakes.

'And you, what did you do?'

The Hamiltons looked at each other. 'You drove to the station, to fetch Adam, didn't you, darling?' said Hamilton.

'Yes.'

'What time would that have been, Mrs Hamilton?' Thanet sensed the heightening of Lineham's attention, quite rightly. Any mention of either of the Hamiltons driving anywhere the previous evening could be highly relevant.

'I must have left about twenty-five past seven. Adam's train was getting in at seven-thirty and it takes about five minutes to get to the station.'

Thanet remembered what Doc Mallard had said. *Say between six o'clock and four A.M., then, to be on the safe side.*

'So you would have arrived back about twenty to eight?'

'Something like that, yes.'

'And you didn't pass your brother on the way, either going or coming back?'

Delia Hamilton's eyes snapped. 'Don't you think I would have said so, if I had? I told you, I didn't see him at all after dinner.'

'What about you, Mr Hamilton?'

'I was working in the office. I usually do, in the evenings.' Hamilton's eyes narrowed. 'Look, why all the questions about what we were doing?' His voice grew a little more strident. 'For that matter, now I think about it, why all the questions about what Leo was doing during the day yesterday? What possible relevance can it have? I appreciate that you need to find out about his movements last night in order to discover how the accident happened, but surely it should be enough for us to say that the last time we saw him was at dinner?'

'I'm afraid it's not quite as simple as that.'

'Why not?'

'Yes, why not?' said Delia Hamilton.

They both stared at him, waiting for a reply.

Thanet hesitated. How much should he say, at this stage?

'Well?' said Delia Hamilton impatiently.

Thanet shrugged. 'A man has died, Mrs Hamilton, and it's our job to find out how and why. I can't tell at this stage what information might be relevant.'

'But it was a simple hit and run, surely,' said Hamilton. 'Unless you're suggesting . . . ?'

'It's a little difficult,' said Thanet carefully, 'to see how Mr Martindale could have landed in that ditch in the position in which he was lying without, shall we say, a little help.'

'"A little help" . . .' said Hamilton. 'My God, Inspector, you're surely not suggesting that someone *put* him there?'

Thanet shrugged. 'I'm afraid I can't say any more at present.'

'But—'

'Look here—'

Again, they spoke together. Delia Hamilton deferred to her husband with a glance.

'Are you saying,' he said incredulously, 'that Leo was *murdered*?'

Thanet was saved from a reply. The door, which must have been unlatched, was pushed open and a head appeared.

'Sorry, couldn't help hearing. Why the surprise, Dad? You always did say Uncle Leo would have come to a bad end.'

It was a boy of fourteen or fifteen, though you would never have guessed it from the way he was dressed. Hair slicked down with brilliantine, he was wearing a navy-blue pin-striped suit, white shirt and narrow knitted tie. A white silk scarf hung loosely around his neck and he was carrying a trilby hat tucked under one arm and a silver-topped walking stick. Coming further into the room he posed with one hand on the stick, the other shoved into his trouser pocket.

There were further shocks to come. 'Sounds interesting,' said a female voice, and a girl of seventeen followed him into the room. She, too, was apparently making a statement of some kind by her appearance, though Thanet couldn't quite make out what it was. Rebellion against her upper-crust background, perhaps? She sported hair in stiff porcupine spikes, skull-like make-up with hollowed cheek-bones and shadowed eye-sockets and an all-black outfit of high heels, tights, sweater and mini-skirt so short that it was more of a frill than a garment.

Thanet sent up a silent prayer of thankfulness that so far Bridget's adolescent revolt had gone no further than a mild flirtation with heavy eye make-up.

With a glance at Thanet, Hamilton stood up. 'Were you two listening at the door?' he said angrily.

'Oh come on, Dad,' said Adam. 'Eavesdropping will get you everywhere, you know that.' He gave Thanet an amused look. 'As in this case. You're the fuzz, I suppose?'

'As you say,' said Thanet drily, casting a warning glance at Lineham. The sergeant, ever-sensitive to insults to his superior, had stiffened. PC Yeoman's expression, he noticed with amusement, was suitably wooden.

'Out!' said Hamilton, advancing menacingly on his off-spring. But they stood their ground.

'Stop coming over the heavy father, Dad,' said Tessa

languidly. 'We've merely come to offer our assistance, like good citizens. I should've thought you would approve. You're always trying to get us to conform.'

'That's enough,' said their mother sharply. 'You heard what your father said. Off you go. Now!'

Reluctantly they began to turn away. 'Just when the conversation was getting interesting,' muttered Adam.

Thanet looked at the Hamiltons. 'I'm sorry, but would you mind very much if I did have a word with them? They might be able to help.'

'Great!' said Adam, dropping his pose and displaying a child-like eagerness to be in on the action.

The Hamiltons exchanged glances.

'How can they possibly help?' said Delia.

'Oh Mum!' Tessa was scornful. 'How can he tell unless he tries to find out?'

And without waiting for further permission they crossed to a settee at right angles to the one on which their parents were sitting and sat down, looking at Thanet expectantly.

Hamilton stood up. 'I'm going!' he said in disgust. 'If you don't mind,' he added sarcastically.

Thanet waved a hand. 'Fine.'

'But I've got to go too!' said his wife. 'There are masses of things to be done.'

But her objection was too late. Hamilton had already left.

'I don't think there's anything else I want to ask you at the moment, Mrs Hamilton,' said Thanet. 'So if you'd prefer to leave . . .'

She shot her children a furious glance, clearly torn between her need to attend to her duties and a reluctance to leave the young people alone with the policemen, for fear of what they would say. 'No, I'll stay a little longer.'

'He won't eat us, Mum, you go,' urged Tessa.

Delia pressed her lips together, shook her head and settled back into her chair. Her children exchanged glances, rolled their eyes and sighed.

'Oh *Mum*,' said Adam.

'Well now,' said Thanet, and introduced himself and Lineham. 'PC Yeoman you already know, no doubt.'

They glanced at Yeoman and nodded.

'Actually,' said Thanet, 'I'm not sure whether you can help us much, Adam.'

The boy's face fell. 'Why not?'

'Well, I gather you didn't get home until twenty to eight last night, so unless you saw your uncle after that . . . Did you?'

Adam shook his head reluctantly. 'No. I did go and knock on his door some time during the evening, but there was no reply.'

'What time was that?'

He frowned. 'Let me think. I had something to eat, then I went up to my room and unpacked . . . It must have been between half-past eight and nine.'

'Was the door locked?'

'Yes.' A defensive glance at his mother. 'I tried the handle because I thought he might have been in the bathroom, and not heard me.'

And he might have been, thought Thanet, and locked his door against just this type of eventuality. So they were no further forward.

'And now, of course, I'll never know what he was like.'

It sounded like genuine regret. To a boy of Adam's age the mysterious wicked uncle who disappeared into the blue never to be seen or heard of again was no doubt an intriguing figure.

He turned on his sister, 'And you can stop looking so smug! Just because you happened to be here—'

'Adam!' said his mother sharply.

'What about you, Tessa?' said Thanet.

But before she could reply there was a knock on the door.

'Come in,' said Delia, with evident relief.

A maid entered. 'Sorry to interrupt, ma'am, but a lot more policemen have arrived.' A glance at Thanet. 'They're asking for the Inspector.'

'Thank you,' said Thanet. 'Tell them I'll be out in just a few minutes.' He turned back to Tessa and raised an expectant eyebrow. 'Did you see your uncle last night?'

'Not last night, no. But I did have a natter with him earlier.'

'Oh, when was that?' said her mother sharply.

'I ran into him on my way downstairs yesterday morning, so naturally I introduced myself and he suggested coffee in the conservatory.' She rolled her eyes. 'He was real dishy.'

'Tessa!'

'Well, he was! So smooth and . . . well, he was *interesting*. I mean, he'd travelled all over the place, seen everything, done everything . . .'

'And everyone!' murmured Adam, *sotto voce*.

'What was that?' snapped his mother. 'What did you say?'

Adam and his sister flicked amused glances at each other. 'Nothing, Ma, no need for convolutions of the undergarments.'

'Adam!'

Lady Bracknell couldn't have put more disapprobation into those two syllables, thought Thanet.

'I would remind you,' she said furiously, 'that this is an official interview.' She cast a disgusted look at Lineham's notebook. 'So just watch what you are saying, if you don't mind.'

'Don't worry, Mrs Hamilton, I have teenaged children of my own,' said Thanet. He could imagine Ben's comments if he saw these two. 'Couple of *posers!*' Ben would say.

He turned back to Tessa. 'Did he give you any details of his activities over the last few years?'

She shook her head and the black spikes quivered. 'Not really, no. Just that he'd been living in the South of France.'

'Did he say what he'd been doing for a living?'

Tessa gave a shout of laughter. 'Work, you mean? You must be joking. Dear Uncle Leo was what Grandmother's generation would have called a lounge lizard.'

'Tessa!' Her mother again.

'Oh, come off it, Ma. What's the point of pretending? I'd guess he lived off women, rich widows mostly, I should think.'

Delia Hamilton stood up, propelled by the force of her indignation. 'That's enough, Tessa! I won't hear your uncle slandered in this way. The interview is over, Inspector. Come on you two, out. And this time I really mean it.'

'But Ma,' Tessa protested, 'that wasn't slander. Slander is false report and that was—'

'ENOUGH!' said Delia. 'Just go, will you?'

And this time, they went.

4

'So what d'you think, Mike?'

They were eating sandwiches provided for them by Mrs Hamilton while awaiting the arrival of the housekeeper, Mona Byfleet. PC Yeoman had been despatched to the village to help Thanet's men in the house-to-house enquiries, while others had been detailed to locate and examine all the vehicles at Longford Hall in an attempt to find the grey one suspected of running Martindale down. DC Bentley had been allocated the task of interviewing the guests, DC Swift the rest of the staff.

'No one's exactly broken-hearted, that's for sure. Mmm, these sandwiches are good.' Lineham lifted the upper layer of bread and peered inside. 'Tuna, sweetcorn and mayonnaise, I'd say. Good combination. I'll have to tell Louise.'

'If you could drag your attention away from the ingredients of your sandwich, Mike, I'd be interested to hear if you think there might be a case to answer.'

'Sorry, sir.' Lineham shrugged. 'As you would say, it's early days yet. But it seems to me that Martindale wasn't exactly the type to endear himself to people, was he? And there is the question of a nice juicy inheritance at stake.'

'Quite.'

'It'd be interesting to know whether the matter was actually discussed.'

'Exactly.'

'I mean, I can't see the Hamiltons being overjoyed at the prospect of going halves in the hotel and presumably

34

the estate, can you, sir, whatever Mr Hamilton says about there being plenty to go around.'

'For that matter, from what we've heard of Martindale I can't really see him being happy to relinquish half of what was rightfully his, however much work his sister and brother-in-law had put in over the last few years.'

'No. And leaving the financial aspect aside, I shouldn't think Mr Hamilton would be too pleased to lose his position as squire, so to speak. He looks the type who rather enjoys the role.'

'I agree. It'll be interesting to see what Swift learns from the staff. In a place like this they'll be pretty thick on the ground, I should think. They might well have picked up some interesting snippets.'

'True.' Lineham yawned. He was looking tired, Thanet noticed.

There was silence while they finished the sandwiches and mulled over what they had learned.

'About time that housekeeper turned up,' said Thanet, draining his coffee cup. He would have liked to smoke his pipe but there wasn't time. He stood up. 'Let's go and see where she's got to.'

They went into the entrance hall, which was empty of guests. It was now 1.15 and they were presumably at lunch. A man in formal butler's uniform of black jacket, striped trousers, white shirt and black tie was just disappearing through a door at the far side.

They crossed to the receptionist's desk.

'D'you know if anyone's managed to locate Mrs Byfleet yet?' said Thanet.

'Yes, we have. She does know you want to see her, she'll be here as soon as she can.' An apologetic smile. 'A minor crisis with one of the guests. Perhaps you'd like to wait by the fire . . . ?'

'You may be able to help us.' Thanet smiled back at the girl, who was in her early twenties, small and well-spoken with a cloud of dark hair and bright dark eyes. She looked intelligent and observant. 'Were you on duty when Mr Martindale arrived, the day before yesterday?'

'Yes, I was.'

'It was about 6.15, I believe?'

'That's right. He turned up out of the blue, with no warning. I thought he was just another guest, though they usually book ahead, of course. He asked if we had a room for the night, and I booked him in. Then he asked for Mrs Hamilton.'

'What did he say, exactly?'

'Just said, "Is Mrs Hamilton around?" And when I said yes, I could find her if he wanted to speak to her, he said yes, he'd like to. And then he said, "Tell her her brother is here." I was surprised. I didn't even know she had a brother.'

'Did you see them meet?'

'Yes. When I gave Mrs Hamilton the message on the phone she sounded very taken aback, then she said, "I'll be down right away."'

'Did she seem pleased to see him?'

'Yes, she did. Though . . .' The girl hesitated, then bit her lip.

'What?'

She shook her head. 'Nothing.'

Thanet guessed that she had noticed a certain falseness in Delia's professed pleasure at her brother's arrival.

'What was Martindale wearing?'

She shrugged. 'Sports jacket, I think. And a black-and-white checked tweed overcoat. I remember that because he took it off and laid it across the corner of my desk.'

'Did he say anything else?'

She shook her head. 'I don't think so. Oh, there was just one thing . . .'

'Yes?'

'While he was waiting for Mrs Hamilton—just before she arrived, in fact—Mrs Byfleet came out into the hall from the drawing-room with a young man, and he nodded at them and said, "Who's that?" So I told him, it was Miss Hamilton's boyfriend. He was just going to say something else when Mrs Hamilton arrived.'

'This young man, who is he?'

'Toby Fever. He's local. His father has a business in the village, he's a haulage contractor.'

Not quite Tessa Hamilton's class, thought Thanet. He wondered why Martindale should have been interested.

'Did you see Mr Martindale talk to him at all?'

'No.'

'Or anyone else, for that matter? You must see all the comings and goings, here.'

'He passed the time of day with one or two of the guests, that's all. Ah, there's Mrs Byfleet now.'

Thanet and Lineham turned to look at the woman coming down the staircase. Delia Hamilton hadn't been too pleased at the prospect of their interviewing her. 'She's not been too well lately, and I don't want her upset. She's . . . well, she's pregnant, with their first child, and she's in her thirties, she's finding it hard going. And I don't want to lose her. She's very efficient and hardworking, she'd be very difficult to replace. It's not easy finding suitable staff for a place like this.'

It was true that Mrs Byfleet didn't look well, thought Thanet. She was, he guessed, about six months pregnant, though her long, dark green dress in some stiff silky material was well cut to conceal the fact. But her narrow face was pale, her short brown hair, despite its good styling, dull and lifeless.

'Mrs Byfleet?' He stepped forward to introduce himself. 'Perhaps we could go into the small sitting-room we've been using . . . ?'

After a brief word with the receptionist she accompanied them back into the little blue-and-gold room, choosing an upright armchair into which she sank with a little sigh.

'Hard morning?' said Thanet with a smile.

'One of the guests had a fall. She's all right, though, thank heaven, just twisted her ankle. She's lying down now. But I shall have to go up and see her again shortly.'

'We won't keep you long. We just wanted to ask you if you could give us any idea of Mr Martindale's movements yesterday.'

'Let me see . . .' She passed a hand over her forehead as if to collect her thoughts. 'Well, he had breakfast in his room at nine, then I next saw him in the conservatory. He was having coffee with Tessa, Miss Hamilton. Then I saw him go out—for a walk, I assumed. He came back for a light lunch with Mr and Mrs Hamilton, then he went out again, to the village, that time.'

'He told you he was going to the village?'

'Yes. I was in the hall and he stopped for a chat, said he was going to see how much it had changed. I told him I thought probably very little. That was all. Then . . .' She faltered.

'Then.'

She shook her head. 'I was just trying to think. I'm not sure when he got back, but he had dinner with the Hamiltons again.'

'And afterwards?'

'I don't know what he did afterwards.'

Alerted by some evasiveness in her tone, Thanet persisted. 'Did you see him again at all, after he'd had dinner?'

'No.'

She met Thanet's eye almost defiantly. She was lying, Thanet was sure of it. But what about? Had there been an incident she didn't want to tell him about, out of loyalty to the Hamiltons?

'Were Mr and Mrs Hamilton pleased to see him?'

'Of course.'

But there was a note of falsity in the affirmation.

'It was a shock to them, of course, they thought he was dead, it would have been a shock to anyone . . .'

'You didn't see any sign of . . . shall we say, disharmony, between them?'

She shook her head. 'No.' Her tone lacked conviction, but she obviously wasn't going to go back on what she had said.

'You like working here, Mrs Byfleet?'

For the first time a genuine smile gave warmth to her response. 'Yes, I do. It suits us very well—my husband and I have a flat over the old stables, he looks after maintenance, and acts as chauffeur when necessary. It's a lovely house to work in, so many beautiful things, and Mrs Hamilton is a good employer, very fair. She expects you to work hard, but she works just as hard herself, so you don't mind.'

'How long have you been here?'

'Just over three years.'

And according to Giles Hamilton, Delia's father had died four years ago. She hadn't wasted much time in getting things moving. With an estate like this there must have been considerable legal battles to be fought, in view of the fact that the heir was missing, before she got permission to proceed with her plans.

'And you opened two years ago, I believe?'

'That's right.'

'So you helped get it off the ground, so to speak?'

'Yes. Mrs Hamilton worked like a slave; we all did.'

'It must be very satisfying to see it become such a thriving business.'

'Oh yes, it has been. We're quiet at the moment, of course, mid-February isn't exactly the most popular time for a break in the country, but we've built up a very good reputation, I think, and for most of the year we're pretty busy.'

Which explained why the housekeeper clearly felt such a fierce loyalty to her employer. Having been in on the project since the beginning, she must feel an almost proprietorial interest in its success.

Thanet rose. 'What I should like to do now is take a look at Mr Martindale's room. It's all right,' he added, seeing the hesitation in her face, 'Mrs Hamilton has given permission.'

'Of course.' She rose, a little clumsily, pushing herself up on the arms of her chair. 'I'll take you up.'

'You've worked in the hotel trade long?' said Thanet conversationally, accommodating his pace to hers as she led them up the graceful staircase.

'All my life, you could say. My parents ran a hotel. Not like this one, of course.' And she glanced around at the profusion of expensive hot-house flowers, the oil paintings on the walls, the gleaming antiques and rich variety of decorative objects.

'Forgive my asking, but aren't the guests ever tempted to walk off with any of these?'

'Not the guests,' she said wryly.

Meaning that the staff were, thought Thanet. Scarcely surprising, really. With so much on display there must be a temptation to think that the odd piece of porcelain or silver might not be missed.

'The guests are usually overwhelmed by it all,' she went on. 'Especially the Americans. They've never actually stayed anywhere quite like this before and they often walk around in a sort of daze for a day or two, just looking and looking.' She gave a little laugh. 'It's interesting, in a very old house like this there are bound to be inconveniences you wouldn't find in a modern hotel, but in all the time I've been here I've never had anyone complain. They just accept it as part of the general, well . . .'

'Ambience?' supplied Thanet.

'That's right. They're almost, well, in awe of it, I think, and either complaining or stealing anything would be a sort of sacrilege.'

At the top of the staircase they had turned left along a broad landing and at the third door along she stopped. 'Here we are. I put Mr Martindale in the Chinese suite.' She pushed open the door and stood back. 'And now, if you don't mind . . . ?'

'Ah yes, your invalid. Just one other point before you go. Staff. How many are there?'

'Theoretically there should be thirty in all. I say "theoretically" because in practice it's very difficult to recruit staff for a place like this, so we're always a few short—we're rather isolated here, you see, there's nothing for them to do when they're off duty, and many of the younger ones can't afford cars, so they get bored and leave.'

'So at the moment you're how many, in all?'

'Eight in the kitchen, we're two short there, and seventeen in the house, we're two housemaids and one parlourmaid short.'

'So apart from the kitchen staff you have a butler, a footman—'

'A head footman,' she corrected him, 'then a footman, six housemaids, four parlourmaids, two receptionists, my husband and myself. Then outside there's the gardener—groundsman rather, I suppose you'd call him—and his assistant.'

'And how many of those live in?'

'Ten, excluding my husband and myself.'

'I see. Thank you, you've been very helpful.' Thanet dismissed her with a nod and a smile.

Inside the Chinese suite Lineham looked around and said, 'Wow! Some hotel room!'

There was only one word to describe it, thought Thanet: sumptuous. His living-room would have fitted into it three times over and there was so much for the eye to feast upon that it was difficult to take it all in. He pivoted slowly, looking.

Predictably the wallpaper was Chinese, in a pale celadon-green with a delicate design of bamboo and herons etched in cream. On the wide, highly polished oak floorboards lay a silky cream carpet with a green and rose design, and the elaborate hangings of the four-poster bed and the long draperies at the windows were in deeper shades of green and rose. On either side of the bed stood low round tables covered with circular floor-length rose-coloured cloths topped with smaller cloths in creamy lace. Half the room was furnished as a sitting-room, with deep, soft sofas and armchairs grouped around a leaping log fire protected by a brass fireguard. There were a number of paintings, including two Chinese scroll paintings of misty mountain landscapes and a series of framed prints of ancient Chinese costumes. Various pieces of antique furniture, including a slender writing desk supplied with headed notepaper and envelopes, were scattered around the room. Everywhere were small personal touches: apart from the ubiquitous television set and a fine enamelled clock, there were pot plants; two arrangements of fresh flowers, in various tones of cream and pink to match the decor; a small wicker basket of wrapped sweets; a bowl of fruit with plates, damask napkins and fruit knives beside it; a tray of drinks; a pile of books both nonfiction and fiction, the latter all recently published novels; and an array of new magazines.

'Wow!' said Lineham again. 'Wonder how much it costs to spend a night in a place like this?'

'We'll pick up a brochure on the way out,' said Thanet.

'I'm serious!' said Lineham. 'If I started saving now, for our wedding anniversary . . . Louise would love it!'

Thanet rather wished he'd had the idea himself and

irritation that he hadn't made him terse. 'Come on, Mike, just remember why we're here, will you? Let's see what we can find out about Martindale.'

It looked as though Martindale had intended to stay some time. The old-fashioned leather suitcase plastered with airline stickers which had been stowed on top of the wardrobe was large, and the wardrobe and chest of drawers were full of clothes, all expensive if somewhat the worse for wear. As well as a dinner jacket, there were several tailor-made suits and Thanet looked into an inside pocket for the tailor's label: *Filligrew and Browne, Sporting Tailors. Conduit Street 21.9.72.* Quickly, he examined the others. None was more recent than 1981. The shoes, six pairs, all Church's, were well-worn, some of the shirts were beginning to fray at collar and cuffs and the underclothes definitely needed replacing.

'Looks as though he was a bit short of the ready,' said Lineham. 'He must have nearly fallen out of that barber's chair with delight when he read that article.'

'Quite. Short of the ready but definitely not at his wits' end. If he had been he would have pawned those long ago.' Thanet nodded at the objects scattered on the chest of drawers: a pair of silver-backed hairbrushes, silver hip-flask, and gold cufflinks.

'True.'

Thanet wandered into the bathroom which displayed the same attention to detail: bowl of potpourri; cut-glass dish of cotton puffs; posy of cotton buds; little basket of toiletries—shower caps, shampoos, foaming bath oil, and a selection of Floris soaps. The towels were thick, soft and in plentiful supply and two luxurious towelling robes with *Longford Hall* embroidered across the pockets hung behind the door. Martindale's possessions were scattered about: razor, shaving cream, badger shaving brush, aftershave, toothbrush, toothpaste. His sponge bag held supplies of paracetamol, Rennies, Alka-Seltzer, and antiseptic cream.

'Nothing much here, Mike.'

There was no reply and it occurred to Thanet that all sounds from next door had ceased. Raising his eyebrows he returned to the bedroom to find that Lineham was asleep on the sofa in front of the fire.

'Mike!'

Lineham awoke with a start. 'Oh, sorry, sir. I must have dropped off. The fire . . . '

'You did drop off. And I'm the one who's sorry. Sorry that you are so tired you actually fall asleep in the middle of a murder enquiry!'

'We don't know that it's a murder enquiry yet, sir.'

Thanet waved a hand irritably. 'A potential murder enquiry, then. You know perfectly well what I mean. And stop avoiding the issue.'

'I really am sorry . . . '

'It's an explanation I want, Mike, not an apology.'

Lineham rubbed his eyes. 'It's my brother-in-law.'

Thanet gave an exasperated sigh and sat down in an armchair facing the sergeant. 'What's that supposed to mean?'

Lineham yawned. 'I was up half the night talking to him. He's having problems with his marriage and he just turned up on our doorstep last night with a suitcase.'

'Left his wife, has he?'

Lineham shrugged. 'Temporarily, anyway.'

'Look, Mike, I'm sorry your brother-in-law is having marital problems and I don't want to appear unsympathetic, but this really will not do, you know. I simply cannot have you dozing off in the middle of an investigation, murder or otherwise.'

'Yes, I realise that, sir. It won't happen again.'

'Won't it? Leaving the question of your brother-in-law aside, I've noticed that you seem to have been looking very tired lately. So what's wrong?'

'Nothing, sir. Not *wrong*, exactly. It's just that Richard still hasn't settled at school yet. I don't think he gets on with his teacher, she seems to have taken against him. So he isn't sleeping very well, wakes up every night crying, that sort of thing. We take it in turns to get up, but it's pretty tiring, never getting a decent night's sleep. Last night put the lid on it, I think.'

'OK, I understand, I've got something similar going on at home myself, as a matter of fact. Ben's just changed schools, as you know, and he's finding it pretty difficult having much stiffer competition. At his last school he could just coast along, but now ... Anyway, I appreciate your difficulty. But Mike, you're going to have to do something about it. Discuss it with Louise, go and see the Headmaster, but do *something*. And as far as your brother-in-law is concerned, well, I'm sure you'll find a tactful way of ensuring that any discussions you have are before bedtime. Right?'

'Yes, sir, of course. Really, it won't happen again, I promise.'

'I hope not. Now, what have you got there? Is that the key to Martindale's suitcase?'

Dangling from Lineham's hand was a tiny key on a leather thong. 'I should think so. It was in the toe of one of his socks.'

'Let's take a look.'

'Ah,' said Lineham with satisfaction as it turned sweetly in the lock.

'Now this looks a bit more interesting,' said Thanet.

Inside was Martindale's passport and a large brown envelope which looked much handled and which crackled when he picked it up. They sat down side by side on the sofa to examine their finds. The passport didn't tell them anything useful. It had been issued only a year ago and bore no stamps; if Martindale had done any travelling since then it had presumably been in the European community, most of whose member countries no longer bothered to stamp the passports of internal travellers.

There remained only the envelope. Thanet tipped out its contents. These looked more promising: an address book, a bundle of letters and postcards, and another, smaller envelope of photographs.

Lineham picked up the address book and flicked through it. 'We're going to have our work cut out if we have to check all these.'

Thanet split the bundle of letters in two. 'Take a quick look at these, will you? We'll go through them thoroughly later. Put them in chronological order, if you can read the date stamps.'

They were all, they discovered, from women and almost all of them were addressed to hotels or readdressed from one hotel to another. The theme was almost always the same, regret that the sender had not heard from Martindale as she had hoped to, coupled with anxious requests for news of him. Several of them delicately referred to 'loans' made to him, and one or two were more strongly worded requests for information about 'investments' made by him on the sender's behalf.

'Love 'em and leave 'em was certainly his motto,' said Lineham.

'Preferably with a pocket full of cash, by the look of it.' Thanet tapped one of the postcards, most of which were of the 'wish you were here' variety. 'Looks as though this one was the last.'

The card was date-stamped 10.11.84 and was a photograph of the Byron Hotel in Worthing. The message on the back read, *Room ready for your return. Roll on the 23rd.* It was signed 'B' and addressed to the Hôtel Paradis in Nice.

'Looks as though at some point he spent some time in Worthing,' said Lineham. 'It'd be a good hunting ground for Martindale's type, I should think.'

'You're assuming the room she's talking about is in the Byron Hotel. But it could simply mean that the sender was staying in the Byron when she wrote the card, and that the room she's referring to is in her own home.'

Lineham pursed his lips. 'It could, I suppose. But isn't the other interpretation much more likely?'

'No way of telling. In any case, after this there are no more letters or cards.'

'Perhaps it was at the Hôtel Paradis that Mr Martindale met this Frenchwoman he's supposed to have been living with.'

Thanet shrugged. 'Who knows? But I agree, it's a possibility. Pity there's no indication of who she is or where she lived.' He bundled the letters up and emptied out the envelope of photographs. Predictably, these were almost all of women, either alone or with Martindale, posing against varying backgrounds. A few, though, were obviously older, smaller, of poorer quality and with curling corners. Thanet picked these up and studied them more closely. 'I think this must be Martindale and his sister, look.'

They were recognisably the same pair, both wearing riding breeches and sitting on the steps leading up to the front door of Longford Hall; Delia with a cloud of dark hair framing those classically beautiful features, Leo handsome and carefree, one arm resting lightly across her shoulders.

'And these must be their parents,' said Lineham.

Tea on the lawn this time, the man lounging in a deck chair, the woman elegantly erect, caught in the act of pouring tea. They were a handsome pair, and Thanet, always interested in the quirkiness of genes, noted that it was her father Delia resembled, and Leo his mother. He wondered how the Martindales would have reacted to this present situation: with dignity and the famous British stiff upper lip, he imagined.

'Pretty pathetic, really, isn't it?' said Lineham, gesturing at the letters, the photographs.

'What do you mean?'

'Well, presumably this stuff, the stuff that's here, in this room, is all the gear he had.'

'I imagine so, yes.'

'I mean, someone like him, with his sort of background... What went wrong, I wonder?'

'What made him leave it all behind, you mean?'

'Yes.'

'With any luck, we'll find out.'

But Lineham was right, it was pathetic. And something more, too. Thanet couldn't believe that this small pile of letters represented the sum total of Martindale's correspondence over twenty years or so, or that there hadn't been many more photographs than this. No, in his view, they were the end result of a fairly ruthless weeding-out process. What had been Martindale's criterion? One letter or card, one photograph per woman? What Thanet was holding, he realised, were the trophies of one man's amorous past. He had a sudden, vivid picture of Martindale sitting in a chair, glass of whisky in hand, poring over them with a small, self-satisfied smile on his face. With a shiver of distaste he began to bundle them all back into the envelope. Later he would sort out which leads were worth following up, if any.

There was a knock at the door.

'Come in.'

It was one of the DCs, accompanied by a housemaid.

'What is it, Markham?'

The girl turned away and the constable shut the door behind him before saying, with understandable triumph, 'We think we've found the car, sir.'

Thanet stood up. 'Oh?'

'Well, a van, actually, sir. It was parked at the back of the hotel. A 1981 Bedford HA. It's grey, going rusty and we found a couple of threads which look as though they might match the victim's overcoat snagged on a piece of flaking metal just beside the front offside headlight.'

'Excellent. Who does it belong to?'

'The hotel, sir.'

'Right. Let's go and take a look, shall we?'

5

Thanet and Lineham returned to the lobby near the front door to put on their boots. While they were doing so Tessa Hamilton passed through with a young man in tow, presumably the one in whom Leo Martindale had shown an interest. What had Mrs Byfleet said his name was? Fever, that was it. Toby Fever. Thanet caught no more than a glimpse of him, but there was something vaguely familiar about his features. Could he have a record, perhaps?

As the three policemen stepped outside the young people drove off in a newish Ford Escort, its wheels skidding on the packed snow of the drive.

After the warmth of the house the icy air was a shock to the system and Thanet turned up the collar of his sheepskin jacket, casting an apprehensive look at the sky which had that ominously leaden look which heralds snow.

'Looks as though we might get some more,' said Lineham.

'Hope not.' Thanet raised his voice to speak to Markham who was leading the way along the front of the house like an eager dog guiding its master to a particularly exciting find. 'This van. Who normally drives it?'

Markham slowed down. 'Chap by the name of Tiller, apparently, sir. He's the groundsman. This way.'

They turned right, along the side of the house.

'Ah yes.' Thanet remembered Mona Byfleet mentioning him. 'He's got an assistant, I believe.'

'I don't know about that, sir. Someone's gone to fetch Mr Tiller, he should be there by now. Your Land Rover's back, by the way, sir.'

'Good.'

They rounded the back corner of the house and a large cobbled yard opened out before them, surrounded on three sides by a range of low, picturesque buildings in brick and tile. At the far side, standing around a small grey van, was a group of policemen stamping their feet against the cold. Amongst them was a man in boots, parka and cloth cap.

'Yes, that'll be him,' said Markham with satisfaction.

As they drew closer Thanet saw that Tiller was in his sixties, a burly figure with weatherbeaten face and angry blue eyes.

'Mr Tiller?' said Thanet.

The man thrust his chin forward aggressively. 'You in charge of this lot? What the hell's going on?'

'I'm sure you've heard about Mr Martindale's . . . accident, by now, Mr Tiller. We need to ask you some questions. Perhaps we could go somewhere a little warmer? A garage, perhaps, or a stable?'

Tiller stood his ground. 'Why?'

Thanet walked around the van and inspected the spot indicated by one of his men. It looked as though they were right and this was the vehicle they were after. A couple of threads of cloth were caught up in a snag of rusty metal. Thanet looked closer. Yes, black-and-white tweed by the look of them. He nodded at Lineham and the sergeant took out a pair of tweezers and a plastic sample bag.

Thanet straightened up.

'Mr Martindale appears to have been run down by a vehicle and it seems possible that it was this one. As you are apparently in charge of it—'

'Now just a minute. Are you suggesting . . . ?' Head down like an angry bull, Tiller appeared ready to charge.

Thanet sensed the tension in his men. The situation must be defused. He smiled. 'I'm not suggesting anything, Mr Tiller. I merely want to ask you some questions. I'm sure you're as anxious as we are to get at the truth of the matter.' He turned to one of the policemen. 'Arrange for the van to be towed in, for inspection.'

Tiller hesitated, his eyes searching Thanet's face for any

sign that he was being misled. Abruptly he turned away. 'This way,' he said gruffly.

He led the way to one of the outbuildings and pushed open the door. It was a storage shed for gardening equipment, with tools, work bench stacked with flower pots and other clutter, sacks of peat, fertiliser and compost leaning against the walls and several motor mowers of assorted shapes and sizes. It was only marginally less cold than outside.

Tiller leaned against the bench and folded his arms. 'Well?'

No point in beating about the bush or attempting to soften the man's mood. Thanet glanced at Lineham to check that he was ready to take notes. 'Tell us about the van.'

'What d'you want to know?'

'I understand you're in charge of it?'

'Sort of.'

'Meaning?'

'Everybody uses it. So why pick on me?' Tiller was becoming belligerent again.

'Please, Mr Tiller, do understand that I'm not accusing you of anything.' *At this stage, anyway.* 'I'm merely trying to find out who drives it, when and for what reason, that's all. And the sooner I find out the sooner this interview will be over. So if you could just give me the information...'

'Mr and Mrs Hamilton, Mr Talion, Mr and Mrs Byfleet, Andy—the lad who helps me. That's it.'

Thanet's heart sank. 'I see. All of them have keys to it?'

'Yes—except for Andy. He borrows mine, when he needs it. The van stands out there in the yard, and whoever wants to use it uses it.'

'Mr Talion. He's...?'

'The farm manager.'

'I thought Mr Hamilton managed the estate.'

'Mr Hamilton *administers* the estate. It's Jack Talion who actually runs it.'

'I see. And where does Mr Talion live?'

'In Home Farm.'

'And where is that?'

Tiller waved a hand. 'Over the other side of the Hall.'

'And you?'

'Where do I live, d'you mean?'

Patience, Thanet told himself. 'That's right, yes.'

'Here, in the stable yard. They converted one of the outbuildings,' he added grudgingly.

'I see.' Thanet did see. This meant that everyone who had keys to the van lived sufficiently close to have had access to it last night.

'So, did any of them use the van last night?'

'How should I know?'

Thanet sighed. It looked as though every drop of information was going to have to be squeezed out of Tiller. He signalled to Lineham to take over.

'What about you, Mr Tiller? Did you use it?'

'What if I did? I had every right, didn't I?'

'No one is saying you didn't. But in the circumstances...'

'Why don't you come right out with it? You think I ran him down, don't you? Go on, admit it.'

'Mr Tiller, as Inspector Thanet has explained, we have no preconceived ideas about what happened last night—'

'Don't give me that guff. In that case why aren't you talking to the rest of them, eh? Go on, tell me why.'

'Because,' said Lineham with admirable restraint, 'we have only just discovered that it is likely to be this particular vehicle that was involved in the... accident.'

'You did it too, didn't you?' said Tiller triumphantly.

'Did what?'

'Paused before you said "accident".' His eyes flicked at Thanet. 'Just like he did, just now. Go on, admit it, you don't think it was an accident at all, do you? You think it was deliberate.'

'Mr Tiller, can't you understand that at this stage we really don't know what happened? We are, I repeat, merely trying to find out. We shall of course,' said Lineham, raising his voice as Tiller again opened his mouth to interrupt, 'be talking to all the other people who have access to the van, but as you are nominally in charge of it we came to you first. So if you could just tell us if you did use it last night, where you went and what time...'

Tiller was shaking his head in disbelief and shifting impatiently from one foot to the other.

'Very well, Mr Tiller,' said Thanet. 'If you don't choose to tell us at present, that is your prerogative. But we must have this information, so if you'd be so kind as to accompany us back to headquarters we can all wait in greater comfort until you are ready to give it to us.'

Tiller was nodding his head with satisfaction. 'Just as I thought. Arresting me, aren't you?'

'Not at all.' Thanet was holding back his exasperation with difficulty. 'In fact, if you'd just give us the information we need we'd all be able to get on with our work that much quicker.' Then, as the man still remained silent, regarding him suspiciously through narrowed eyes, 'Come on, man, let's get it over with. As I said before, the sooner you tell us, the sooner we'll be finished, can't you see that? If you have nothing to hide there's nothing to worry about.'

Tiller gave a contemptuous snort and turned his back on them to gaze out at the yard through the cobwebbed window.

Silence.

Then, just as Thanet was about to give up and hand the man over to be taken back to Sturrenden to cool his heels for a while, Tiller swung around. 'I suppose you're right,' he said reluctantly. 'If I've nothing to hide...'

Thanet nodded. 'That's right,' he encouraged.

Tiller hesitated a moment longer. 'As a matter of fact I did use it last night. I went to the pub.'

The atmosphere eased. 'Good,' said Thanet.

'What time was that, Mr Tiller?' said Lineham.

'Half-past eight or thereabouts.'

Tiller, it seemed, usually spent Tuesday evenings in the village pub with a woman friend called Sonia Rankle, who also lived in Sutton-in-the-Weald, half a mile out on the Sturrenden road. He would pick her up soon after 8.30 and take her home at around 10.30 before returning to his own quarters at Longford Hall.

'And this was what happened last night?' said Thanet.

'Yes.'

'Now think very carefully, Mr Tiller. Did you, either on your way to the pub or on the way back, see Mr Martindale at all?'

The answer, of course, was predictable.

'No, I did not!'

A thought struck Thanet. 'You do know who I'm talking about, don't you?' To the groundsman Martindale might just have been one amongst a number of guests.

'I know him.' Tiller's response was wooden, arousing Thanet's interest.

'You mean, you know him because you've seen him around over the last couple of days, or because you knew him when he used to live here?'

'I'm local. I knew him before.'

Thanet strained to catch the overtones in Tiller's voice which, in contrast to all his previous responses, continued to be strictly neutral.

'And you're absolutely certain you didn't see him when you were out last night?'

Suddenly the man's belligerence returned in full force. 'I've bloody told you, haven't I? I knew you wouldn't believe me.'

'Is there any reason why we shouldn't believe you, Mr Tiller?'

'No! There is not!'

'In that case, we'll get on with our work. Come on, Sergeant.'

Tiller unfolded his arms as it dawned on him that the need to be on his guard was over. 'You mean, I can go?'

'Certainly. Thank you for your cooperation.'

They left him gazing after them in apparent disbelief.

6

'Interesting,' said Lineham, as soon as they were outside.

'What, specifically, Mike? The fact that he was so on the defensive or the fact that he clammed up when I asked if he knew Martindale before.'

'Both. I'd say he definitely has something to hide, wouldn't you?'

'No doubt about it. But it won't do any harm to let him stew for a bit while we find out if anyone else drove the van last night.' Thanet frowned. 'Pity so many people had access to it, though.'

'Who're we going to see first?'

'Out of courtesy it'd better be the Hamiltons. We'll start with him, I think. Presumably he is officially its owner.'

They went back into the house to find out where Hamilton was and were told that in the afternoons he usually worked in the Estate Office, which was in the stable block at the back of the house.

Retracing their steps Lineham said suddenly, 'So did Mrs Byfleet, for that matter.'

Like the partners in a long-established marriage, able to take up and lay down a thread of conversation without ever having to spell it out, Thanet knew at once what Lineham meant. 'Yes. I suspect she's either seen or heard something which she thinks would present the Hamiltons in a bad light.'

'She obviously feels a very strong loyalty towards Mrs Hamilton, at least.'

'Quite. That's an interesting point, actually. She hardly mentioned him.'

'Don't suppose she sees much of him, it'd be Mrs Hamilton she works with.'

'True.'

'There's the office, over there.'

Preoccupied earlier with Tiller and the van Thanet had not noticed the tastefully discreet OFFICE sign screwed to the wall beside one of the doors in the stable block. Guests at the hotel presumably shouldn't be made to feel that this was too much of a commercial enterprise.

Hamilton was seated at his desk dealing with paperwork. 'Ah, Inspector.'

'Sorry to trouble you again, Mr Hamilton.'

'Not at all, I was hoping for a word with you.' He waved a hand. 'Please, sit down.'

It was an attractive place in which to work, thought Thanet as he and Lineham sat down on a couple of upright chairs facing the desk. The original brick stable walls had been painted white, the overhead beams sandblasted to a smooth honey, the old granite floor sets cleaned and polished. Sturdy pine furniture and a huge map of the estate added to the atmosphere of prosperous country living. Even on a day like today the room was comfortably warm.

'I saw your men towing away our van. Do I gather that you think it was involved in the accident?'

'It seems possible,' said Thanet carefully. 'That's why I wanted to see you.'

'Oh?'

'We're trying to find out who drove it last night, and I gather that a number of people have keys to it, yourself included.'

'That's true.' Understandably, Hamilton's tone was now guarded.

'Did you, in fact, drive it last night?'

Hamilton hesitated only for a moment, presumably realising that sooner or later the truth was bound to emerge. 'Yes, I did, as a matter of fact. I went to pick up my daughter from Ashford, at about, oh, it must have been a quarter past eleven.'

Well within the time limit set by Doc Mallard.

'She doesn't drive?' Thanet was surprised. He would have expected a girl like Tessa to have taken her driving test soon after her seventeenth birthday, and he wouldn't have thought that there would be a shortage of vehicles for her to borrow, if she hadn't already been given a car of her own. Perhaps she was younger than she looked.

'Yes, of course she does. And last night she borrowed the Range Rover. Unfortunately, when she was ready to come home, she found it wouldn't start. So naturally she rang to ask if someone could come and collect her.'

'It seemed to be working all right this morning.'

Hamilton shrugged. 'It's a bit temperamental some-times. Last night it was a very simple matter. When I got there I checked the sparking plugs'—he gave a self-deprecating smile—'that's about my limit as far as me-chanical failure is concerned. Anyway, I was in luck, one of them was loose and she was able to drive it home.'

'You'll understand that I must now ask if you saw your brother-in-law either on your way out or on the way back.'

'No I didn't. Anyway, what on earth do you think he would have been doing, wandering around outside at that hour on a freezing night like that?'

Thanet shrugged. 'What time did you get back?'

'Around ten past twelve.'

'Was it snowing then?'

'It was just starting as I turned into the drive.'

'Do you know of anyone else who drove the van last night? Presumably, when your wife went to pick up your son from the station, she would have used her own car.'

Hamilton's lips tightened. It was obvious that he had been expecting this. 'As a matter of fact no, she didn't.'

'She used the van?'

'Yes. The car she usually drives, the BMW, is in for repair. Some idiot backed into it when it was parked in the Stoneborough Centre in Maidstone last week. And of course, Tessa had the Range Rover.'

'And the BMW is the only car you have, apart from the Range Rover?'

'Well, there's the Rolls, but that's used strictly for business, to meet hotel guests or ferry them about. It's one of the luxury services we offer. She certainly wouldn't use it to pick Adam up from the station. Anyway, it wasn't here. Byfleet had driven it to Gatwick, to pick up the Americans, and he didn't get back till eight.'

The door opened and Delia Hamilton came in with a flurry of cold air. 'Giles, what's all this I hear—' She broke off when she saw Thanet and Lineham. 'Ah, Inspector. Why have they taken the van away? Is it anything to do with my brother's accident?'

Patiently, Thanet went over it all again, the strong possibility that the van had been involved, the necessity of finding out exactly who had driven it last night.

Delia had crossed to stand behind her husband, one hand on his shoulder as if to draw strength from the physical contact. 'Giles, have you told them that I . . . ?' She faltered.

'That you drove it last night?' He reached up to lay his hand reassuringly on hers. 'Yes, I have. So did I, if you remember.'

She paled, the beautiful bone structure of her face suddenly accentuated, briefly almost skull-like. 'Oh my God, so you did. To fetch Tessa.' She put up the other hand and pressed her fingers into her temple as if to ease a sudden onset of pain. 'I'd forgotten.'

'It's unfortunate that so many people have keys to the van,' said Thanet. 'I understand that apart from yourselves and Mr Tiller, who presumably uses it most, both the Byfleets drive it and so does the farm manager, Mr Talion.'

'Jack! Oh God, he used it last night too! I didn't bother to tell you,' she said to her husband, 'because it didn't seem of any importance at the time.'

She and Hamilton exchanged a look full of unspoken messages which Thanet tried to read and failed. One thing was certain, however. For some reason the farm manager's name had some special significance for them, in this context. 'Jack? Would that be Mr Talion?'

'Yes.' Delia was still looking at her husband. 'Just after I got back from the station with Adam someone rang to say that some of our sheep had got out on to the road near the Linklaters' house—that's close to the junction with the Ashford Road,' she explained to Thanet. 'Jack—Mr Talion—

had walked across from Home Farm to join us for a drink before dinner, he often does, and he said he'd attend to it. Of course, he didn't have his car with him so he went in the van.'

'That would have been at what time?'

She shrugged. 'Five minutes or so after I got back.'

'And that was about twenty to eight, you say? So, say a quarter to eight.'

'Something like that, I suppose.'

'And how long was he away?'

'I haven't the faintest idea. You'll have to ask him.'

'He's been with you long?'

'For years. He was farm manager in my father's time, and stayed on when my husband took over.'

'How many years?'

Delia frowned. 'I'm not sure, exactly. He came when I was a child. Twenty-five, thirty years, something like that. Again, you'll have to ask him. Or I suppose we could look it up in the records.'

'No, it doesn't matter. As you say, I can ask him.'

But it was interesting to learn that Talion, too, would have known Leo Martindale before he left the area.

'I didn't ask before, but why, exactly, did your brother go away?'

Delia gave an embarrassed laugh. 'I'm afraid my father's patience ran out. Leo was always a bit wild and Daddy was forever having to bail him out of one scrape or another. In the end, after he'd paid off his debts for the umpteenth time, he gave him a final warning: if he didn't mend his ways he would be out on his ear, no allowance, nothing.' She shrugged. 'Leo didn't pay any attention to the warning and out he went.'

'I assume your father therefore also cut your brother out of his will.'

Delia looked uncomfortable. 'Well no, he didn't. He couldn't. The Hall is entailed.'

'I thought most of those old entails were broken long ago.'

'Yes, most of them were, in 1925 I think Daddy said. But unfortunately ours was a little more complicated than that.'

'In what way?'

'I can't see how all this can possibly be relevant,' said Hamilton.

'It may well not be, Mr Hamilton. But I'd be grateful if your wife could explain, all the same.'

Delia Hamilton looked at her husband and he gave a reluctant nod.

'Well, it's a question of something called an entailed trust, actually, and as a matter of tradition the arrangement has been continued from one generation to the next, right from the time Longford Hall was first built. What happens is this. On the twenty-first birthday of the heir, the trust would in each generation be renegotiated so that before anyone actually inherited it, it was tied up for the generation beyond.'

'So that if, in fact, the heir ever wished to sell it, he couldn't?'

She nodded. 'That's right. Because it would be impossible to know exactly how many children he's going to have until he's dead. It's a very unusual arrangement, but it's what we've always done.'

'So you're saying that the trust had been renegotiated with Mr Martindale on his twenty-first birthday?'

'Yes.'

'And once set up it couldn't be broken?'

'That's right.' She sighed. 'Of course, no one envisaged a situation in which the heir couldn't be found. As it was, obviously someone had to administer the estate so the trustees allowed us to do so in my brother's absence.'

'And if he hadn't turned up by the time seven years had passed he would presumably have been assumed dead and the estate would have come to you?'

A tight nod.

No doubt they were all thinking the same thing, thought Thanet. *As it now does.*

'I see. Well, there's just one more question I must put to you.' And in the circumstances it was very difficult to think of a way of putting it tactfully. 'If it does turn out, as seems likely, that it was your van that ran your brother down, is there any reason why any of the people who have access to it wouldn't be sorry to see him dead?' *Apart from you, of course, with the king-sized motive which you've just handed to us.*

His delicacy was wasted. They were intelligent people and saw at once what he was asking, and its implications. They stared at him, in apparent disbelief.

'Let me get this straight,' said Hamilton at last. 'I asked you earlier if you were suggesting that Leo might have been murdered. I couldn't believe then that you were serious and I can't believe it now. But you are, aren't you? What you're really asking is whether or not any of these people—including us, I presume, as we also drive the van—had a motive for killing him?'

'This is crazy!' said his wife, clutching her head. 'I can't believe what I'm hearing. My brother has a perfectly straightforward accident and before we know where we are we're accused of murdering him!'

'No!' said Thanet. 'You're jumping to conclusions. I'm accusing no one of anything at the moment, I'm merely looking at all the possibilities. That is what I'm paid to do. And you must see that—'

There was a knock at the door.

'Come in,' called Hamilton, a little too heartily; relieved, no doubt, at the interruption.

It was Bentley. 'Sorry to disturb you, sir, but . . .' It was obvious that he had come across something interesting.

Thanet stood up. Clearly he wasn't going to get anything more out of the Hamiltons at present. 'All right, Bentley, we've finished here for the moment.'

Outside the light was fading and it was beginning to snow. Thanet turned up his collar again and pulled on his woolly hat. No point in freezing in order to look dignified. 'What is it?'

'One of the guests told me that he was out for a walk yesterday morning and he saw Mr Martindale having a blazing row with somebody.'

'Who?'

'He couldn't remember his name, though he had heard it—he saw him again last night when they were having drinks before dinner, and they were introduced. Anyway, he says he's the farm manager.'

'Talion,' said Lineham. 'Well well. I noticed the look

Mrs Hamilton gave her husband when his name came up, didn't you?'

'Yes. Was this guest close enough to hear what the row was about?'

Bentley shook his head regretfully. 'No, unfortunately. But he did say that there was another man nearby, a tractor driver. Apparently the farm manager and this man were talking when Mr Martindale joined them. The farm labourer moved a little way away, tactful-like, and soon afterwards the row started.'

'But your witness thinks this tractor driver would still have been close enough to hear what was said?'

'Yes, sir.'

'In that case,' said Thanet, 'perhaps it would be a good idea to have a word with him first, before seeing Talion.'

He glanced at his watch. Ten to four. With any luck they might catch the tractor driver before he finished work for the day. Presumably the place to look for him would be at Home Farm.

Sam Tiller was crossing the yard carrying a shovel, heading for the storage shed in which they had interviewed him earlier, and Thanet called him over. To get to the Home Farm, they learned, they could either walk through the grounds of the Hall, a distance of about half a mile, or drive down to the road and take the first turning on the left.

With a glance at the leaden sky and the thickening snow Thanet decided to take the easy way out. After a word of thanks to Bentley he and Lineham headed for the Land Rover.

7

'Marvelous, isn't it?' said Lineham gloomily as they set off down the drive. 'Not only do we discover that six people had keys to the van, but that four of them actually used it last night. And we haven't asked the Byfleets yet.' He slowed down as they reached the main road. The red Ford Escort with Tessa Hamilton and her boyfriend inside turned into the drive as he pulled away.

Thanet lifted a hand in response to her wave.

'Those two young Hamiltons could put you off parenthood for ever,' said Lineham.

Thanet laughed. 'Bit late for that, isn't it, Mike?'

'All I can say is, I hope Mandy doesn't look like that when she's seventeen. . . . Anyway, the whole thing seems pretty hopeless to me. Even if we do suspect who was actually driving the van when Mr Martindale was hit, we haven't got a hope of proving it. No witnesses, nothing.'

'Come on, Mike. It's early days yet. You never know what the house-to-house enquiries will turn up and there's always forensic. If Martindale was actually put into that ditch as we suspect . . .'

'Hmm. Ah, here we are.'

He swung the Land Rover into a lane with HOME FARM stamped in black on a wooden sign. There were well-maintained wire fences on either side of the road, with snow piled against them where tractors had no doubt cleared the way. Ahead was a cluster of farm buildings and in a few hundred yards the track divided, one arm entering a drive leading to a red brick-and-tile farmhouse, the other widening out as it entered a broad yard surrounded by barns and sheds.

Over to the left a tractor with a forage box attached was moving very slowly along the wide central aisle of a long cattle shed. Thanet and Lineham walked across, hunching their shoulders and keeping their heads down against the swirling snow. At the entrance to the shed they stopped. On either side were stout iron barriers behind which black-and-white cattle on thick beds of straw were lined up munching the silage feed being spewed out of the forage box into the pens along a narrow conveyer belt.

Lineham wrinkled his nose. 'Phew! What a stink! How do these farmworkers stand it?'

'I suppose they're used to it.'

The tractor had now reached the far end of the aisle and with a roar it accelerated, described a wide arc in the open space beyond the shed and headed back towards them at a fair speed, its task presumably now completed. They stepped back as it approached and Thanet held up a hand. The driver stopped and switched off the engine.

'Yes?'

The sudden silence was a relief. Thanet stepped forward. 'We're from Sturrenden CID.' He introduced himself and Lineham. 'We're looking into the death of Mr Martindale, from the Hall.'

'Oh yeah.' The driver remained firmly planted in his seat, one hand on the steering wheel and the other on the ignition, as if ready to take off again at any moment.

'Was it you who was with Mr Talion yesterday, when he had that row with Mr Martindale?'

'Cor, was that him? I didn't realise.'

'Would you get down, please? We'd like a word.'

With a practised movement the man swung around and jumped down beside them. 'Why?'

He was in his forties, Thanet guessed, with the weathered skin of a man used to working out of doors, wearing a bulky ancient parka the colour of mud and an incongruously cheerful bobble cap in red and white stripes. A large dewdrop hung from the tip of his fleshy nose and he wiped it away with the back of his gloved hand. Almost immediately another began to form.

The smell of silage, whether from the forage box, the cattle pens or the man's clothing, was overpowering.

Thanet stamped his feet. 'Is there anywhere a bit less exposed where we could talk, Mr . . . ?'

'Mardy. Jim Mardy. I can't hang about. I got work to do.'

'It won't take long.'

Mardy hesitated a moment longer and then, without speaking, led the way across the yard to a small shed constructed of tarred weatherboarding and pushed open the door. There were no windows and inside it was very dark. Mardy twisted a switch and a single, feeble electric light bulb strung up on one of the rafters revealed a row of nails on which hung several pairs of overalls and an assortment of scruffy coats. Spaced out around the walls on a floor of beaten earth were a number of bales of straw on three of which lay plastic lunch boxes and Thermos flasks. Mardy crossed to one of the bales, picked up a Thermos, sat down and poured himself a cup of steaming liquid. Thanet and Lineham watched enviously, Thanet making a mental note to make sure that tomorrow, if the case continued, he would come well supplied with hot drinks. Lineham, he was sure, would be making a similar resolution.

Mardy was watching him expectantly over the rim of his mug. Thanet sat down on one of the bales and signalled to Lineham to begin.

Lineham remained standing, shoving his hands deep into his pockets. 'We understand that you were talking to Mr Talion when Mr Martindale arrived.'

''Sright. Some of the fencing needs renewing, we'd gone to take a look at it.'

'What time was this?'

'Just before me dinner break. Getting on for twelve o'clock, it must've been.' Mardy wiped away another dewdrop.

'Could you tell us what happened?'

The glint in the man's eye told Thanet that Mardy had now realised the purpose of this conversation. The question was, would he be cooperative or obstructive? It all depended, Thanet guessed, on Mardy's character and on his relationship with his employer, whether loyalty would win over the desire to give an account of the drama.

'What d'you mean?'

The man was playing for time, still hadn't quite made up his mind. Thanet opened his mouth to intervene then closed it again. It wasn't fair to Lineham to jump in whenever the going became sticky.

Lineham had noticed and gave Thanet an uncertain glance. Thanet looked at the ground. *Go on*.

'We thought you might be able to tell us what the row was about.'

Mardy shrugged. 'No idea.'

'You heard what was said, though.'

'Some of it.'

'Perhaps you wouldn't mind telling us what you did hear.'

Silence. Mardy took another slow, deliberate swig from his cup, then screwed it back on to the Thermos. 'Why don't you ask Mr Talion?'

'We shall.'

'In this case,' Mardy stood up, 'there's no point in me telling you, is there?'

For a few minutes longer Lineham persisted but it was useless. Now that Mardy had made up his mind nothing would shake him.

'Very well,' said Lineham eventually. 'Just tell me one thing. How long did this conversation last?'

Mardy hesitated, weighing up the pros and cons of answering this question and apparently deciding that it was harmless. 'Not more 'n a few minutes.'

'And would you say they'd met before, recently?'

Again a hesitation. Then Mardy shook his head. 'The other bloke, Mr Martindale, started off by saying, "Hullo Talion. Long time no see."'

'And what did Mr Talion say?'

Realising that he was imperceptibly being drawn into giving away information he had decided to withhold, Mardy headed for the door. 'I gotta get on.'

Thanet and Lineham returned to the Land Rover and watched him roar off on his tractor into the gathering dusk.

'I blew it, didn't I?' said Lineham. 'Sorry, sir.' He thumped the steering wheel in frustration before turning

on the windscreen wipers to clear the thin film of snow
which had built up while they had been talking to Mardy.
'I jumped in too quickly. If I'd begun as I ended, I might
have got somewhere.'

'No point in worry about it now. The main thing is, you
can see where you went wrong. And those last two
questions were very useful.'

'I just thought it would be interesting to know how long
they'd been talking before the row broke out,' said Lineham
eagerly. 'And whether or not it was the continuation of a
recent row.'

'Quite. And apparently it wasn't. The implication being...'

'That whatever the issue between them, it was a pretty
powerful one. I mean, you don't meet someone after an
interval of twenty odd years and plunge straight into a row
unless you've got a very good reason.'

'Also, it sounds as though it might have been Talion who
had the grudge. Martindale's greeting sounded friendly
enough.'

'Mr Talion now, then?'

Thanet nodded and they drove out of the farmyard and
into the driveway of Home Farm. Inside the house a dog
started barking as they approached the front door. The
barks grew louder and the man who answered their knock
made no attempt to stop the noise until Thanet had
introduced himself.

'All right, Rhett. Enough!'

The dog, an Alsatian, at once fell silent but remained
wary, watching the two policemen for any threatening
move.

'You'd better come in.'

Talion opened a door to the right of the small hall,
switching on the light, and they followed him into a cold
gloomy dining-room furnished with heavy oak table and
chairs, carpet square and skimpy unlined curtains patterned
with orange and yellow flowers. The room looked as
though it was rarely, if ever, used and as if no one had
cared what it looked like for a very long time.

'What is it?' He was in his sixties, short and stocky,
dressed in well-worn corduroy trousers, pullover and tweed
sports jacket. He looked like a man who had long ago

forgotten how to smile; all the lines in his face drooped and there were deep creases between his eyebrows. He did not invite them to sit down and agreed only reluctantly when Thanet asked if they may. The dog flopped down at Talion's feet and buried its nose in its paws.

The door was pushed open and a woman came into the room. 'Who is it, Jack?' She was small, pale and thin, her clothes nondescript, her grey hair pinned back in a meagre bun.

At once his whole demeanour changed and in a flash he was up out of his chair and putting an arm protectively around her shoulders. 'It's all right, Meg, it's only business, it won't take long. You go back in the warm.' Gently, he urged her into the hall and through the door at the far side.

'I don't want my wife upset,' he said as he came back in, shutting the door firmly behind him. 'Her health isn't too good. Heart trouble.'

'I'm sorry to hear that.'

Thanet was sincere, but Talion gave him a sceptical glance as he sat down again. 'Well, what did you want?'

'You'll have heard of Mr Martindale's death?'

A flicker of—what? Satisfaction? Some even stronger emotion?—in Talion's eyes. He nodded. 'Hit and run, wasn't it.'

Statement, not question, Thanet noticed. And still no hint of regret, false or otherwise.

'That's what we're trying to find out.'

Talion was looking disconcerted. 'What do you mean?'

'What I say.' Thanet paused. 'It looks as though he was knocked down by the Ford van they use at the hotel as a general runabout.'

He watched Talion apparently assimilate this information and remember that he had used the van himself last night.

'So?'

'So naturally we are talking to everyone who drove it last night. As I understand you did.'

'Yes, that's true. I did. What of it?'

'Mrs Hamilton tells us that you had to go to check on some sheep that had got out on to the road.'

'That's right.'

'You left at about a quarter to eight, I believe. What time did you get back?'

Talion shrugged. 'I wasn't away long. Twenty, twenty-five minutes, perhaps.'

'So you were back by, say, ten past eight?'

'I suppose. What does it matter?'

'I'm just trying to get a clear picture of the van's movements last night. And naturally I have to ask you if you saw Mr Martindale, while you were out.'

'No, I didn't.'

'You'd seen him earlier in the day, though, I understand?'

'Who told you that?'

'One of the hotel guests saw you together.'

Talion said nothing.

'He said that you were arguing.'

Still no response.

'Having a row, in fact?'

'What of it? Aren't I entitled to have an argument with someone without the police taking an interest?'

'Not,' said Thanet, 'if that someone happens to be killed later on that same day.'

Talion stood up and, as if pulled by an invisible string, the dog rose too. 'Now just a minute . . . What are you suggesting?'

The dog's hackles were rising, Thanet noticed. 'Nothing, Mr Talion. Merely enquiring. What, exactly, was the row about?'

'It's none of your bloody business!' he snarled.

Lips curling back from teeth, dog and master looked remarkably alike. A low growl issued from deep in the animal's throat.

'That's not true, I'm afraid,' said Thanet mildly. 'Everything to do with Mr Martindale is police business now. A suspicious death means a complete loss of privacy for everyone concerned.'

Talion laid a hand on the dog's head. 'All right, boy, it's all right. Lie down.' He sat down himself as the dog subsided and for several moments remained silent, staring at the table. Eventually he stirred. 'I suppose,' he said, 'if

I don't tell you now, you'll be back, until you get what you want.'

Thanet said nothing. He guessed that Talion was remembering that there had been a witness to the argument and, unaware that they had already interviewed Jim Mardy without success, was thinking that it would be best to get in first with his own version.

'So I might as well tell you. Mr Martindale told me that he was thinking of staying on for good, now he'd come back. I told him that he'd do better to take off again, the sooner the better as far as everyone around here is concerned.'

'He was that unpopular?'

Talion shrugged. 'Let's just say he had a knack of getting up everyone's nose.'

'And that's it?'

'Well, he wasn't very pleased, naturally. Said after all this time we ought to be able to let bygones be bygones. I couldn't agree and said so.'

'You make it all sound very calm, very rational. But it wasn't, was it?'

Talion said nothing, just shrugged again.

'Our witness was some distance away, but it was obvious to him that you were having a heated argument.'

Talion's mouth set in a stubborn line. 'That's all that was said.'

Now for the really important part. Thanet didn't think that he was going to get anywhere, but he had to try. 'I can't believe that you were concerned only in a general way, for the good of the community. I assume that if Mr Martindale said you ought to let bygones be bygones you had a personal reason for being so against his settling here again?'

The silence stretched out, became protracted. Thanet waited. And waited.

Eventually Talion stood up. 'Sorry, but I've said all I'm going to say.' He thrust his chin forward and his voice rose. 'And as I said before, it's really none of your bloody business. So get out, will you?'

The dog was on his feet again, barking this time, the fur along his back standing up in ridges.

It was pointless to persist. Slowly, almost casually, giving the dog no cause for alarm, Thanet rose. Lineham followed suit and they left. Outside, Lineham released pent-up breath. 'Phew. I thought he was going to set the dog on us in the end, didn't you?'

'Doesn't look as though either of us is doing too well at the moment, Mike.'

Back in the Land Rover Thanet looked at his watch. Four-thirty. If he was to report back to Draco as ordered at five they would have to get a move on. And he was chilled to the bone. The thought of home, warmth and hot food was irresistible.

He decided to call it a day.

8

As usual, however, the lure of home had to be resisted. By
the time Thanet had reported to Draco, chewed over the
day's findings with Lineham and written up the 'detailed,
literate and accurate' reports upon which Draco invariably
insisted, it was nearly nine o'clock. Fortunately the
threatened heavy snowfull had not materialised and all the
main roads were relatively clear. Thanet hoped that they
would stay that way.

His own street looked unfamiliar, its pavements lined
with humps of piled-up snow where householders had
tossed it aside to clear their driveways.

Inside the house the warmth and savoury smell of food
were like a benediction. He shrugged off his sheepskin
jacket and hung it in the cupboard under the stairs, his
stomach rumbling in anticipation.

Joan had heard him and came out into the hall. She was
wearing a new jumpsuit which they had chosen together
the previous Saturday, in a soft, misty blue which enhanced her delicate skin tones and hair the colour of clear
honey.

'Mm,' said Thanet as they kissed. 'You look gorgeous.
Smell gorgeous, too.'

'I just had a bath.'

'What are you doing?'

'Nothing much. I'm giving myself an evening off.'

'Were you watching something you wanted to see, on
television?'

'Nothing special.'

71

She led the way into the kitchen, took his supper out of the oven and put it on the table where his place was laid. 'I had it on a very low heat but it's a bit dried up, I'm afraid.'

'Looks delicious,' said Thanet. It was steak and kidney pie, his favourite. 'Just what I need.'

'I thought of you today, tramping about in the snow. Was it grim?' She knew how he hated the cold.

Thanet grimaced. 'This morning was.'

'How did you get on with Superintendent Draco breathing down your neck?'

She poured the tea then sat down opposite him and they chatted about the day's events while he ate. When he had finished telling her about the case she sat thinking for a while. Eventually she stirred. 'He sounds a pretty sad sort of person. The victim.'

'That wasn't the impression I got from the people I talked to.'

She shook her head. 'No, I don't mean the impression he gave other people, I mean what he was really like, underneath.'

'You mean, because I said that no one has yet shown any sign of sorrow over his death?'

'Partly, I suppose. It must be awful to think that there isn't a single person who cares if you're alive or dead.'

'We don't know that that's how it was with him. There might be other people, in other places . . . No, well, I admit it does seem unlikely. He was very much a rolling stone, by the sound of it. But if you'd seen the pile of letters—carefully hoarded—from all his conquests, perhaps you wouldn't feel quite so sorry for him.'

'Oh, I'm not trying to defend all that. I'm just saying it must be sad to feel so alone.'

Thanet laid down his knife and fork. 'He certainly seems to have succeeded in making himself thoroughly unpopular in the area. And now . . .'

'What?'

'I'm just trying to work it out. Yes, I feel as though they're all drawing closer to each other in a tight circle to prevent me from finding out the truth.'

'And what d'you think the truth is?'

Thanet shrugged. 'No idea.'

'You're not suggesting that it was a communal plot to get rid of him!'

'No. Oh no, nothing as bizarre as that. It's just that I'm beginning to suspect that everyone is really rather relieved that he is dead and therefore feels a degree of gratitude to whoever was at the wheel of that van when it happened. So there's a . . . well, a conspiracy of silence, if you like, to protect that person. No one wants to be suspected himself, but he's going to make sure he doesn't point the finger at anyone else. So far the only useful leads we've had are from outsiders.' He sighed. 'If it continues like that, it'll be hard going. Any more tea in the pot, love?'

She took his cup and he watched her pour it, grateful for a relationship in which each performed such small services for the other when they needed it without a second thought. It had taken them a long time to reach that plateau. For many years he had, while paying lip service to Joan's need for a satisfying career of her own, inwardly been the original male chauvinist pig he outwardly professed to despise. But now . . . He caught her hand, kissed it. He was a lucky man.

'The house is very quiet tonight. Bridget out?' He knew that it was her evening off.

'Yes. And Ben's doing his homework.'

'Still?'

They grimaced at each other. The days of Ben's skimping his homework had long gone. The higher academic standards and level of attainment in his new school had seen to that. At first Thanet and Joan had been delighted at his new seriousness over his work but by now they were becoming concerned about it. They'd had enough trouble over Bridget, when she sat her GCSEs, to be concerned lest Ben should go the same way.

'I'll pop up and say hullo.'

Ben was sitting at his desk, hunched over his books. Thanet sat down on the bed. 'Still at it?'

'Yes. I've nearly finished.'

Ben looked tired, Thanet thought, remembering anew with a lurch of anxiety how obsessive Bridget had become over her work last year, how it had nearly ended in disaster. Questions he longed to ask, things he longed to say, tumbled through his mind but he held them back. He and Joan would stick to their original resolution, to give Ben six months to settle down in his new school before reviewing the situation. He stood up. 'Good.'

Ben looked up. 'There's a chap in my class, Fellows ... He's asked if I'd like to go ice-skating at Gillingham on Saturday. His brother's got a car.'

With difficulty Thanet refrained from asking how old the brother was, how long he'd been driving, how many of them would be going. This was the first time Ben had mentioned a specific friend at the new school. He smiled. 'Sounds fun.'

Downstairs he flopped down on to the settee beside Joan and told her about the proposed expedition.

'Oh good! I am pleased. I think that's what he's found hardest of all, having none of his old friends at the same school.' She frowned. 'Though I'd like to have known how long it is since the brother passed his test. Still, as you say, it really will do him good.'

'Did you have the chance of a word with Bridget about last night?'

She shook her head. 'No. She was in the bathroom, as usual, when I got home and then she came down in a tearing hurry, said she was meeting Diane at seven.'

'Where were they going?'

'I didn't have a chance to ask. She was gone practically before I could open my mouth.'

Thanet frowned. 'I don't like not knowing where she is.'

'I know.'

'And it's not the first time it's happened. She's got to realise she must always let us know who she's with and where they're going.'

Joan sighed. 'I have tried. But she just says how can she tell me if she doesn't know herself? She says they never decide in advance, just see how they feel when they meet.'

'I can understand the difficulty but all the same, it's not good enough. We really must try and work out some system.' She could be anywhere, Thanet thought. How would we begin to know where to look for her, if she just didn't come home?'

'Perhaps it would be better if you spoke to her, Luke. She's so touchy with me these days. If ever I say anything like that to her she just says, "Oh Mum, don't fuss", or "Other people's mothers don't go on like that".'

'I don't care what other people's parents do,' said Thanet grimly. 'While she's living under our roof we do have a right to know where she is. I'll see what I can do.'

'Don't be too heavy-handed, will you? We don't want her saying, "If that's how you feel I'm moving out."'

'D'you think she would?'

Joan considered, head on one side. 'No, I don't think so. No, I'm sure she wouldn't. After all, on the whole, we get on pretty well. If you think of some of the problems other parents seem to have with their children . . .'

Thanet sighed. 'I suppose that's true. It's just that there always seems to be something . . .'

Joan grinned. 'At the risk of sounding hackneyed—*C'est la vie.*'

Thanet smiled back. 'That's one of the things I love about you. Your truly original mind.'

She raised a provocative eyebrow. 'What are the others?'

'Which would you prefer?' said Thanet, putting an arm around her. 'Demonstration or exposition?'

She snuggled closer. 'Oh, demonstration, definitely.'

Next morning Thanet set off for work early. There would be a stack of reports to read from Bentley, Swift, and the men who had been working on the house-to-house enquiries, and he wanted to skim through them before the morning meeting with Draco at 8.45. He hated facing the Super's early morning ebullience ill-prepared. He was thankful to note that the temperature had risen and the snow was beginning to thaw. He'd remembered to make two large flasks of coffee but it looked as though it wouldn't be quite as miserably cold today.

Lineham had not yet arrived. Thanet hoped that the sergeant had managed to sort out his problems with his brother-in-law and get a good night's sleep. He lit his pipe, considerately leaving the door open so that Lineham would not be greeted by a smoke-filled room, and settled down to read.

A number of interesting points had emerged.

One of the guests had seen the housekeeper, Mona Byfleet, coming out of Martindale's room at 7.15 on the night he died. This meant that she was, so far, the last person to have seen him alive. Thanet sat back and gazed up at the coils of smoke lazily intertwining above his head, remembering.

'I don't know what he did afterwards.'

'Did you see him again at all, after he'd had dinner?'

'No.'

And he distinctly remembered knowing that she was lying and wondering why. At the time he had thought that perhaps she had overheard some snatch of conversation, some argument, even, between Martindale and the Hamiltons, but now he wondered. Had she simply not wanted him to know that she had seen Martindale again after dinner? But why not?

Thanet shook his head. No, it was much more likely either that she had been making a routine check on the room or that Martindale had called her in to solve some small domestic problem, and the incident had been so trivial that it had slipped her mind.

He picked up the next report.

The Byfleets claimed that neither of them had driven the van last night, Byfleet stating that he had left the Hall at 5.30 in the Rolls to pick up some guests from Gatwick Airport and had arrived back just before eight. The guests had confirmed this. All very well, thought Thanet. That still meant that apart from the time when Tiller had been using the van to go to the pub, they had both been free to drive it later on in the evening, if they had so wished.

He moved on to the house-to-house reports.

The landlord of the village pub had mentioned Tiller and Mrs Rankle, his woman friend, as being among the regulars who had been in that night. They always came on Tuesday evenings, he said, and had arrived at their usual time, around twenty to nine. Also... Thanet's eyes widened.

'Morning, sir.' It was Lineham, looking, Thanet was pleased to see, somewhat fresher this morning.

'Listen to this, Mike. The landlord of the pub says that Mrs Rankle—Sam Tiller's girlfriend—always borrows his van some time during the evening to nip home. Apparently she's got a handicapped son and she likes to check that he's OK.'

'And did she borrow it on Tuesday?'

'Apparently she went out for a short while as usual, and he assumed that was where she'd gone. She's usually away for twenty minutes or so.'

'Wonder what sort of driver she is. The roads were pretty icy that night.'

'Quite. We'll have to go and see her, obviously.'

Lineham picked up a batch of reports and sat down. A few minutes later he looked up. 'Sir! This is interesting...'

It was the report of an interview with a Mrs Doreen Victor, who lived in the village. She claimed to have seen Martindale (identified by his distinctive black-and-white checked overcoat) twice that afternoon. On the first occasion he had been talking to Mrs Fever, wife of a local businessman (and mother of Toby Fever, Tessa Hamilton's boyfriend, Thanet wondered?) who had been filling her car up with petrol at the garage. On the second occasion Mrs Victor had seen him having what appeared to be a heated exchange with Mrs Rankle, Sam Tiller's friend. Unfortunately they had been on the other side of the street and she had been unable to hear what the argument was about

'An argument,' said Thanet thoughtfully. 'You don't walk up to a perfect stranger in a village street and have an argument with her, do you?'

'He must have known her before,' said Lineham eagerly. 'When he lived here. And she drove the van that night...'

'Quite... What about this Mrs Fever? Did the witness have the impression Martindale knew her too?'

'She doesn't say,' said Lineham regretfully.

'Did you happen to notice if the petrol pumps at the garage are self-service, Mike?'

'No, I didn't. You mean, there might have been an attendant, who could have overheard the conversation?'

'It's possible. A lot of the smaller garages in the villages haven't switched to self-service yet. We'll check.'

Lineham made a note.

Thanet was now glancing through Swift's reports of interviews with the staff at Longford Hall. 'Ah, listen, Mike. One of the housemaids saw Martindale having a row with a Mr Fever—this woman's husband, I presume—at about a quarter past six that evening. She was in the library, checking that everything was in order, and Martindale was there. Fever apparently came barging in and laid into him, telling him to keep away from his wife.'

'What did Martindale say?'

'He was very cool apparently, tried to play it down, laugh it off. Said there was no harm in saying hullo to an old acquaintance, was there? Fever nearly went through the roof.'

'What happened?'

'Mrs Hamilton came in and shooed the girl away, so she didn't hear any more.'

'So Mrs Hamilton knew about this and didn't say a word.'

Thanet sighed. 'It's just as I thought. I was saying to Joan last night, I suspect we're going to have our work cut out trying to get people to talk. Our main hope is through outsiders like this Mrs Victor, or the pub landlord, and this housemaid.'

'They're not exactly outsiders.'

'By outsiders I mean people who didn't know Martindale before.'

Lineham pulled a face. 'You may be right. If so, as you say, it'll be hard going.'

Thanet checked the time. Eight-thirty-five. 'Let's just glance through the rest of these. I'd like to be up to date before the meeting, and know roughly what our plans are for today.'

They hurried through the remainder of the reports. The only other item of any interest was Swift's account of an interview with another member of staff, who had overheard Sam Tiller delivering an ultimatum to Delia Hamilton: if Martindale stayed, he, Tiller, would go.

'Mr Martindale certainly wouldn't have won a popularity poll around there!' said Lineham.

'No.' Thanet shuffled the papers together. 'Right, Mike.

Go over these again while I'm in the meeting, check we haven't missed anything. We'll have to interview a lot of these people again, see if we can get any more out of them—that's Mrs Byfleet, Mrs Hamilton, Mr Tiller. And we must also try and fit in Mr Tiller's girlfriend, Mrs Rankle, both the Fevers and of course this Mrs Victor, in case she can tell us anything more. It sounds as though she could be an interesting source of gossip, perhaps we ought to try and see her first. So ring and get the interviews set up.'

Thanet glanced at the clock again. 'Sorry, must dash.' One minute to go. If he was late Draco would be furious and they'd waste half the meeting listening to a lecture on the importance of punctuality.

9

Thanet made it to the meeting with ten seconds to spare. He slipped into his seat and noted Draco's customary glance at the clock. After murmured greetings all round Draco picked up the sheaf of papers lying exactly in the centre of the blotter on his desk and cleared his throat.

Apart from Draco and himself there were two other men in the room: Chief Inspector Tody, who acted as Draco's deputy should the Superintendent be unavailable; and Inspector Boon, Thanet's long-time friend and colleague. Each was watching Draco in characteristic manner, Tody with an ingratiating half-smile, Boon with an ironic twinkle in his eye.

There was a sense of expectation in the air, Thanet realised. Something was up. He looked at Draco again and yes, the signs were there: the familiar glint of self-satisfaction overlaid by missionary fervour, the almost audible crackle of energy which emanated from him. It looked as though the long-rumoured new campaign was about to begin. Mentally, Thanet braced himself. What now?

'Good morning, gentlemen. Incidently, I think that we should soon try to amend that state of affairs. There should, if we are to keep abreast of the times, be at least one woman present. That is, however, not what I want to talk to you about this morning. This morning I want to talk to you about a scheme for further improving the efficiency of our police force here in Sturrenden. Oh, I know what you're saying to yourselves.'

Draco's Welsh accent was becoming more pronounced,

80

Thanet noticed, a sure sign that he was getting into his stride. He often felt that the Superintendent's style was more suited to the pulpit than the police force.

'You're saying, "Haven't we had enough changes for the moment? Don't we need—indeed deserve—a bit of a break?"'

Draco brought the flat of his hand down upon his desk, making everyone jump. 'No! That is the very moment, I tell you, when standards begin to slip. Complacency is our enemy. It leads to lazy minds, lazy work practices and, above all, lazy policing.'

Draco sat back, tucking his thumbs into the armholes of his waistcoat, and deliberately looked at each man in turn. 'Now I'm not denying that you've all worked very hard to make this a more efficient force over the last year, and the results show, as I'm sure you'll agree. But I think you'll also agree, when you've heard my new proposals, that there are a number of areas in which there is room for further improvements.'

You had to admire the man's enthusiasm if nothing else, thought Thanet. Must remember to give those cards and letters to Swift, he reminded himself, concentration flagging as Draco carried on in the same vein, see if he can track down any of Martindale's old girlfriends. Not that at this stage there would appear to be any urgent reason for doing so, but it was a lead, however unpromising, that ought to be followed up.

Draco was still on his preliminary speech. Oh, do get on with it, you Welsh windbag, Thanet urged silently.

He was thinking about Martindale, about how extraordinary it was that anyone could arouse in so many people such a degree of animosity that it could survive apparently undiminished an interval of more than twenty years, when, with a loving glance at the papers in his hand, Draco finally came to the point.

'After considerable thought I have identified the three main areas in which improvements need to be made. Organisation, Delegation and Documentation.' He spelt it out letter by letter. 'O-D-D. Which, as you'll no doubt realise, spells, " Odd".' He waited for the small ripple of amusement before smiling himself. 'Yes, I thought you'd

appreciate that. And if the acronym affords the men some
light relief, then that's all right by me. I don't in the least
mind appearing a figure of fun so long as they buckle down
and get on with implementing my proposals. It will, of
course, be up to you to see that they do.'

He stood up and handed a sheet of paper to each of them.
'Here they are. I'd like you to take them away and study
them and come back to me tomorrow with comments—
constructive, of course. No, don't read them now, there's
no time, you'll all be wanting to get back and get on with
your work. So, briefly, could we have your reports, please.'
He sat back, folding his hands over his waistcoat.

Although he made it as succinct as possible Thanet's
report was of necessity the longest, the finding of Martindale's
body in the ditch being by far the most important of
yesterday's events. He wondered if Draco was going to
raise any objections to an intensive investigation, but
apparently the discovery of the fibres on the van had
convinced the Superintendent that for the moment at least
Thanet and his team were justified in devoting their
energies to finding out exactly what had happened.

'I might even pop out to Sutton myself later on,' said
Draco, causing Thanet's heart to sink. 'You'll be needing
to see several of these people again, as well as interviewing new witnesses. I suggest you begin with the chap who
barged into the hotel and had a row with Martindale—
what's his name? Fever, was it? And with this woman
Rankle.'

Thanet forbore to say that by now Lineham should
already have a series of appointments set up. If Draco
came looking for them, with any luck he wouldn't find
them. If this made the Superintendent mad, too bad.
Hoping that he wouldn't have to waste too much time in
elaborate games of hide and seek with Draco, he made his
way back upstairs to his office, where he found Doc
Mallard talking to Lineham. As usual the little police
surgeon was looking spruce and cheerful and was scarcely
recognisable as the sardonic scarecrow of a man he had
become after the lingering death of his first wife. Thanet
never ceased to marvel at the miracle which remarriage
had wrought in his old friend.

'Ah, Luke. Just telling Lineham here that the PM is set for this afternoon. I'll let you know the findings as soon as I can.'

'Thanks, Doc.'

'How's it going?'

Thanet shrugged. 'All right, so far. Did Lineham tell you we found the van?'

'Yes. Belongs to the people at Longford Hall, I gather. Does the plot thicken?'

'I'm not sure, yet. It could have been a simple hit and run.'

'As non-committal as ever,' said Mallard, twinkling at Thanet over his half-moons. 'How you ever have the nerve to complain when I can't be too precise about time of death I don't know.' He picked up his bag. 'Well, I'll be in touch later, then. Happy hunting.'

When Mallard had gone Lineham gestured at the paper in Thanet's hand. 'Anything interesting, sir?'

'The Super's latest campaign.' Thanet handed it over. 'Haven't looked at it myself yet.'

Lineham took it eagerly. 'Thought something was brewing.' He grinned. 'Does he realise . . . ?'

'Oh yes. ODD. It's his crafty way of taking the sting out of it all.'

Lineham, reading, groaned.

'Don't tell me,' said Thanet. 'I'm not going to read it until I'm feeling stronger.'

'At this rate we're going to end up doing so much paperwork there won't be any time for policing. Do you realise . . .'

'Mike, I said, don't tell me. At the moment I don't want to know. Now, did you get those interviews set up?'

'All except the ones with Sam Tiller and Mr Fever. I'm still trying to get hold of them.'

'Right. You carry on while I have a word with Swift. I want to put him on to tracing some of Martindale's former girlfriends. Are we seeing Mrs Victor first?'

'Yes. At eleven.'

'Fine.'

By 10.30 they were on their way. The sky had cleared, the sun had come out and in the town the few remaining

areas of blackened slushy snow were thawing fast. Out in
the country it was a different matter. Along the sides of the
lanes, where the sun had not yet penetrated, the snow still
lay in drifts, piled up against tangled brown hedges on
which there was as yet no hint of green. In the open fields
it had melted in patches, stippling the brown of ploughed
earth and tender green of winter wheat with random
frostings of white. Tall trees stood winter-stark against a
sky the milky blue of opals.

'What I can't get over,' said Lineham, pulling into the
side of the road to allow a lorry to pass, 'is the degree of
bad feeling against Martindale. Sam Tiller obviously felt so
strongly about him that he threatens to leave if Martindale
stays on, Jack Talion tells him bluntly he isn't wanted, this
Mr Fever barges up to the Hall and has a row with him
because Martindale passes the time of day with his wife,
and even Sam Tiller's girlfriend launches straight into
some kind of argument when she bumps into him in the
village. It's incredible! Really makes you wonder what
he'd done.'

'I was thinking the same thing myself, earlier. I'd really
like to know just what all these people had against him.
And was it the same thing, or did they all have different,
individual grudges? The trouble is, I suspect it's not going
to be easy to find out.'

'Perhaps it doesn't matter, sir. Perhaps it'll turn out to
be a simple accident. Someone ran into him by chance—
the roads were very icy that night, remember—and couldn't
face owning up. So when they discovered he was dead
they just dragged him into the ditch and left him there.'

'Could be. Though in that case we haven't a chance of
finding out what happened unless a witness turns up or
someone actually walks into the police station and confesses.
Still, we'll just have to see. What did you say the Victors'
house is called?'

'Casa Mia. And it's a bungalow, at the far end of the
village. There's a For Sale sign outside, apparently.'

They were just entering Sutton and Lineham slowed
down. Like so many of the smaller villages in Kent it had
no obvious centre and consisted of a straggle of houses, a

pub, a garage, a church and a village school, now converted
into a private dwelling.

The severe shortage of building land in the South-East
meant that Casa Mia, like most new houses in rural areas,
had been squeezed into what had evidently been the
garden of the older house next door. It had been built,
Thanet guessed, by someone who had cherished the dream
of a villa in Spain and had had to settle for the next best
thing. Its Moorish arches and wrought-iron embellish-
ments looked as out of place in this very English setting as
a tart at a vicar's tea party.

Lineham parked the car in the road and they got out.
The inappropriately tall iron gates were flanked by brick
pillars topped with stone pineapples.

'Delusions of grandeur,' murmured Thanet.

A curtain twitched as they walked up the drive and
Thanet just had time to realise that the doorbell chimes
were playing 'Home Sweet Home' before the door opened.

'Mrs Victor?'

The woman patted her towering beehive of dyed blonde
hair and gave a coy smile, revealing suspiciously white and
even teeth. She was, he guessed, in her late fifties, and
many sessions on either sunbed or beach had tanned her
skin to a deep, rich brown, unfortunately drying it to the
texture of a prune in the process. She was carefully if
heavily made up and was wearing unsuitably youthful
clothes—tight trousers and flower-strewn sweater. Thanet
gave her a warm smile as he introduced himself. She
looked exactly as he had hoped she would, a woman with
too much time on her hands and little to do but take an
interest in her neighbors' affairs.

She peered anxiously over his shoulder down the drive
before inviting them in. 'I'm expecting my hubby home
any moment.'

It was clear that she didn't want the interview to begin
until he arrived. In the living-room the Spanish theme
continued, with heavily carved furniture in dark oak,
incongruously juxtaposed with the ubiquitous dralon three-
piece suite, and a garish painting of a Spanish flamenco
dancer over the synthetic dressed stone fireplace. Mrs
Victor fussed about, settling them comfortably and insisting

on providing them with unwanted cups of coffee. 'It's all ready, it won't take a tick.'

'Wonder if her husband was due home anyway?' said Lineham, when she had left.

'Or if she rang him after you set up the appointment, you mean?'

'And if so, why?'

Thanet shrugged. 'Perhaps she's the little woman type, doesn't feel comfortable unless her husband is at hand to give her moral support.'

Lineham's lip curled. 'I thought that sort of attitude had gone out with the ark.'

'I can't see why you're so surprised at the idea. There must be thousands of women— Isn't that a car in the drive?'

Lineham half rose to glance out of the window. 'Jaguar, E reg. Must be doing well.'

Outside in the hall footsteps went past towards the front door and there was a murmur of voices.

Of all the many different aspects of his work interviewing was the one Thanet enjoyed most and it was with a keen sense of anticipation that he stood up as the Victors entered the room.

10

'Inspector Thanet?' Hand outstretched, Victor advanced, picture of an honest citizen eager to do his duty.

Thanet, experienced in encounters of this kind, sensed a secret bubble of excitement in the man. Was it merely that Victor was relishing the drama of being involved, however peripherally, with the death which must be the talk of the village, or was there something more?

Short and burly with sparse curly hair and copious side-whiskers, he was formally dressed in dark suit and discreetly striped shirt. Only his tie, vividly patterned in orange and mustard-yellow whorls, betrayed the taste which had bought and furnished Casa Mia.

'The coffee's all ready,' murmured his wife, and by the time the three men were seated she had brought it in.

Victor began conventionally enough. 'Naturally the wife was wondering what you wanted to see her about.' He took a cautious sip of the scalding liquid. 'I mean, she told the policeman who called yesterday everything she knew about this Mr... What was his name?'

'Martindale.'

'That's right, yes. Which wasn't much. I mean, she'd never set eyes on him before Tuesday afternoon and at the time, of course, she didn't realise who he was. It was only when his coat was mentioned...'

'Black-and-white checked tweed,' said Mrs Victor, entering the conversation for the first time. 'Very nice, too.'

'Yes, Dor, we know that.' A hint of impatience, there. He turned back to Thanet. 'So...?'

'We just wanted to clear up one or two points, sir. Clarify your wife's impressions.'

'I see.'

Obviously he didn't, but he pressed gamely on. 'Well, any way we can help, of course . . .'

And there was that glint of excitement again, as if Victor was hugging some secret knowledge to himself. Thanet began to wonder if the man's presence had nothing to do with his wife and he was really here because he had a titbit of information to impart. If so, no doubt he would come out with it in his own time.

'Thank you. Now I understand, Mrs Victor, that on Tuesday afternoon you saw Mr Martindale twice?'

'Yes.' She put her coffee cup down on the low carved oak table beside her and looked at her husband, waited for his encouraging nod. 'I had to go to the post office, see, to get some stamps. It's at the far end of the village so of course I had to pass the garage. That was where I first saw this man, this Mr Martindale. At least, I suppose it was him?' She glanced doubtfully at her husband.

'Tell the Inspector what he looked like, Dor,' said Victor, as if encouraging a child who lacked confidence.

'He was in his late forties, early fifties, I should say. Medium height, brown curly hair, going a bit thin on top.' An involuntary glance at her husband's own sparse locks before she hastily averted her eyes. 'I didn't see him all that clearly then; it was later, after he'd been talking to Mrs Rankle, he passed quite close to me.'

Victor glanced at Thanet for confirmation and he nodded. 'Sounds like him.'

'I noticed him,' said Mrs Victor, getting into her stride, 'because of course he was a stranger and we don't get many around here, we're a bit off the beaten track. So naturally I wondered who he was. Especially . . .' She pulled herself up. 'Well, no, not especially, I suppose . . . But anyway, he was talking to Mrs Fever.'

Thanet, intrigued, tried an oblique approach. 'Mrs Fever is a friend of yours?'

'Oh no! It's just that . . .' She stopped, looked at her husband for help.

He sniggered and said, 'Fever has a reputation for being

jealous as hell. His wife can't so much as look at another man without him going off the deep end, so she tends to avoid little tête-à-têtes with anything in trousers.'

Interesting. 'You've actually seen him lose his temper over this?' Thanet wondered if Victor had made a pass at Mrs Fever himself, and had learnt about Fever's possessiveness the hard way.

'Not exactly. We don't mix much, in the village.' He glanced at his wife and gave a bitter little laugh. 'To be honest, they're not exactly a welcoming lot around here. Keep themselves to themselves and if you're a newcomer... Doreen and me've got fed up with it. We've decided to move back to Maidstone.'

'So how did you find out that Mr Fever was inclined to be jealous of his wife?'

'That was me,' said Mrs Victor. 'One day when my car was in for repair I had to go into Sturrenden on the bus and I heard two of the women from the village talking...'

'But you can tell by the way he watches her,' said Victor. 'We've been to one or two dos in the village, the church fête and that, and he never takes his eyes off of her.'

'So when you saw Mr Martindale talking to her on Tuesday afternoon, Mrs Victor, you were naturally intrigued?'

She nodded. 'Yes. That was another reason why I specially noticed him.'

'I see. Were you close enough to hear what they were saying?'

She shook her head with a tinge of regret. 'No.'

'She was filling her car with petrol, I believe you said?'

'That's right. Well, she wasn't actually doing it herself, Bert was. The garage attendant.'

'I see.' Good. With any luck Bert would be able to tell them more. 'And they were just passing the time of day, so far as you could tell.'

'Well, I'm not sure. I wouldn't put it quite like that. He seemed to be doing the talking and she was shaking her head.'

'As if he was trying to persuade her to do something?'

'Could have been. Something like that, anyway.'

'Were they talking long?'

'Just while her car was being filled up. I looked back when I got to the post office and she was just driving off.'

'Did you have the impression they knew each other?'

'Oh yes. Definitely.'

Thanet glanced at Lineham and raised his eyebrows. *Anything else?*

Lineham shook his head.

'Right, thank you. Now, I assume that it was when you came out of the post office that you saw him again, this time talking to Mrs Rankle?'

'That's right. When I went in Mrs Rankle was there, being served. She went out, I bought my stamps and when I went out again there they were, having this argument.'

'Where was this? Were they on the same side of the road as you?'

'Yes. He must've crossed over while I was inside.'

'How far away from you were they?'

She screwed up her face in concentration and glanced at her husband as she said doubtfully, 'Fifty yards?'

'Dor's not very good at distances,' said Victor with an apologetic little laugh.

'It doesn't matter. Were they near enough for you to hear what they were saying?'

'Not really, not most of it, anyway. But you could tell they were arguing. And I did hear Mrs Rankle say, "How you've got the cheek to show your face here again I just don't know."'

'She raised her voice, presumably? Yes. Did you hear any more?'

Mrs Victor shook her head regretfully. 'I was sticking the stamps on my envelopes before posting them and if I'd gone back along the pavement the way I'd come, well, I'd have had to pass quite close, you see, and it was so obvious they were rowing . . . It would have been embarrassing, trying to pretend I couldn't hear. And it would have looked a bit obvious if I'd crossed the road just to avoid them. I didn't know quite what to do, so in the end I just stayed where I was and made out it was taking a long time to stick the stamps on.'

'Yes, I see.' Pity, but still . . . 'So then what happened?'

'She went off, well, flounced, really, I suppose you'd say, in a temper. And he came on towards me and went into the post office. That was when I got a better look at him.'

'Did he seem upset?'

'Yes, he did a bit. Well, I mean, it'd be understandable, wouldn't it, after being told to your face you're not wanted.'

She and her husband exchanged glances. *We know all about being not wanted.*

'Is there anything else you can recall?'

A shake of the head. 'No, I don't think so.' Then another glance at her husband, a slight lift of the eyebrows. *Are you going to tell them?*

Might as well make it easy for him, Thanet decided. 'I believe you were out yesterday, when our man called, Mr Victor?'

'That's right, yes.'

'So is there anything you can add to your wife's statement?'

'Well there was something, as a matter of fact. Though I don't know if it's of any importance . . .'

'If you could tell us anyway . . .'

Victor passed the tip of his tongue over his upper lip and leaned forward, relishing his moment centre stage. 'I was in the pub on Monday night—'

'Sorry to interrupt, but I just want to make sure I've got this straight . . . You're talking now about the night before Mr Martindale had his accident?'

'Yes.'

Thanet remembered Delia Hamilton saying that Martindale had gone down to the pub that first evening, and had got back about nine. 'Go on.'

'Dor'd gone to her Keep Fit class in Ashford, so I went along for a drink, about eight it must've been. Place was pretty crowded, there was a darts match on. Anyway, this chap was at the bar, by himself.'

'Mr Martindale, you mean?'

'Yep. Though I didn't know it was him, if you get my meaning. At first I thought he was a stranger, just dropped in for a drink as he was passing through the village, then I began to realise there was more to it than that.'

'What do you mean?'

'Well, after a while it dawned on me that all the locals,

the older ones, anyway, were avoiding him. It was unnatural, like. They didn't look at him and when they wanted a refill they'd deliberately go to the end of the bar away from him.'

'How did he react?'

'Just sat there drinking as if he didn't notice what was happening. I wondered if I was imagining it at first, but after a while I was sure I wasn't and I began to feel sorry for him. I'd just made up my mind to go and stand next to him, have a chat, perhaps offer to buy him a pint, when Sam Tiller came in—he's groundsman up at the Hall.'

'Yes, I know. Go on.'

'Well, he comes in and goes straight to the bar, to the space next to this man. Martindale looks round and says, "It's Sam, isn't it? Sam Tiller! How are you?" Tiller looks at him and sort of freezes . . . I swear, if looks could kill . . . Tiller doesn't say a word, just moves away, to the other end of the bar. No one says anything, but all the locals were watching, to see what Martindale would do.'

'And what did he do?'

'Just finished up his drink and left.'

So, a public snub, thought Thanet. And more than that, a warning?

'What happened after that?'

'Sam paid for his drink and went across to join some of his pals.'

'Nothing was said, that you could hear?'

'No. But one of them clapped him on the back and said something, and they all laughed.'

'I see. Well thank you very much, both of you. You've been very helpful.'

'There's just one point . . .' said Lineham, as they all stood up. 'When you came home on Monday night, Mr Victor, did you happen to mention this incident to your wife?'

'Yes, I did. Well, like I said, I felt sorry for him.'

'I was just wondering why you didn't mention it to the PC who interviewed you yesterday, Mrs Victor?'

She looked confused. 'I don't know. I didn't think . . . He said they were trying to trace Mr Martindale's movements during the day he died, so I just told him what I'd seen.'

'But when I got home from work and heard what had happened,' said Victor, 'that this chap was dead and the police had been round asking questions, I thought perhaps I ought to tell you. If you hadn't made this appointment I was going to give you a ring.'

'Quite right, too,' said Thanet. 'We need all the help we can get.'

In the car Lineham said, 'What d'you think, sir? Think Mrs Fever was an old flame of Martindale's?'

'Possibly. Anyway, it certainly confirms that both Fever and Tiller have some explaining to do, doesn't it? What time is the appointment with the Fevers?'

'Twelve-fifteen.'

Thanet glanced at his watch. Twenty to twelve. 'Just time for a word with that mechanic first.'

11

The local garage did nothing to enhance the meagre charms of Sutton, being no more than a large weatherboarded hut tacked on to the end of a row of cottages in the centre of the village. At some point the peg tiles had been stripped off the roof and replaced with green-painted corrugated iron. Outside were two antiquated petrol pumps with a notice saying PLEASE HOOT FOR SERVICE, inside was the usual acrid smell of oil and metal.

Business did not appear to be thriving. There was only one car in the workshop and one pair of legs sticking out from beneath it. Bert, presumably.

Lineham advanced. 'Bert?' He stooped, peered underneath the car. 'Sorry, I don't know your surname.'

The legs slid forward, a torso emerged clad in mechanic's overalls, then a head.

'Seller.' The man squinted up. 'What d'you want?'

He was in his thirties, Thanet guessed, with longish, greasy black hair and pinched ferrety features.

'Police, Mr Seller.' Lineham held out his warrant card.

The man glanced warily from Lineham to Thanet and back again. 'If it's anything to do with the business you'll have to wait for Mr Stake. He's gone into Ashford to pick up a spare part.'

'No, it's nothing to do with the business. It's you we wanted to see.'

'Oh . . . ?' Seller scrambled to his feet as Lineham introduced himself.

Thanet was intrigued by the overtones of wariness in Seller's voice. Had Lineham noticed?

Seller crossed to a bench, put down the spanner he was holding and wiped his hands on an oily rag.

'We're looking into the death of a Mr Martindale, the night before last.'

'The hit and run.'

'Yes. During the afternoon he was seen talking to Mrs Fever here at the garage.'

He was nodding. 'That's right. She'd stopped for petrol, and he came over.'

'Could you tell us about the conversation, please?'

'Well . . .' He squinted into the middle distance, considering. 'I was just starting to fill Mrs Fever's car when he came across.'

'Across the road, you mean?'

'Yeah. He was walking towards the post office, on the other side of the road. I'd noticed him because he was a stranger and we don't get many around here. Anyway, he must've spotted Mrs Fever because suddenly he stops, looks, and then crosses the road. He nods at me then he bends down and says through the car window, "It is Yvonne, isn't it?" Well, she looks up and goes white as a sheet. She doesn't say a word, but it's obvious she'd recognised him and he says, "Yes, it's me. Leo."

'She still doesn't say nothing, but she opens the door and gets out, and moves away a bit with a look at me as if to say, "I don't want him to hear this."' Seller grinned. 'Out of luck, wasn't she? Hear a pin drop at fifty yards, I can.'

'So what happened then?' said Lineham.

Seller glanced from one to the other, obviously gratified by their rapt attention.

'The chap runs after her, doesn't he? "Aren't you pleased to see me?" he says.'

'Where on earth have you sprung from, Leo?'
'Oh come on, 'Vonne. What sort of a welcome is that?'
'Why have you come? What do you want?'
'Which question would you like me to answer first?'
'Leo, please!'

'It's quite simple, my sweet . . .'

'Don't call me that!'

'Very well. It's quite simple. I've come home for good.'

'Oh God, no . . . But why? Why now, after all these years?'

'Shall we say I recently learned something to my advantage?'

'You mean, you didn't know your father was dead?'

'Not until last week.'

'I'd finished filling up with petrol by then and Mrs Fever asked me how much it was. She paid me and I had to go into the office to fetch her change,' said Seller regretfully. 'Then the phone rang and I had to answer it. When I went out again he was trying to persuade her to go to tea with him. For old times' sake, he said.'

'Did she agree?'

'No. He was still trying to get her to change her mind when she got into the car and drove off. Pretty upset she looked, too.'

'Then what?'

'He looks at me, grins, shrugs and says, "Ah well, you can't win 'em all." Then he crosses the road and goes on his way towards the post office.'

Thanet was surprised that Seller had been so forthcoming. Initially he had thought that Lineham might have problems in getting the man to talk. He remembered Seller's uneasiness when Martindale was first mentioned. Was all this loquacity a smokescreen for something else? He watched carefully as Lineham continued the questioning, and became convinced that the man was hiding something. Seller had apparently worked in the village for only two years and at first had had no idea who Martindale was.

'When did you find out?' said Lineham.

'I mentioned it to Mr Stake when he came back.'

'Mentioned what, exactly?'

'That this Leo character had been chatting Mrs Fever up.'

'And he knew who he was, straight away?'

'Oh yes. Said, "Leo Martindale back? I hadn't heard. That's a turn-up for the book."'

'Mr Stake has lived here a long time, presumably.'

'All his life. His dad had the garage before him.'

'How old is he?'

Seller looked surprised, shrugged. 'Fiftyish?'

Contemporary with Martindale, then, thought Thanet.

'What else did he say, when you told him?'

'Not much. Just said he hoped he wasn't going to start causing trouble again.'

'What sort of trouble?'

'He wouldn't say.'

Lineham glanced at Thanet, raised his eyebrows.

'Mr Seller,' said Thanet, 'did you by any chance mention this incident to anyone else?'

On target! Seller's expression changed and he shuffled his feet, looked uncomfortable.

'Yes, Mr Seller?'

Seller was still hesitating.

'Let me guess, then,' said Thanet. 'You thought you might stir things up a bit by telling Mr Fever, didn't you?'

'He's such a prick!' Seller burst out. 'Always throwing his weight about, thinks he's so great! I thought it would do him good, take him down a peg or two. How did I know he'd react like that?'

'Like what? When was this?'

'Outside the Drovers. I went along for a pint, after work. I ran into him in the car park.'

'So what, exactly, did you say to him?'

'Nothing much! Just said I'd seen an old friend of his wife's, that afternoon. The man's a nutcase!'

'What did he do?'

'Grabbed me by the collar and said, "What the hell do you mean by that?"'

'And?'

'I tried to back-pedal, play it down, but he wouldn't have it. He made me tell him what I'd heard.'

'And then?'

'He got straight back into his car and drove off.'

'In the direction of the Hall?'

Seller nodded sullenly. 'Like I said, he's a nutcase.'

Thanet considered that after such deliberate malice Seller had been lucky to get away so lightly. He said so to Lineham, outside.

'I should think Fever was much more interested in tackling Martindale, sir. He must have rushed straight up to the Hall to have it out with him.'

'Sounds like it. But in any case Martindale was alive and well for some time after Fever tackled him at—what time was it? Six-fifteen?'

'Yes! he had dinner with his sister and Hamilton after that.'

'Of course, it's always possible that Fever went back later. Though that still wouldn't put him behind the wheel of the van.'

'We're still not a hundred per cent sure that it was the van, are we, sir? When d'you think forensic will come up with the confirmation?'

'The Super said this afternoon, if we're lucky. If not, tomorrow morning. I'd be very surprised indeed if it doesn't turn out to be the vehicle we're after. Anyway, we'll see what Fever has to say for himself. It's nearly a quarter past, we'd better get a move on.'

The Fevers lived in a large modern house set in generous gardens next to the dilapidated range of farm buildings from which he ran his haulage business.

'Wonder how on earth he got planning permission for that,' said Lineham as they parked on the wide gravelled sweep of drive. 'Bet a bit of palm-greasing went on there.'

'Not necessarily, Mike. If you look at the centre section you'll see the brick is older than the rest. I think it's an ambitious conversion.'

'Pretty well done, then,' said Lineham grudgingly.

Thanet awaited the sergeant's next remark with an inward smile. It came.

'Can't be short of a penny,' said Lineham. 'There must be money in haulage.'

'Thinking of buying a lorry and setting yourself up?' Thanet rang the door bell and this time was rewarded with a rendering of the opening bars of 'My Old Man Said Follow The Van'!

'Very appropriate,' said Lineham with a grin.

The door was opened by Toby Fever, Tessa Hamilton's boyfriend. 'Come in.'

A good-looking young man, thought Thanet, nagged once again by the feeling that he might have seen him somewhere before. He wondered what the two families thought of Toby and Tessa's friendship. For various reasons, not much, he imagined.

'I'll tell Dad you're here.' Toby opened a door to the right of the hall, ushered them into the room then went off towards the back of the house.

It was a large sitting-room, at least twenty feet square, with windows, overlooking the garden on three sides. It had considerable potential, Thanet thought, but whoever chose the furnishings had played too safe with neutrals and pastels; although the thick carpet, heavy curtains and three-piece suite were of good quality the effect was dull and lifeless. Mrs Fever, he guessed, lacked sufficient confidence in her own taste to indulge it.

'Inspector Thanet?'

For the second time today Thanet was greeted by an outstretched hand. In the case of a man at whom the finger had been pointed, like Fever, such bonhomie invariably made him suspicious.

And Fever himself was a surprise.

It was interesting, Thanet thought, how one could build up an image of someone through other people's accounts of him, and how completely wrong one could be. He'd had a very clear picture of Fever as a great lumberjack of a man, overpowering as much by his physical size as by the force of his personality. Apart from his age, which Thanet guessed to be around fifty, the reality was completely different. Fever was at most five five in height, and wiry as a whippet. He was wearing expensive casual clothes— slightly baggy gaberdine trousers and high-necked cashmere sweater over soft-collared shirt. Beneath the surface affability he was, Thanet thought, distinctly wary.

A woman had come into the room behind him.

'And this is my wife! I believe you did want to talk to her as well?'

Like the Princess in the fairy tale guarded by a dragon,

Thanet had expected Mrs Fever to be beautiful and she did not disappoint him. Well, perhaps not exactly beautiful, he corrected himself, but very attractive, certainly. She was perhaps an inch or two taller than her husband, with a beautifully proportioned figure, a cloud of dark hair and soft deep-velvet-brown eyes. She seemed to exude not sex-appeal but something much more subtle, a fragrant femininity enhanced by the flared suede skirt which flowed about her as she walked, the high-heeled shoes and silk blouse. She might not give her husband cause for jealousy but Thanet could understand his fear of losing her to another man.

They all sat down, Fever and his wife side by side on a settee.

'As you've no doubt realised, we're looking into the death of Mr Leo Martindale,' said Thanet. 'And at the moment we're trying to build up a picture of his movements on Tuesday.'

'Excuse me interrupting, Inspector,' said Fever. 'But why? By all accounts it was a hit and run accident. Surely you ought to be concentrating on motorists passing through the village that night?"

'Among other things, yes, we are. Unfortunately it looks as though it might not be as simple as that. It's difficult to see how Mr Martindale could have got into the position in which he was lying without, shall we say, a little help.'

Mrs Fever's eyes widened as she understood the implications of what he was saying and her hands, clasped together in her lap, tightened their grip on each other. Thanet saw the knuckles whiten.

Fever's eyes narrowed and he sat forward. 'Now wait a minute. What are you saying? Are you implying that it wasn't an accident, that . . . ?'

'We're just trying to find out exactly what did happen. It's possible that it was an accident, that the driver panicked when he got out to investigate and discovered that Mr Martindale was dead, moved the body into the ditch to prevent anyone else running over him.'

'But it's also possible that he was deliberately run down. That is what you're getting at, isn't it?'

Fever was becoming agitated.

Here we go again, thought Thanet. The interview was already beginning to follow a pattern that had become all too familiar over the last couple of days. 'Anything is possible, Mr Fever. You must see that at this stage we have to keep an open mind...'

'Don't give me that guff!' Fever sprang up and began to pace about. 'That's really why you're here, isn't it? You heard I had a bit of a barney with Martindale on Tuesday and you want to pin his death on me!'

Mrs Fever made an inarticulate little sound of distress then put out her hand towards her husband and said, 'Lewis, please.'

Fever ignored her. 'Well you won't get away with it! If every time two men had an argument one of them is accused of murder, the place would be littered with corpses!'

'We're only interested in one corpse, Mr Fever, Mr Martindale's. As I say, we're not yet satisfied that his death was an accident and we are only doing our duty in trying to find out precisely what did happen.'

'Duty! Is this what you call duty, coming into a man's home and accusing him of murder!'

'Mr Fever!' Thanet was capable of showing steel when he wanted to and had no intention of being browbeaten into going away without what he had come for. 'I am accusing no one of anything. Would you please sit down and allow us to have a rational conversation, or—'

Fever ran his hands wildly through his hair. 'Rational! What's rational about—'

For the second time in two days, Thanet was driven to a course of action he normally regarded as the last resort. He stood up. 'Very well. If that's the way you want it. I shall have to ask you to accompany us back to headquarters, for questioning.'

Mrs Fever jumped up and grasped her husband by the sleeve. 'Lewis, please, they're only doing what they have to...'

He shook her off and stood glaring at Thanet.

There was a tense silence and then he plumped down on the settee, folding his arms belligerently across his chest. 'I don't seem to have much choice in the matter, do I?'

'On the contrary,' said Thanet, sitting down again. 'The choice is yours. Here . . . or there.'

'Here, there, what's the difference? In any case I have nothing to hide, so for God's sake let's get on with it, shall we?'

In the event, there was little more that they could add to what Thanet already knew. Mrs Fever confirmed the substance of the conversation with Martindale at the garage, studiously avoiding looking at her husband while doing so, and Fever, keeping his volatile temper barely under control, gave a brief account of his visit to warn Martindale to keep away from his wife, to frighten him off.

'You've all known each other for years, I gather, since before Mr Martindale went away?'

Fever's face went curiously wooden. 'That's right, yes.'

Mrs Fever cast an anxious little sideways glance at him. 'You were friends, at that time?'

'Friends! Leo didn't have any friends, believe me.'

'Why not? what did people have against him?' Thanet didn't have much hope of an honest answer and he didn't get one.

'Let's just say he had the knack of putting people's backs up.'

And Fever gave a smile that was more a baring of the teeth, reminding Thanet of Jack Talion's reaction.

Thanet stood up. 'That sounds like an understatement to me.'

They all rose. 'Think what you like,' said Fever. 'That's the way it was. But if you're looking for a scapegoat, Inspector, you won't find him in this house.'

'Charming,' said Lineham, when the front door had slammed behind them. 'D'you think he's our man, sir?'

Thanet shrugged. 'As I said before, not unless we can put him behind the wheel of that van. And even then . . . I don't know, Mike. I suppose I can see him running Martindale down while he was still all steamed up, but not calmly sitting about considering it and going back to do it in cold blood. We'll just have to see. What's next on the agenda?'

'Mrs Hamilton at 1.30.'

It was now 12.45.

'Time we visited the local, I think, Mike.'

12

Like so many country pubs the Drovers had suffered from modernisation in the sixties and seventies. The ancient floorboards had been covered with heavily patterned carpets, sections of wall faced with synthetic boarding and the bar tarted up with a collection of dangling keyrings. At this hour on a weekday there were only three other customers. The food, however, was good and the beer acceptable.

Thanet took an appreciative mouthful of roast beef sandwich seasoned with French mustard. 'What did he say?'

Lineham had been deputed to ask the landlord why he had not mentioned Martindale's ostracism by the locals on Monday night.

'Same old story. "Nobody asked me..."' Lineham loaded his crusty French bread with butter, cheese and pickle. 'Think the Super will turn up?'

Thanet grimaced. 'Hope not.'

Lineham grinned. '"Perhaps there'll be a mini crime wave in Sturrenden and he'll be too busy.'

'I'll pretend I didn't hear that remark, Mike.'

Lineham chewed thoughtfully for a while and then said, 'What about this van, sir? Think there's any hope of proving which of them was driving it?'

'Ridiculous, isn't it? Six people have keys and we already know four of them drove it on Tuesday night—as well as Mrs Rankle, who borrowed it to check on her son.'

Lineham ticked them off on his fingers. 'Mrs Hamilton

went to fetch Adam from the station at 7.25. When she got back at about 7.40, Mr Talion used it to check on the sheep that had got out. He took about—how long did he say?'

'Twenty-five minutes or so.'

'So he would have got back at around ten past eight. Then it stood idle for twenty minutes or so until Sam Tiller went to pick up Mrs Rankle. Then at 9.15 or thereabouts she borrowed it . . .'

'Passing the entrance gates of the Hall on her way. And she wasn't exactly on friendly terms with Martindale, by the sound of it. I wonder what she had against him?'

'Think there's any hope of finding out?'

'Not much, the way things are going. It's like trying to get blood out of a stone, trying to find out why they were all so anti Martindale, isn't it?'

'Never mind. As you would say, it's early days yet.'

Thanet grinned. Lineham's unfailing optimism was one of the reasons why he enjoyed working with him. 'True. Anyway, you were saying . . .'

'Sam Tiller drove it next, to take Mrs Rankle home and then go home himself. Leaving the pub at . . . ?'

'Ten-thirty, I think.'

'And finally Mr Hamilton used it at 11.15, to go and pick up Tessa, when the Range Rover wouldn't start. Think that's true, sir?'

'We must check with her. But I shouldn't think he'd risk involving her in lying for him.'

'So really its movements are pretty well accounted for, except for twenty minutes or so between ten and half-past eight and the three quarters of an hour between 10.30 and 11.15. Time enough in both cases for any one of them to have driven it down to the gates and back.'

'Yes, but who? Let's see, what did they all claim to be doing between those times, Mike?'

'Mr Hamilton said he was working in his office during the earlier period. He must have been alone or he would presumably have mentioned that someone was with him. He could easily have slipped out. He and Mrs Hamilton stood to lose a packet, if Martindale had claimed what was rightfully his. Say Hamilton looked out of the window and happened to see Martindale leaving the house, to go to the pub, perhaps...'

'I doubt that he would have gone to the pub, Mike, after getting the cold shoulder the night before.'

'Oh, I don't know. He sounds pretty thick-skinned to me. Anyway, he needn't have been going to the pub. He could have been meeting someone...'

'Who, for example?'

'I don't know. I'm only making suggestions, sir.' Lineham was beginning to sound plaintive. 'He could just have been going for a walk.'

Thanet shrugged. 'True. All right, Mike, go on.'

'So,' said Lineham, leaning forward eagerly as he warmed to his theory, 'Hamilton sees the perfect opportunity to get rid of him. Everything's quiet, the guests are at dinner... He gets to the van without being seen and drives off. He catches up with Martindale at the bottom of the drive and runs him down. He gets out to check that Martindale is dead, then drags him into the ditch so he won't be found by anyone else coming in or out of the Hall gates that night. Into the van, up the drive, back into his study and he's home and dry. It need only have taken ten or fifteen minutes in all. What d'you think, sir?'

Thanet took out his pipe, tapped it, inspected it, blew through it and began to fill it. 'Unless it was a straightforward accident, I should think it must have happened like that. But the trouble is, you could apply the same scenario to any one of them. We don't know what Mrs Hamilton was doing just then, or Sam Tiller, or Jack Talion...'

'Or the Byfleets, for that matter,' Lineham conceded gloomily. 'He's supposed to have got back from Gatwick about eight, so they were both around between ten and half-past eight as well. And the van stands near where they live in the stable yard.'

'Unfortunately the van was conveniently accessible to the lot of them,' said Thanet with a sigh. 'We've got a tremendous amount of checking to do, Mike. It would help if we had some idea what time Martindale was knocked down, but as yet we haven't a clue. After that early dinner, which was over by about seven, no one seems to have seen him.'

'Except for Mrs Byfleet. She was seen coming out of his room at 7.15, remember.'

'I know, but it could just have been a routine check. The room might well have been empty.'

'We both thought she was lying about something.'

'I know. Ah well, come on Mike, drink up. I don't think Mrs Hamilton is the type to appreciate being kept waiting.'

'Don't suppose we'll get much out of her,' grumbled Lineham.

'You never know. We have got one or two cards up our sleeve, remember,' though Thanet wasn't feeling too optimistic about the coming interview. Mrs Hamilton wouldn't easily be manoeuvred into telling them anything she didn't wish to divulge.

In the car park Thanet came to a sudden halt. 'It's just occurred to me . . .'

'What?'

'The van. Apart from the twenty minutes or so when Mrs Rankle used it, it was standing out here in the pub car park all evening, between say 8.45 and 10.30. During that time anyone could have borrowed it and unless they were actually spotted no one would have been any the wiser.'

Lineham groaned.

Delia Hamilton was waiting for them in her office, a pleasant, sunny little room tastefully furnished with antiques and country house chintzes.

She rose to greet them. 'I hope this won't take too long, Inspector. How are you getting on? Have you found out what happened?'

She was as immaculately groomed as ever, her hair in a smooth chignon today, wearing a simple, elegant dress of raspberry-coloured wool with long sleeves and a cowl neck. Pearls and a beautiful enamelled antique fob watch completed the English country lady image.

'Not yet, ma'am. But don't worry, we shall.'

She waved them to two upright chairs already in position in front of her desk and sat down behind it. She raised her eyebrows expectantly. 'Well?'

'One or two things have emerged . . .'

'Such as?'

'I understand that there was an argument that night, between a Mr Fever, who lives locally, and your brother.'

'So I believe.'

'Can you tell us anything about it?'

'I wasn't present, so no, I'm afraid I can't.'

'Can you think of any reason why Mr Fever should have been so angry with your brother?'

'I haven't the faintest idea.' She waved a hand, dismissing the matter as of no importance. 'Fever has the reputation of having what is commonly called a short fuse. I suppose Leo had done something to annoy him. I shouldn't place too much importance on it, if I were you.'

'Mr Fever's wife, Yvonne . . .'

Delia Hamilton's delicately arched brows rose again. 'What about her?'

'Your brother seemed to know her. We understand they met in the village on Tuesday, and he greeted her like an old friend.'

'Sutton is a very small community, Inspector. Yvonne Fever has lived here all her life. As children we all knew each other.'

'Was there anything special between them?'

'Special?'

'Was she his girlfriend, before he went away?'

Delia laughed. 'I wouldn't put it quite like that. Let's just say that Leo was a very attractive young man and I've no doubt that at one time or another he took most of the local girls out. But a special girlfriend . . .' She shook her head. 'It wouldn't have been suitable.'

Because of the difference in class, presumably. A rather naïve view, Thanet felt. He was pretty certain that if Leo had fancied a girl he wouldn't have hesitated to break the rules. Besides, he suspected that the question had made Delia Hamilton uneasy. Because of Yvonne Fever, or had there been another scandal to do with Leo and a local girl? Sam Tiller's daughter, perhaps, if he had one? Or Jack Talion's?

'So to your knowledge there is no particular reason why Mr Fever had a grudge against your brother?'

She shook her head. 'No.'

'What about Sam Tiller?'

'Sam Tiller?' Briefly, she looked disconcerted.

'Someone overheard Sam Tiller telling you that if your brother stayed, he would leave.'

A flash of anger, quickly suppressed. At being put in the difficult position of having to explain, presumably. 'You shouldn't listen to gossip, Inspector. You can't believe half of what you hear.'

'You deny that this conversation took place, then?'

'I didn't say that.'

'Or that Sam Tiller did in fact present you with this ultimatum?'

'I'm the one who presents ultimatums around here, Inspector.'

'You haven't answered my question.'

She hated being pinned down like this, obviously wasn't used to having anyone press her for an answer which she didn't want to give.

'What question was that?' But there was the beginning of resignation in her eyes. She could see he wasn't going to let her wriggle out of it.

Thanet was rather enjoying this duel of wits. 'Did Sam Tiller tell you that if your brother stayed, he would have to hand in his resignation?'

'What if he did? What possible relevance could it have?'

'Did he, Mrs Hamilton?'

Anger sparked in her eyes as she capitulated. 'If it's so important for you to know . . . Yes, he did.'

But the battle was only half won. Thanet still had to find out what he really wanted to know. 'Why was that?'

She shrugged, lifting elegant shoulders. 'How should I know?'

'*Do* you know?' he pressed.

'I've no doubt he had his reasons.'

'What were they?'

Her self-control was admirable but her fury and tension showed in the unnatural rigidity of her posture, the clenching of the muscles along her jawline.

Thanet waited. Was she going to tell him, would he have to press her further or would she lie? It was, he felt, absolutely crucial that he win this battle. It would be the first crack in the barrier of silence which everyone who knew Martindale seemed to put up when being questioned about the general hostility towards him.

He allowed the silence to prolong itself for a little while longer then sighed. 'Mrs Hamilton,' he said gently. 'You're not really asking me to believe that if you didn't already know, you wouldn't have asked why Sam found the idea of working for your brother so unacceptable?'

'I'm not asking you to believe or disbelieve anything.'

Thanet tried a different tack. 'I'm beginning to wonder if you really do want us to find out about your brother's death.'

That had stung. Her lips tightened. 'You can't fool me, Inspector. You don't believe anything of the sort. You're just trying to goad me into telling you what you want to know. If it's so important, why don't you ask Sam himself?'

'If you don't tell me, I shall. But I assume that as you're so keen to protect him you really don't believe he can be involved. In which case you would be doing him a good turn by telling me, instead of my having to ask him straight out. I assume that it is a matter which has caused him some distress, in the past?'

Still no answer.

'I shan't give up until I find out, you know.'

Silence. She rose with an exasperated sigh and went to stand looking out of the window with her back to them.

Thanet waited, glancing at Lineham, who grinned and raised a triumphant thumb. Thanet pulled down the corners of his mouth and shrugged. *We mustn't count our chickens...*

Finally she turned to face them, leaning back against the windowsill. Sunlight haloed her hair. 'Just why is it so important?'

'We don't know that it is. It's just that it could be.'

'Because you suspect Sam of running Leo down.'

'It's one possibility among many.'

She gave a wry smile and returned to her seat. 'Well, Inspector, I can see that as you say you're not the type to give up. As you will have gathered, I don't like talking about my employees behind their backs. In my view loyalty is a two-way process. But I suppose you might as well hear the truth from someone who will give you an unbiased account of it.'

And a vested interest in diverting attention away from herself, Thanet reminded himself as she began to speak. But he had won!

'Sam wasn't always in such a . . . well, menial position. He once ran his own farm. It was only a small farm, but it had been in his family for several generations. . . . He also had a passionate and life-long ambition, to breed a prize bull. Oh, you may well smile, Inspector, but believe me there was no more serious subject in the world to Sam.

'Well, to skip all the years of trial and error, of complete failure and near misses, and to cut a long story short, in the end he did it. His bull won the prize of Supreme Champion at the Royal Show at Stoneleigh. It's the most prestigious prize of all and Sam was walking on air. Stud fees, he knew, would make him a rich man, but best of all was the knowledge that he had done it, he alone by his own efforts had made it. You understand what I mean?'

Thanet nodded.

'The week after the show my dear brother left open the gate of the field in which the bull was kept. I don't know if you've ever seen one of these creatures, Inspector, but believe me they are massive. It was unfortunate that an articulated lorry happened to be coming along at the time. The bull ran straight out into its path. The animal wasn't killed outright but it was so badly injured that it had to be put down. You can imagine how Sam felt.'

'It was carelessness on your brother's part?'

'Oh I don't think it was deliberate, if that's what you mean. But it was carelessness, yes, sheer, criminal, absolutely inexcusable carelessness. My father paid heavily in compensation, tried to smooth things over, but of course it couldn't make up to Sam for all those years of singleminded endeavour. It just about broke his heart, finished him. He couldn't face starting all over again. He let things slide, the money dwindled and dwindled and in the end he went bankrupt. Just about then his wife died and he went to

live with his daughter. For years he got occasional jobs as
tractor driver or farm labourer, and then when my father
died and I decided to turn this place into a hotel I needed
someone to look after the grounds. There was accommoda-
tion available in the stable block and I felt an obligation to
Sam . . . He took some persuading but by then there was
friction with his son-in-law and he was tempted, as I
hoped he might be, by the prospect of independence.
He's been here ever since.'

'I see.' Thanet did see. Long years of bitterness could
shrivel a man's soul. To Tiller the prospect of working for
the man who had ruined him would have been unendurable.
Faced with having to abandon for the second time the life
he had built for himself and presented with the opportunity for revenge he could well have succumbed to temptation.

"Oh, I know what you're thinking, Inspector. It's why I
didn't want to tell you. You're thinking that if the opportunity presented itself Sam might well have been tempted to
run Leo down. But he's not like that. He's a good man,
kind . . .'

Remembering Tiller's defensiveness, his aggression and
hostility, Thanet wasn't so sure. He said as much to
Lineham, outside.

'I agree. Though how we'd ever be able to prove it, if it
was him—' Lineham broke off. 'Oh, no . . .'

Thanet turned to look. A police Land Rover was coming
up the drive. It was just close enough for him to recognise
the passenger.

Superintendent Draco had arrived.

13

Draco sprang out of the Land Rover and came bouncing towards them across the gravel. Energy emanated from him in almost visible waves. 'Ah, there you are, Thanet. How's it going?'

'We're just going to have a word with the groundsman, Sam Tiller, sir.'

They waited while two of the guests, a middle-aged couple dressed for a country walk in wellington boots and anoraks, came out of the hotel and passed them, casting curious glances. Then Thanet gave a brief account of the conversation with Mrs Hamilton.

A delighted smile spread across Draco's face. 'That's a new one. Revenge for the death of a prize bull, eh? Thought I'd heard them all, but this really takes the biscuit.'

They headed for the stable yard.

'Even if Tiller did run Mr Martindale down we're going to have a hard time proving it. Have you heard anything from forensic yet, sir?'

'No. I was on to them again just before I left. Usual story, snowed under with work etc. But they promise the results by tomorrow.'

Draco was glancing about curiously as they walked. He looked as though he was thoroughly enjoying himself.

Thanet again remembered wondering, when Draco first came, how long the Superintendent was going to tie himself to his desk. He hoped this visit wasn't heralding a new era of involvement on the Superintendent's part in the day-to-day progress of cases in his division.

'There was one point, though.' Draco fished in his pocket, produced a piece of paper. 'Bentley thought you might be interested to know that Mr . . .' He consulted the paper. 'Mr Talion had sacked a farmhand a couple of weeks back. Here's his name and address.' He handed the paper to Thanet. 'He thought it might be useful to interview him, in view of the fact that Talion and Martindale had had a row and you hadn't been able to find out why. He thought the man might possibly know the reason for any animosity between them and if he's still feeling sore he might be tempted to talk. I told him to go ahead. I hope that's OK by you.'

It wasn't. Thanet did not appreciate Draco giving his men orders. Who knew where it would end? He swallowed his resentment and said non-committally, 'It could be useful.' But again, it might not. It depended, Thanet thought, on how long the man had lived in the area and how much he knew about the grudge which Talion evidently harboured against Martindale. Still, he admitted reluctantly, Draco was right, it was worth following up.

The stable yard appeared deserted.

'He may be in the outbuilding where we interviewed him yesterday,' suggested Lineham.

They walked across and knocked. A moment later the door opened. Tiller scowled. 'Oh, it's you again. What d'you want this time?'

'Another word, if you don't mind. This is Superintendent Draco.'

Was that a flash of fear as Tiller glanced at Draco? If so, it was immediately replaced by the old sneering belligerence. 'Come to arrest me, have you?'

'Just a word, as I said.' Thanet was at his most benign. Grudgingly, Tiller stood back.

He had been cleaning his tools, sharpening a spade with a whetstone. Not much could be done outside in this weather, Thanet supposed. It was a good time for ensuring that equipment was in good order for the rush of work when spring arrived.

Draco's arrival had given Thanet little time to consider

how he was going to tackle Tiller. He felt inhibited by the Superintendent's presence, despite the fact that Draco had tactfully withdrawn into the background and was pretending to examine the tools arrayed on hooks on the walls. With an effort he tried to put the Superintendent out of his mind, pretend that he wasn't there.

He decided to take the bull by the horns. Suppressing a wry smile at the appropriateness of the metaphor he said, 'You told Mrs Hamilton that if Mr Martindale stayed on here, you would leave.'

Tiller leaned back against his work bench and folded his arms. 'So?'

'We know why, Mr Tiller.'

A spasm—of what? anger? fear?—briefly contorted the man's features. 'If you're so clever I don't know why you bother with pretending you want to talk to me. Go on, admit it, you've made up your minds I ran him down, haven't you?' His gaze encompassed all three policemen then focused again on Thanet.

Thanet sighed. 'If my mind were as closed as yours, Mr Tiller, I'd have a string of false arrests to my credit. And that's not the way I work. I repeat, we're merely trying to find out the truth. And I would like to point out that if you were not involved in Mr Martindale's death it is in your own interest for you to cooperate with us as fully as possible.'

Silence while Tiller considered the logic of what Thanet had said. Finally he unfolded his arms and took a pipe from his pocket.

Thanet immediately wanted to follow suit. If Draco hadn't been present he might in fact have done so. Such a small act of sharing a mutual enjoyment could create a common bond and lower the emotional temperature of a difficult interview by several degrees. Once again he cursed Draco's presence.

Tiller was stuffing tobacco into the bowl with practised fingers, taking matches from his pockets. He waited until he had lit up and then, gazing up at the coils of smoke swirling lazily above his head, said, 'You could have a point there.'

Thanet knew when to keep silent and he continued to

wait patiently, acutely conscious of Draco behind him. He could rely on Lineham, but the Superintendent was a different matter. Patience was not his strong point and if he said or did anything at this crucial moment . . . He wouldn't, surely? Thanet reminded himself that Draco hadn't reached his present rank without good reason.

Tiller's gaze slowly descended to linger on Thanet's face. 'All right, then. What d'you want to know?'

There was a distinct easing of the atmosphere. But they were not there yet. Slowly now, Thanet warned himself. 'We're still trying to check the movements of the van last night. You said you left here at 8.30 to pick up Mrs Rankle?'

Tiller nodded, puffing rhythmically at his pipe.

'And left the pub at around 10.30, to take her home before returning here?'

Another nod.

'When did you last use it, earlier in the evening?'

Tiller considered, then took his pipe out of his mouth. ''Bout five o'clock. To run Andy home—the young lad who helps me. He usually cycles, but his bike's out of commission at the moment.'

'And after that the van stood out in the yard, as usual?'

''S right.'

'Do you know of anyone else who used it, that night?'

Tiller hesitated.

No point in reversing the man's mood and making him dig his heels in again out of mistaken loyalty to Delia Hamilton. 'Mrs Hamilton told us she used it to fetch her son from the station just before half-past seven. Also, Mr Talion used it to check on some sheep that had got out on to the road, some twenty minutes later. After that it stood idle until you left at 8.30, so far as we know . . .'

No response.

Thanet tried again. 'Do you know if anyone used it either before Mrs Hamilton or during those twenty minutes between ten and half-past eight?'

Tiller was shaking his head. 'Not so far as I know. Someone could have, of course.'

'Does your cottage overlook the yard?'

Tiller nodded, eyes narrowing.

'Even if you didn't actually see anyone getting into or out of it, or driving it, did you happen to glance out at any point and notice that it was gone?'

Tiller considered. Finally he shook his head. 'Earlier on I was having my tea in the kitchen at the back of the house. Then I watched telly until about eight, when I went upstairs to have a shave and get ready to go out. And it was dark, of course, the curtains was drawn.'

Pity. 'Did you hear anything, then, while you were in your bedroom? An engine start up?'

'Nah. Had the radio on.'

'What about later on, after you got home? Did you hear anything then?'

Tiller started to shake his head again, then stopped. 'There was something,' he said slowly.

'When was that?'

'Soon after I got into bed. I was just dozing off. Must have been about a quarter past eleven. I heard a car start up.'

'Ah, yes, that was probably Mr Hamilton. Miss Hamilton had borrowed the Range Rover and she couldn't get it to start. Mr Hamilton went to help her. You might have heard them come back.'

'Not me. Went out like a light, I always do.'

'What about earlier, before you went to bed?'

Another shake of the head. 'Sorry.'

Dead end, there. Move on, then, to the more delicate topic of Mrs Rankle borrowing the van. Would it be best to try to get Tiller to volunteer the information, and risk arousing his anger again if it was necessary to press him, perhaps catch him out in a lie, or to ask him outright? Either way he was likely to erupt. Marginally better, perhaps, to avoid putting him in the wrong.

'I understand that when you and Mrs Rankle go to the pub she usually borrows the van some time during the evening to go and check that her son is all right. He's handicapped, I believe?'

Tiller's reaction was instantaneous. Ignoring the last question he took his pipe from his mouth and straightened up, glaring at Thanet. 'So what? I've got every right to lend it to whoever I like.'

'I'm not questioning your right to lend it . . .'

'I should hope not. Because you ask Mrs Hamilton. Go on, ask her. I wondered about Sonia driving it because of the insurance, see, I wasn't sure who was covered, so I asked Mrs Hamilton's permission and she told me the cover was comprehensive and I could use it as I liked. "Off duty you must treat the van as yours, Sam," she says. "Just use your own discretion."'

Thanet held up his hand. 'All right, all right. I accept that. I told you, I'm not questioning your right to lend it to whoever you want to lend it to. All I'm trying to find out is whether Mrs Rankle drove it on Tuesday night.'

If Tiller had been playing a game of Statues he couldn't have frozen into immobility more quickly. Only his eyes seemed alive, small black burning coals in an expanse of paralysed flesh. Then a hiss escaped through his slightly parted lips, his left eyelid twitched and he took a deep breath. 'Just what,' he said through his teeth, 'are you implying?'

The waves of antagonism emanating from him were so powerful that it was with difficulty that Thanet stood his ground. 'Asking, Mr Tiller. Not—'

Tiller took a step forward and Thanet sensed Lineham tense beside him. 'Just leave Mrs Rankle out of this, d'you hear me? LEAVE HER OUT OF THIS!'

'That may not be possible, Mr Tiller.'

Tiller made an inarticulate sound that was almost a growl and, bunching his hands into fists, took another step forward.

Lineham also moved forward and Thanet was suddenly conscious of Draco flanking him on the other side. Three against one, he thought. Not very fair. He suppressed a desire to laugh. How impressed the Super must be with his handling of this one!

He was opening his mouth to speak when Draco intervened. 'Come now, Mr Tiller. That wouldn't be very sensible, would it? Assaulting a police officer and all that?'

'Look,' said Thanet, humiliated and seething, trying to ignore the fact that Draco had spoken at all, 'I can imagine how you feel . . .'

'Can you?' snarled Tiller. 'How would you like it if

someone you knew died in an accident and before you could turn round you're suspected of murdering him? Or if not you, your girlfriend or wife, perhaps. Just think about it! How *would* you feel?'

'If I were innocent—furiously angry, outraged, helpless, frustrated, hurt, confused, misjudged...'

'Well then!'

'But if I were guilty...' Thanet allowed the pause to lengthen then said softly, 'If I were guilty, then I would put on a good show of feeling all those things, in order to proclaim my innocence.'

Tiller stared at him. Then his shoulders drooped and he turned away. 'I can't win, can I? I can't bloody win!'

'You don't help yourself by getting all worked up like this, that's for sure,' said Thanet gently. 'And I do assure you that we are putting precisely this kind of question to everyone who had access to the van that night. Everyone. Sooner or later the truth will come out. And I meant what I said. If you are not involved you have nothing to fear and everything to gain by cooperating with us in full.'

Tiller made a dispirited gesture. 'I've told you all I know. But if you want to ask questions about other people you'll just have to go and talk to them yourself, because I can't and won't answer.'

There really was no point in continuing. 'Very well, Mr Tiller, I can understand that.' Thanet glanced at the others. *Ready to go?* 'We'll leave you to get on with your work.'

Outside they crossed the yard in a tense, embarrassed silence. After a few moments Draco cleared his throat.

'I owe you an apology, Thanet.'

Thanet said nothing.

'I shouldn't have interfered. I was most impressed by the way you handled him.'

Apologies didn't come easily to Draco and Thanet felt appeased. 'I admit he had me worried for a moment there, sir. I was glad you and Lineham were present.'

'Tricky customer. And no fool. With a chip as big as a mountain on his shoulder. If that's the degree of antagonism Martindale was capable of arousing, it wouldn't surprise me in the least if someone grabbed the opportunity to get rid of him. Think it was Tiller?'

'I just don't know, sir. What do you think, Lineham?'

Lineham was pleased to be included in the discussion, Thanet could see, but the sergeant was as undecided as he was himself.

'If Mr Martindale happened to be walking down the drive when Tiller drove down to collect Mrs Rankle, well, I could certainly see him being tempted. But I don't know that he would deliberately have planned to do it.'

'I agree.' Thanet sighed. 'If only we had a better idea of Martindale's movements . . .'

'What's your next move, Thanet?' Draco was still being conciliatory.

'I thought we might go and see Mrs Rankle."

Thanet held his breath, praying that Draco wouldn't say he would accompany them.

They had reached the front drive and Draco stopped. 'Right, I'll leave you to it, then, I've got to be getting back.'

Relief. 'Right, sir.'

One foot in the Land Rover, Draco turned. 'And as I said, Thanet, well done.'

Thanet raised a hand in acknowledgement and watched the Land Rover drive off.

'Think he'll give you a medal, sir?' said Lineham.

He ducked as Thanet threw a mock punch at him and tension dissolved into laughter.

14

'Pretty uphill work, isn't it?' said Lineham as they set off down the drive.

'I feel as though I'm swimming against the tide most of the time,' Thanet admitted. 'I can't ever remember a case in which we've had so many hostile witnesses. I just wonder...'

Lineham glanced at him. 'What?'

Thanet shrugged. 'I was wondering if this means we're barking up the wrong tree. That it was after all just a simple hit and run accident.'

'I'm not quite with you, sir.'

'Perhaps I'm being fanciful, and I don't quite know how to put this, but... Well, if someone had killed Martindale, his anger against him would be defused. It wouldn't still be around. But most of these people, they're still so angry it's like handling a lot of unexploded bombs. D'you see what I mean? It's almost as if...'

Lineham raised his eyebrows.

Thanet gave an embarrassed little laugh. 'It's almost as though their hostility towards Martindale has been redirected, at me.'

'Are you suggesting we should abandon the investigation?'

'Absolutely not. In fact, the harder it gets the more determined I become to find out the truth.'

'I wonder if there'll be any response to the TVS appeal.'

They had arranged for a request for all motorists passing through Sutton-in-the-Weald between the hours of seven p.m. and two a.m. on Tuesday night to come forward.

'We'll just have to wait and see.'

'That'll be Mrs Rankle's cottage, I think.'

Lineham pulled up in front of a pair of semi-detached cottages. In the garden of one of them, a youth, warmly wrapped up in rug, anorak and bobble hat, was sitting in a wheelchair parked in front of a rapidly thawing snowman. He was leaning forward and patting it.

'Hullo,' said Thanet, smiling.

The youth's head swung around and Thanet saw that he was much older than Thanet had thought, in his late twenties, perhaps, with the vacant stare of the mentally handicapped. He looked upset, on the verge of tears.

'What's the matter?' Thanet squatted down in front of him.

'No gone.' The words were barely intelligible.

Thanet frowned, trying to understand.

'Who are you? What do you want?'

The voice was shrill with alarm. A woman was standing at the open door of the cottage. She started towards him as Thanet stood up.

'Mrs Rankle? Sorry, we didn't mean to startle you.' He introduced himself. 'Your son seems upset.'

She was in her late fifties or early sixties, thin and slight, with untidy brown hair and a worn, lined face. There were deep creases between her brows and she looked as though she carried the sorrows of the world on her bowed shoulders. She wore no make-up and was dressed in a shapeless brown skirt and fawn jumper matted by many washings. She fished a handkerchief out of her pocket and briskly wiped the young man's cheeks. 'He's upset because the snow is melting, aren't you, Vince? You thought it was lovely, didn't you? Come on, we'd better go inside, you're getting cold.'

She turned the chair and began to push it across the soggy lawn. It was hard going and Thanet said, 'Let us do that for you.'

Between them he and Lineham manoeuvred the chair on to the path and in through the front door. Mrs Rankle went ahead of them, along a short passage. She flung open the door. 'In here.'

It was a squarish kitchen-cum-living-room, old-fashioned

but adequately furnished with central table, china-clay sink, gas cooker and antiquated refrigerator. A small coal fire burned in the black cast-iron grate and there was a wooden armchair beside it, complete with cushion and curled-up cat. It should have been comfortable enough, cosy even, and yet... Thanet, ever-sensitive to atmosphere, looked about, searching for clues to his unease. The place felt curiously empty, bleak. Perhaps it was because the room was not only spotlessly clean but immaculately tidy. There was none of the clutter that Thanet associated with living—books, newspapers, magazines, plants, and no signs of any kind of activity on the part of either Mrs Rankle or her son. What did they do all day in this small bare cell?

Stupid question, he realised. Mrs Rankle had been removing Vincent's hat and coat and now she went to the huge television set, which Thanet had noticed but not really registered, and switched it on. A gardening expert was explaining how to care for pot plants. Then she manoeuvred Vincent's wheelchair so that it was positioned squarely in front of it. 'All right, love?' She ran her hand over his hair in a gesture of affection before turning to Thanet. 'What did you want?'

'May we sit down?'

She looked around. 'We need another chair.' She started towards the door. 'I'll get one from the front room.'

'No, don't bother,' said Lineham. 'I can stand.' He went to lean against the sink.

'You're sure?' She sat down in the armchair, Thanet in the single upright chair beside the table. Didn't they ever have visitors? he wondered.

'As you've probably guessed, we're looking into the death of Mr Martindale, on Tuesday night.'

He paused. What was the expression that had flitted across her face? Satisfaction?

'And one of the things we're trying to do is piece together his movements during the day.' He gave her no chance to ask him why. 'You were seen talking to him in the village that afternoon... Having an argument with him, in fact.'

No response.

'We wondered why ... Why you were arguing with him, that is.' He waited for denial, prevarication, outright refusal to discuss the matter. It would only be par for the course.

She glanced at Vincent who was apparently absorbed in how to take geranium cuttings, her mouth settling more firmly into bitter lines. 'No reason why I shouldn't tell you. If I don't, you'll hear soon enough from someone else, I've no doubt...'

She gestured at her son. 'Leo Martindale did that to Vince.'

Thanet was shaken. What did she mean?

'You'd never believe it to look at him, would you, but until he was nine he was a perfectly normal, healthy little boy.' Briefly the sour lines around her mouth slackened, then tightened again. 'One day, nearly twenty-five years ago, we were visiting my mother, in this cottage. We didn't live here then. We had a council house in Cranbrook... While we were here Vince went out to play. We'd told him not to go out on the road but you know what boys are. The first we knew, there was a squeal of brakes and a crash... We went rushing out. Vince was lying in the road and Leo Martindale's sports car was slewed across, nose in the hedge.'

In a brief, vivid flash of memory Thanet remembered the heart-stopping moment when Ben, aged about nine himself, had been knocked off his bicycle by a tractor. His stomach clenched as it had then and he was not surprised that as she recalled the incident, even now after all this time, Mrs Rankle's hands were moving in desperate wringing movements painful to watch and her eyes had filled with tears. She dashed them angrily away. 'He'd been drinking,' she said bitterly. 'There was a girl with him. They were both all right, of course, but Vince...' She glanced at him again, immobile in front of the flickering screen. 'We thought he was going to die. He was in a coma for weeks, and when he recovered...' She shook her head and gave a cynical little laugh. 'Recovered! Not a very good choice of word, as I think you'll agree.'

What could he say? What did one say, in such circumstances? 'It must have been a terrible time for you.'

'I can't tell you . . .' She glanced at him assessingly, as if suddenly aware of whom she was talking to, and he could see her wondering whether to continue. Strictly speaking, of course, he had got at least part of what he wanted, the fact that she had a powerful motive for wanting Martindale dead: revenge. He could understand now that look of satisfaction earlier, when he had mentioned Martindale's death. Even if she hadn't been at the wheel of the van herself there must be for her a delicious irony in the fact that he had himself been killed in a road accident similar to that in which he had maimed her son. Thanet knew that he should now go on to question her about her use of the van that night, but something held him back. There was more that she wanted to tell him, he was sure of it. It occurred to him that it must be rare indeed now for her to have the opportunity to talk about the tragedy that had surely blighted her life. The local people must all know about it and would scarcely welcome hearing the same old story over and over again, and she could hardly go up to a total stranger and buttonhole him like the Ancient Mariner.

'It wasn't as though it was over, when he came out of the coma,' she said in a low voice. 'It was only just beginning. When we found he was permanently brain-damaged and would never walk again, my husband . . . He just couldn't take it, you see. He stuck it out for a couple of years and then walked out.' Her mouth twisted and she snapped her fingers. 'Just like that. One day he was there, the next he was gone. Leaving me stuck . . .' She pulled herself up. 'Not that Vince isn't a good boy, he is. Very loving and obedient, but . . . It's just that there's no relief. You know it's going to go on and on and on, day after day, month after month, year after year . . .'

Her voice was rising and the desperation in her face gave Thanet a glimpse of the endless, unremitting years of selfless commitment she had had to endure. How could she bear it? 'Don't you have any help at all in looking after him?'

'A couple of times a year they take him into residential care while I have a break, but that's all. There just isn't enough manpower to give people like me any help on a regular basis, it's as simple as that—especially in a rural area like this. And the fact of the matter is, that so long as you're coping, you'll be left to get on with it.'

'And you wouldn't want him to go into residential care.' Thanet made it a statement, not a question.

'I've thought about it, often. And I have got as far as making enquiries once or twice when I've been feeling really desperate, but you wouldn't believe the waiting lists, for people in far worse case than Vince. Besides, he's happy here and so long as I'm able to look after him... When you have kids you can't just opt out of your responsibilities when the going gets tough, can you?'

An understatement if ever there was one. Thanet shook his head sympathetically. 'Was there a prosecution?'

She grimaced. 'Yes. All he got was a six-month suspended sentence and his licence taken away for eighteen months . . . It still makes me mad to think about it. Oh, it wasn't so bad when Mum was alive. Vince and me moved in here with her and she used to look after him while I went out to work part-time. But since she died, ten years ago . . . No one can imagine, who hasn't been through it . . .'

And with no prospect of relief in sight, thought Thanet. It wouldn't have been surprising if, hearing that Martindale was back and faced with the opportunity to avenge the long purgatory of looking after a son born perfectly fit and healthy and now reduced to helpless dependency, she had succumbed to the impulse to run his destroyer down. He hoped very much that this was not what had happened. How could he live with his conscience if she were convicted and Vincent's only prop were removed?

Come on, he told himself. You're not here to judge, simply to discover the truth. And whether you like it or not, that's what you have to do.

Closing his mind with difficulty to the rumblings of his conscience he said quietly, 'Mrs Rankle, I understand you borrowed Mr Tiller's van on Tuesday night, to come back here and check that Vincent was all right?'

She blinked at the change of subject. 'Yes, I always do. It's the only night of the week I go out.' She was on the defensive now. 'I put Vince to bed a bit early on Tuesdays. He can't move about by himself, you see, so he's perfectly safe. But I do like to check he's OK, halfway through the evening.'

'I'm not questioning the care you take of him. It's obvious he's very well looked after, it's just that . . . did you see anybody, on your way here, or on your way back to the pub?'

She frowned, thinking. 'Not so far as I can remember. It was very cold, the roads were icy and I was concentrating on driving, I don't drive much, you see . . . Oh!' Her eyes widened as she realised where this could be leading. 'Just a minute . . . I was wondering why you'd come. You're not trying to tell me it was Sam's van that knocked him down?'

'We're not absolutely certain yet, but it looks that way, I'm afraid.'

'Oh, my God.' She glanced at Vincent then shrank back in her chair, looking near to panic.

Thanet saw her throat move as she swallowed convulsively and she put her hand over her mouth as if she were about to be sick. Her eyes above it were wide and staring. If she were acting, he thought, it was a first-rate performance. He sincerely hoped she wasn't.

Then she sat up again, making a visible effort at self-control. 'You . . .' she whispered, running the tip of her tongue over dry lips. 'Surely you're not suggesting . . . ? Oh God, you are, aren't you? You think I might have run him down.'

'Mrs Rankle, I assure you that at this stage we're not suggesting anything. We're merely trying to find out what happened.'

A thought struck her. 'Sam . . .'

'Several people drove the van that night, Sam included. We're talking to all of them.'

Now that she was over the initial shock she was rallying. He could see it in the straightening of her back, the tilt of her head, the hardening of her expression. She was a fighter, he reminded himself. If she wasn't, she would have given up long ago.

'That's why you were asking about the argument.' Her voice was much stronger, almost belligerent as she said, 'Well let me tell you this. I may have no reason to love Mr rotten Martindale, but that doesn't mean I'd run him down in cold blood. And in case you're wondering, I didn't knock him down accidentally, either.'

Suddenly she leaned forward, eyes gleaming. 'You said, "All of them". That several people had driven the van that night and you were talking to all of them. Does that include Lewis Fever?'

Thanet saw Lineham, behind her, stiffen.

'What do you mean?' It was scarcely surprising that she should try to use diversionary tactics, but this could be an unexpected break for them. If Tiller had lent Fever the van on Tuesday night they had both kept very quiet about it. Presumably Mrs Rankle felt no such loyalty to Fever.

'He borrowed the van that night too. He came into the pub, about . . .' She put her hands to her temples, pressed them as if trying to force her memory to function efficiently. 'Let me think. It was . . . Yes, it was before I came to check on Vince.' The words began to tumble out as she recalled the incident more clearly. 'It must have been about, oh, around a quarter to nine. He came into the pub and asked Sam if he could borrow it. He and Sam are old mates . . . He'd just heard his mother-in-law had been taken ill and he wanted to run his wife over to see her.'

'Why didn't he use his own car, or his wife's—I presume she's got one?'

'Yes, but Toby had borrowed it. They'd set out in his car, Lewis's that is, but as they were driving through the village he realised he'd got a slow puncture. He didn't want to waste time changing the wheel and he saw Sam's van in the car park at the Drovers so he came in to ask if he could borrow it for half an hour. Of course, Sam said yes.'

'Where does his mother-in-law live?'

'Ashford.'

So Fever would have had to pass the gates of the Hall on his way. 'How long was he away?'

'Only half an hour or so, as he promised. As soon as he got back I drove home to see if Vince was OK.'

Outside in the car Lineham said resignedly, 'I just don't believe this. How many more people d'you suppose drove the wretched thing that night?'

'The Byfleets?' said Thanet.

'How much d'you bet?'

'I'm not a gambling man, as you well know, Mike. But the way things are going the odds in favour seem pretty high. We need to find out if she actually saw Martindale that night when she went to his room, anyway, so let's go and ask them, shall we?'

15

On the way back up the drive they passed the middle-aged couple they had seen earlier, returning from their walk, and in the stable yard Adam Hamilton was mooning about, kicking a stone. Thanet scarcely recognised him at first; he had discarded his bizarre outfit of yesterday in favour of jeans and a scruffy sweater—a discard of his father's?—which hung on him in folds and with sleeves so long that they completely covered his hands. He came over as they parked the car.

'Hey, Inspector, how're you doing?'

'Fine, thanks.'

'Found out who dunnit yet?'

'Done what?' Though it was clear what Adam meant.

'Oh come on! Bumped off dear Uncle Leo, of course. It's obvious that, as Eliza Doolittle would say, someone done 'im in.'

'What makes you say that?'

'Stands to reason, doesn't it? I keep my ear to the ground and the word is he really stirred things up in the short time he was here.'

'And who's the popular choice of villain?'

Adam shrugged. 'You pays yer money and you takes yer choice . . . I couldn't care less as long as it wasn't the old man.'

His tone was flippant but briefly Thanet glimpsed the fear behind the façade. Adam, whether he knew it or not, was looking for reassurance that his father wasn't involved. Unfortunately Thanet couldn't give it to him, not at this

130

stage. His own tone was correspondingly light as he said, 'You think it might have been?'

The boy shrugged, looking suddenly very young and defenceless. 'Had a bloody good motive, didn't he?' He rallied, flinging his head back and gesturing theatrically about him. 'The old ancestral acres and all that.'

Thanet took pity on him. 'I shouldn't lose too much sleep over it just yet. As you say, your uncle seems to have stirred up a good many sleeping dogs in the short time he was here and anyway there's no indication yet that it wasn't an accident, pure and simple . . . Look, I wanted a word with the Byfleets. Do you happen to know where they might be at this time of day?'

'Since Mrs Byfleet's been in pod Ma's insisted on her having the afternoon off, so she might be in the flat. I don't know about him, he could be anywhere around.'

'Where do they live, exactly?'

Adam pointed to some windows above a row of stable doors. 'Over there. You go in through the right-hand stable, there're some steps leading up.'

Thanet thanked him and he and Lineham began to walk in that direction. Adam fell in beside them.

'It's pretty boring hanging around here at half-term. Trust me to be away when something really exciting happened for once. So if I can help at all . . .'

'Go on keeping your ear to the ground. And if you come across anything interesting, let me know.'

'Anyone special you'd like me to keep an eye on?'

'Not at the moment, thanks.'

Adam looked disappointed and walked moodily away, hands in pockets, in the direction of the house.

'Poor kid. Must be worried sick,' said Lineham.

'You noticed, then. Yes. But there's not much we can do about it at the moment.'

The door Adam had indicated was propped open with a stone and led into a long building divided off on their left into a series of stalls where horses had once been kept. This end section had been gutted and a sturdy wooden staircase with wide, open treads and a handrail had been fixed to the right-hand wall.

'Pretty dark in here,' said Lineham. 'Wonder if there's a light.'

He looked about and found one, just inside the door. He clicked it on and a bulkhead light fitment at the top of the staircase came on, illuminating the door beside it. Byfleet answered their knock and when he saw who it was stood back without a word. He led them through a tiny vestibule into a large sitting-room which ran the whole depth of the building with windows to front and rear. It was, Thanet thought, a delightful room, the sort of room he would be very happy to live in himself, with beams overhead infilled with rough plaster painted a rich, creamy white. Overflowing bookshelves stood between the windows, and the colours in the flowery chintz curtains were echoed in the comfortable, slip-covered armchairs and the patterned rugs on the wide, highly polished floorboards. There were brightly coloured cushions, plants and flowers and, in addition to a small portable television set, there was a modest stereo system and an extensive collection of records and tapes on specially constructed shelves. A bundle of lacy white knitting lay on one of the chairs and a low table with an unfinished game of chess laid out on it stood nearby. On another table stood a beautiful blue-and-white ceramic bowl heaped with odds and ends—some coloured pebbles, a silver nutcracker, a corkscrew, a pocket diary, a brass doorknob, a screwdriver and a pair of pink baby's bootees. Table lamps cast welcoming pools of light. It was a living-room in the best sense of the word, a room for enjoying life. The contrast with Mrs Rankle's bleak kitchen was almost painful.

'Did you want to speak to my wife?'

'We'd like a word with both of you, actually, Mr Byfleet.'

Up until now Thanet had had little more than an occasional glimpse of the housekeeper's husband and he studied him with interest. Without the bobble hat his ears did not stick out quite as much as Thanet remembered, and the man was younger than he had thought, in his late thirties, perhaps. Divested of his anorak he was even thinner than Thanet expected, a tall, bony, gangling individual whose joints seemed articulated rather than smoothly linked by muscle and tendon. He looked tense, but there was no special significance in that. Most people were tense when interviewed by the police, innocent and guilty alike. And perhaps Byfleet was feeling especially protective towards his wife at the moment, as she'd been having a difficult time with her pregnancy. His next words confirmed this.

'She's having a rest.' He glanced at his watch. 'But she should be up soon. She asked me to call her at a quarter to four.'

The implication was clear. He didn't want to wake her before time. Thanet glanced at his watch. Three-thirty. 'That's fine. We can talk to you first, while we're waiting.'

They all sat down.

Byfleet looked expectantly at Thanet but as prearranged it was Lineham who spoke. 'We understand you picked up some guests from Gatwick Tuesday night, Mr Byfleet.'

'That's right.'

'You took the Rolls-Royce, I believe.'

'I usually do when I'm collecting guests.'

'I bet they love it.'

'They do seem to appreciate it, yes.'

'You're a lucky man. It's one of my life-long ambitions, to drive a Rolls—oh, don't worry, Mr Byfleet, I'm not hinting. But even a humble copper can have his dreams.'

This brought a faint smile to Byfleet's face.

Well done, Mike, approved Thanet. Lineham had done well to get Byfleet to relax even to this degree.

'Anyway,' Lineham went on, 'you got back at around . . .' He pretended to consult his notes.

'Five to eight,' said Byfleet. 'Or thereabouts.'

'Did you meet Mr Talion going down the drive in the van? He had to go and check on some sheep that had got out on to the road about then.'

Thanet was sure that Lineham was well aware that Talion had left a good ten minutes earlier.

Byfleet was shaking his head. 'I didn't meet anything coming down the drive. But even if I had I wouldn't have known Mr Talion was driving. It was dark.'

Lineham shrugged. 'But your headlights would have been on. You might just have recognised someone. Anyway, if you say you didn't meet anything . . .'

'I didn't.'

Thanet missed the next exchange. He was wondering if Martindale had realised that the approaching van was going to run him down. Thanet imagined the scene: Martindale walking through the darkness, the sound of his footsteps crisp in the frosty night. Then, from behind him, the sound of an approaching car, its headlights casting long fingers of light towards the entrance gates. Martindale would have stopped walking, perhaps moved in close to the fence at the side of the road for the car to pass. At what point would he have realised that it wasn't going to, that he himself was its target? Perhaps he never had realised. The tear in his overcoat was in the back. Perhaps he had been hurled all unawares into Eternity. Of course, it was possible that it had been an accident after all. The driver could have seen the pedestrian ahead, braked too fiercely in order to pass him, and found himself skidding on the icy road. And of course the entire incident could have taken place on the main road and not in the drive at all. In any case it was highly unlikely that Martindale would have glimpsed the face of his killer.

Thanet switched his attention back to the interview.

'If you had happened to look out of any of the front windows, would you have been able to recognise anyone crossing the stable yard? How well lit is it at night?'

Lineham had evidently been asking if either of the Byfleets had seen anyone drive the van away.

"Very well lit really. Mrs Hamilton had extra lights installed when a guest twisted her ankle on the cobbles last year.'

'Who is responsible for switching them on?'

Byfleet shrugged. 'Theoretically I am. But if I'm not here when it gets dark one of the others will do it.'

'Were they on when you got back that night?'

'I think they must have been, or I'd have noticed.' He thought for a moment. 'Yes, they were.'

'Your wife was already here when you got back?'

'Yes. She knew I'd be back about eight, so she came over to finish getting supper ready.'

Had Thanet imagined it, or was there a touch of unease

there? Any mention of Mrs Byfleet seemed to disturb her husband. It would be interesting to see them together.

'And you say you sat down to supper straight away?'

In the kitchen, presumably, thought Thanet. There was no dining table in here. Unless they had eaten off trays. He opened his mouth to ask then thought better of it. Perhaps this point had already been covered in the brief snatch of conversation he had missed while thinking about the accident. He mustn't let his attention wander again.

Lineham had noticed and raised his eyebrows. *You wanted to ask something?*

Thanet shook his head.

'How long did you take over supper?'

Byfleet shrugged. 'Not that long. Twenty minutes, half an hour perhaps.'

So, over the crucial period when the van had stood idle Byfleet was claiming that he and his wife were enjoying a cosy domestic interlude.

Lineham hadn't missed this point. 'You usually eat at that time?'

'Generally between eight and half past, yes. By then the guests are usually at dinner, and my wife is free.'

'And she goes back over to the Hall afterwards?'

'For an hour or so, yes. From around nine to ten.'

'She works long hours.'

'She does have the afternoons off. And at least one full day every week.'

Delia Hamilton commanded an astonishing degree of loyalty from her employees, thought Thanet. So far he hadn't heard a single grumble about her.

Lineham glanced at his watch. 'Well, thank you, Mr Byfleet. It is ten to four now, so perhaps you wouldn't mind waking your wife?'

Byfleet frowned then stood up, reluctantly. He hesitated then said, 'Look . . .'

Thanet and Lineham said nothing, waited.

'My wife . . . She's not been well.'

'Yes, Mrs Hamilton told us,' said Thanet.

'I don't want her upset unnecessarily.'

A touch of belligerence there.

'We're not inhuman, Mr Byfleet. We just want to ask her one or two simple questions.'

Byfleet looked embarrassed. 'I'm sorry. It's just that... Well, this baby... it's... We've been married five years and we'd given up hope, you see, and then...'

'I understand.'

Byfleet hesitated a moment longer, as if in need of further reassurance, then turned away and disappeared through a door at the far side of the room, closing it behind him.

'Bit jumpy, isn't he?' said Lineham.

'Mm. I can't make up my mind if he's got something on his mind or if it's just that he's concerned that all this shouldn't upset his wife. He obviously feels very protective towards her.'

'Understandable, I suppose. They're both getting on, for a first baby, and the pregnancy hasn't been straightforward, apparently.'

'Quite. Er... I'm afraid my attention wandered for a few minutes back there, Mike. Where did he say they were while they were having supper?'

'In the kitchen at the back of the building.'

Thanet got up and wandered over to the bookshelves. He was always interested to know what people were reading. The Byfleets seemed to have pretty catholic taste. There was biography, mostly fairly light, a modest collection of poetry, a whole shelf of non-fiction covering topics ranging from travel to do-it-yourself, and row upon row of fiction, both classical and contemporary. On the bottom shelf, below a row of romantic historical novels, were a few children's books. Thanet squatted to inspect them: Alison Uttley, Beatrix Potter and the once despised but now reinstated Enid Blyton. Smiling reminiscently he picked out *The Famous Five Go Adventuring Again*, one of his own favourites. Inside the front cover was written in neat, carefully rounded script:

Mona Taylor
The Limes Preparatory School
Burgess Road
Brighton

Sussex
England
The British Isles
Europe
The World
The Universe.

He smiled and held it out to show Lineham. 'Things don't change much, do they? I remember writing this myself, and I bet you do, too. And so did Ben and Bridget.'

'Yes. No doubt my two'll get around to it in due course. Pretty nice place they've got here, haven't they? Bit unexpected, really. For that matter, he's not exactly your typical handyman, is he?'

'Presumably he likes the life. Perhaps they just enjoy working together.' Thanet was now glancing at the records and tapes. Popular classics, Gilbert and Sullivan, old pop songs, none of the more recent stuff. He could almost hear Ben and Bridget chanting *'boring'*.

'Taking their time, aren't they?' Lineham was getting restless.

'If she's been asleep she'd have to have a few minutes to collect herself.'

'Is the Super expecting you to report in again today?'

''Fraid so.' Thanet returned to his seat.

Lineham groaned. 'It's getting beyond a joke. Think he's going to turn up every day, like he did today?'

'I sincerely hope not! I'm trying to tell myself the novelty'll soon wear off.'

'It'd better, or he'll be having a mutiny on his hands.'

'Now now, Mike. You didn't say that. Or if you did, I didn't hear it. And do stop prowling around like that, you're getting on my nerves.'

'You were prowling yourself until a minute ago!' Lineham plumped down on his chair looking disgruntled. 'I hate hanging about like this.'

'I wonder if they've finished the post-mortem yet.'

'Should have, by now.'

'Doc Mallard said he'd let us know if there was anything interesting and there hasn't been a word, so it doesn't look

as though we're going to get much help there. I'm beginning to think this case might be a nonstarter, Mike.'

'It's not like you to say that. But I see what you mean.
And I agree, there doesn't seem to be much prospect of
proving who did it even if we do find out. Still, we've had
cases before when we've said exactly the same thing and
we've made it in the end—or you have, at least.'

'Mm.' Thanet was beginning to feel drowsy. If he had to
sit in this very comfortable chair much longer he would
fall asleep. The first couple of days of this type of investigation were always very tiring. There were so many
people to see, so many leads to follow up, so many
judgements to make, impressions to absorb. It was fine so
long as you kept going, but once you stopped and lost
your impetus... Abruptly he got up and crossed to the
window in an attempt to rouse himself. 'They are taking a
long time...'

'Perhaps they've knotted sheets and climbed out of the
window,' said Lineham with a grin.

'Ha ha. Very funny.' Thanet peered out into the stable
yard. The sky had clouded over and once again it was
getting dark early. Tiller emerged from his work shed and
crossed the cobbles, trundling a wheelbarrow. From here
there was an excellent view of almost the entire yard,
across to the back of the house. Tiller's house was at the
end of this same side and Hamilton's office in the block at
right angles. All of them would have had a clear view of
Martindale if he had come out of the back door, especially
if the yard had been well lit. Thanet said so.

Lineham came across to look. 'Yes. And in that loud
checked overcoat of his he would have been easily
recognisable. But why come out of the back door, not the
front?'

Thanet shrugged. 'He didn't feel like running into guests
in the foyer? It can't be easy, finding your home overrun
by all and sundry who feel they have as much right there
as you have. Or—'

They both turned as the door opened and the Byfleets
came in. Byfleet's arm was around his wife's shoulders.
She was wearing the same long dark green dress, her
housekeeper's uniform, presumably. Her eyes were still

puffy with sleep and she looked alarmingly pale and fragile.

'Sorry to keep you waiting, Inspector,' she said with a smile. 'I'm afraid it takes me a little while to get going after a rest, these days.'

'It really doesn't matter, Mrs Byfleet. I'm sorry to trouble you again, but I'm afraid there are one or two small points...'

'I understand.'

She and Byfleet sat down. He took her hand. Side by side Thanet noticed that they were already beginning to acquire that uncanny resemblance sometimes found in married couples who are very close to each other. He had noticed it before and wondered once again exactly wherein it lay. In facial expression, attitude, in tiny gestures or habits unconsciously picked up from each other? Did he and Joan have it?

'It's just that we are still trying to piece together Mr Martindale's movements on Tuesday, and when we saw you yesterday you forgot to mention that you had seen him after dinner that evening.'

He watched the slow tide of colour suffuse the pale, almost translucent skin and wondered if she could remember their conversation yesterday as clearly as he did.

'*Did you see him again at all, after he'd had dinner?*'

'*No.*'

She shook her head in embarrassment. 'I expect you're wondering why I didn't mention it before, but...' She glanced at her husband and Thanet saw the grip on her hand tighten as Byfleet nodded.

'It's just that it was so awkward, so embarrassing...'

Surely Martindale hadn't made a pass at her, in her advanced state of pregnancy?

'I was just doing a routine check around the house as I always do at that time, to make sure that everything is in order—lamps lit, curtains drawn, that sort of thing—and as I was walking along the corridor past the Chinese room the door opened and Mr Martindale looked out. He said he wanted a word with me, so I went in. He...' She glanced at her husband again and took courage. 'It was horrible! He began to—well—quiz me, about the hotel.

He began by asking how long I'd been here, whether I liked it and so on and then he started asking very specific questions about the number of staff, about how many guests we had, about staff wages and holidays and things like that . . . I just didn't know what to say . . .'

She was becoming agitated and Byfleet put an arm around her shoulders again. She shook her head. 'I mean, I know he was Mrs Hamilton's brother, but I just didn't feel he had the right . . . I tried to be polite, or pretend I didn't know the answers but he just persisted . . . In the end I said I was sorry, but I just didn't feel I could give him that sort of information without Mrs Hamilton's permission, and he said I'd better get used to the idea that from now on I would ultimately be responsible to him, not to her . . . I asked him if that meant Mrs Hamilton wouldn't be running the place any longer and he said yes, she would, but that he was the owner and everyone was going to have to adjust to the fact. I said that I still felt I would have to get Mrs Hamilton's permission to give him the sort of information he was asking for. I was a bit nervous when I said it—after all, if he really did own the place, he was my employer and I thought he might be angry, ask if I was calling him a liar of something, but he just laughed and said to go ahead and ask her, that he admired loyalty in members of staff and would see me again when I had spoken to her.'

'And did you speak to her?'

'Not immediately. I met a guest on the way, who delayed me for a few minutes, then I found Mrs Hamilton had gone to the station to meet Adam. Then when she got back she went straight into the drawing-room to have drinks with the guests—she always does, before dinner— and then I had to come back here to get your supper, didn't I, Des, so it wasn't till just after nine that I eventually saw her.'

'And she confirmed what he had said?'

'Yes.'

'Why didn't you tell me this yesterday?'

She shrugged. 'It didn't seem relevant.'

Thanet sighed. 'I wish people would let me decide what is relevant and what isn't.'

She bit her lip. 'I'm sorry.'

'Never mind, you've told me now . . . We asked your husband, earlier, if he happened to notice the van drive out of the yard during the evening. He said no, but did you?'

She shook her head.

'What about later on? Sam Tiller drove it back from the pub at 10.30.'

'I didn't notice,' said Byfleet. 'Did you, love?'

Another shake of the head.

'And after that?'

She hesitated. 'I did hear something . . .'

'When?'

'Shortly after we went to bed. Somewhere around a quarter past eleven. I heard a car start up and drive off, and come back some time later.' She gave a rueful smile. 'I don't sleep too well these days.'

Thanet remembered Joan's restless nights during the latter months of her pregnancies. 'No . . . Did you hear one car return, or two?'

'Two, I think.'

'And that was when?'

'I'm sorry, I didn't notice. I didn't think it was important.'

Thanet rose. 'There is just one question I must put to you both. Did either of you, for any reason, drive the van that night?'

They obviously realised the significance of the question. Neither looked at the other as they shook their heads in unison.

'We had no reason to,' said Byfleet stiffly.

Picking their way carefully down the staircase outside Lineham said, 'Did you believe them, sir?'

Outside Thanet took deep breaths of the clear, cold air. He shrugged. 'Difficult to tell. She's so obviously unwell and he's so on edge about her . . .'

'Of course, what she told us does give them some sort of a motive, doesn't it, sir?'

'You mean, they might have been afraid that they would lose their cosy billet if Martindale took over? Bit thin, isn't it? A good housekeeper and chauffeur/handyman can always find a job, surely.'

'When she's pregnant and her health isn't too good? Not as easy as all that, I shouldn't think.'

'Perhaps not.'

As they got into the Land Rover the lights in the courtyard came on. Byfleet was right, the whole area was well illuminated. Had Martindale strolled across this very spot on the way to his death?

As he had said to Lineham, earlier, Thanet was beginning to wonder if he would ever find out.

16

Arriving home at around 8.30 Thanet was surprised to find Bridget in the kitchen with Joan. He kissed them both, then said, 'I thought you were on duty tonight, Bridget.'

'Mandy wanted me to swap with her, so I worked the lunchtime shift today.'

Thanet nevertheless wouldn't have expected to find her in—but managed not to say so. Bridget led such an active social life. At seventeen she was blossoming into womanhood—face and figure were fast losing the plumpness which had bedevilled her mid-teens and she always managed to look stylish when going out even though her wardrobe could hardly be called extensive. Tonight she was wearing jeans, trainers, a collarless man's shirt and a baggy sweater which practically reached her knees, sleeves pushed casually up to just below the elbows.

He plucked at it. 'This looks familiar.'

She flung her arms around his neck in mock humility. 'I knew you wouldn't mind. You don't, do you?'

'Can't call a thing your own in this house, these days.'

'Don't tell me!' said Joan. 'We haven't eaten, by the way. We thought we'd wait till nine to have supper, in the hope that you might be back in time. It's ages since we all had supper together.'

Thanet beamed 'Lovely.' His irregular hours had always meant that family meals were a hit-and-miss affair but when the children were younger he had at least known that if he did manage to get home at a reasonable hour they'd all be able to eat together. But lately, especially since Bridget had left school and begun working in the restaurant, this had become an increasingly rare event. 'What about Ben? Has he managed to last out?'

'I stuffed him with baked beans and toast when he got home from school,' said Bridget with a grin.

'I'll go and wash my hands, then.'

Upstairs he remembered that he and Joan had promised themselves a serious talk with Bridget about late nights and jaunts to destinations unknown, and his heart sank. It would be a pity to spoil the pleasure of an evening together. Perhaps they could put it off to another time? He scowled at himself in the bathroom mirror as he shook his head. No. For his own peace of mind it had to be done. The problem was, how to choose the right moment.

By the time he came down supper was ready.

'This looks good,' said Thanet. 'What is it?'

Bridget looked pleased. 'Chicken with paprika and onions.'

'Bridget cooked it,' said Joan. 'Don't gobble, Ben,' she added.

Ben scowled and went on shovelling food in as fast as he could. 'I've still got homework to do.'

'Don't know how you can taste it when you eat at that speed,' said Bridget.

'It's all right for you. You're finished with all that, aren't you? Nothing to do but enjoy yourself these days.'

'I wouldn't put it quite like that. I do work, you know.'

'Call that work? A few hours a day? I should be so lucky.'

'That's enough,' said Thanet. 'Bridget had to go through what you're doing now, remember.'

Ben laid down his knife and fork. 'Any pud?'

'All in good time,' said Joan. 'We're still eating.'

Ben pushed his chair back and stood up. 'Well I can't hang around. I'll have it in my room, while I'm working.'

'You will not!' said his mother. Then, more gently, 'Look, Ben, it's ages since we all had supper together. Let's just relax and enjoy it, shall we?'

He gave her a black look. 'I'll go without, then!' And he stumped off.

'Ben!' Thanet half rose, then sat down again with a rueful look at Joan. 'May as well let him get on with it. I can quite see he finds it difficult to enjoy a leisurely meal with work hanging over his head.'

'He's absolutely impossible these days,' said Bridget.

'He's finding it difficult settling in to the new school, as you well know,' said Thanet. 'We have to make allowances.'

'But he's always having a go at me! It's my clothes, or my make-up, or I'm taking too long in the bathroom, or—'

'I think,' said Joan, beginning to clear the plates, 'that his nose is put out of joint.'

'Oh, why?'

'Well you used to get on so well together. Now you don't have time for him any more—or so he feels.'

Now Bridget was getting cross. She stood up and picked up the other plates, clashing them together in a way which made Joan wince. 'What am I supposed to do? Take him with me? Who wants a kid brother hanging around their neck all the time?'

She flounced out and Joan gave Thanet an exaggerated shrug of mock despair. 'I always put my foot in it these days. No,' she said as he stood up, 'don't bother to come out. We can manage.'

She and Bridget returned with the pudding, a lemon meringue pie, and the dessert plates. Joan began serving in an uncomfortable silence.

'Look,' she said, 'I'm not suggesting you should let Ben tag along with you, of course I'm not. But he is going through a bad patch and if you could find a little more time for him . . .'

'But he's always working! And if he's not, I'm out.'

Thanet caught Joan's eye and an unspoken message passed between them.

Don't forget we've got to talk to her . . .

I know.

Bridget wasn't stupid. 'What was that supposed to mean?'

'What?' said Joan.

'That look. You and Dad looked at each other.'

Thanet sighed. There wasn't going to be a right moment to discuss this. Should they leave it? But the subject had come up and if he were realistic, he realised, there never would be a right time for what he had to say. Why did adolescents have to be so difficult? But he refused to give in to moral blackmail and fail to broach delicate subjects for fear of provoking an outburst of bad temper.

'Well, now that you mention it . . .'

Bridget rolled her eyes. 'What now?'

'Bridget, I do think that's unreasonable!' Uncharacteristically, Joan was now becoming angry. 'How many restrictions do we place on what you do, where you go, or who you go with?'

'Hah. So that's it!' Bridget laid down the spoon she had just picked up, sat back and folded her arms. 'Well, let's have it. What have I done now?'

Pleasant family meals were evidently a thing of the past, thought Thanet with regret as he said sharply, 'That's enough, Bridget. Your mother and I wanted to have a sensible, adult discussion with you. Please, try to calm down.'

'By "sensible discussion" I suppose you mean you're going to lay down rules that I'm supposed to follow?'

'Well you suppose wrong. I meant exactly what I said, a sensible discussion. That is, a discussion in which both sides put their point of view and a compromise is reached. Now, are you going to listen or are you going to behave like a spoilt adolescent?'

She glared at him. 'Oh, so that's what I am now, is it? A spoilt adolescent?' She pushed back her chair preparatory to getting up.

Thanet put his hand on her arm, detaining her. 'No, Bridget, wait. Just answer me one question.'

'What?' She was still glowering at him.

'Can you honestly say we've been the sort of heavy-handed parents who lay down the law and expect you to accept what they say whether you like it or not?'

Pause. She chewed the inside of her lip, poised for flight yet unable honestly to answer in the affirmative. Eventually, 'I suppose not,' she said grudgingly.

'Well in that case, can't you at least listen to what we have to say, see if you think we're being unreasonable this time?'

Another hesitation, then he felt the rigid muscles in her arm relax. But she was still sulky as she said, 'Go on, then. Let's get it over with.'

Thanet paused for a moment, marshalling his thoughts. He had to get this right first time.

'Can you accept that as your parents we're bound to worry about you?'

'Oh, *Dad!*'

'Yes, I realise you must find that irritating. When you're young you don't want to have limitations put on your freedom—and I want to make it clear that that's not what we're after. We know you, and trust you to be sensible, but at the same time we'd like a little more peace of mind ourselves. So what we're asking is this: if you know you're going to be late, could you give us a ring to let us know, and if you're going out, we would like to know who you're going with and where you're going. That's it.'

'But that's impossible!' Bridget burst out. 'I've told Mum over and over again! How can I tell you where I'm going if I don't know myself?' You don't understand! Say I'm meeting Sue. She may have arranged to meet some other people as well and when we're all together we say, Right, where shall we go tonight? It could be bowling, or to a pub—oh, don't look like that, Dad. It's different nowadays. Everyone goes to pubs and yes, I know I'm under eighteen and I promise you I don't drink alcohol, I really don't, but that's where people get together these days . . . Or we might go to McDonalds or if one of us has a car we might drive over to the Chimneys in Biddenden or over to that Hungarian restaurant in Tunbridge Wells . . . And you needn't worry about that, either. Whoever's driving never drinks. We make sure of that. We don't want to end up in the mortuary, either.'

'Look love, you're wrong in thinking we don't understand. We do. And we do see the problem. We know that that's how things work, and one of the reasons why we've never brought the matter up before is because we really couldn't see any solution to it. But now, well, I think I've thought of a possible answer. But before I see what you think of the idea, I would just like to know if you can understand why we're making a fuss about it. Can't you see that not to know where you are, to think that we wouldn't even know where to begin looking for you if by any chance something went wrong and you just didn't come home—and don't roll your eyes like that! I'm better placed than most people to know just how often these things do happen. If you'd met some of the frantic parents I have . . . But anyway, do you understand what I'm trying to say?'

'I suppose so.'

'Well then, this is what I suggest. That you carry on as usual. You meet your friends, you go wherever it is you want to go, with one small difference. That when you get there you make a phone call, just a brief one, telling us where you are. That's all. It need take only a few seconds and it would help us to stop worrying.'

'Everyone would fall about laughing!' She mimicked a child's voice: ' "Excuse me, everyone. I've got to go and ring my Mummy and my Daddy, to let them know where I am." '

'Would it really be so impossible? You needn't tell them who you're ringing. Or you can make us out to be ogres if you like, lay all the blame on us. We wouldn't mind . . .'

She bit her lip, thinking about it.

What, exactly, would he do if she refused? Thanet wondered. He had no intention of playing the heavy father and laying down ultimatums which it would be impossible to keep. They never worked and would have a disastrous effect on what he liked to think, despite the present problem, was basically a good and sound relationship.

'Look,' he said, as the silence stretched out. 'Would you at least agree to give it a trial run? For a week, say? If it didn't work, and you really did find it too embarrassing, we could think again, see if we can work something else out. Or if you've got an alternative suggestion . . . ?'

She shook her head. 'I can't think of anything at the moment . . .' Suddenly she capitulated. 'OK, then. I'll give it a whirl. Why not?'

The sense of relief was overwhelming. Thanet felt as though he'd just run an exhausting race. 'Good! Terrific!' He looked at his untouched piece of pie. Now he would be able to enjoy it. And afterwards, he'd take a slice up to Ben.

He and Joan usually did the washing up together after supper but tonight Bridget insisted on doing it all.

'Go on, relax while you can! I'll bring you in some coffee later.'

Thanet and Joan plumped down side by side on the settee. 'She's OK really, isn't she?' said Joan. 'If you look about you and see the sort of mess so many young people get into, we're very lucky.'

'So far.'

'So far. It's just that at the moment I seem to get on her nerves all the time.'

'Perhaps she's too like you to be able to forgive you your faults at present. She'll grow out of it, later on.'

Joan sighed. 'I suppose so. Yes. I remember someone telling me once about his daughter. Apparently, in her late teens, she was absolutely impossible, made life hell for them. And a few years later, when she was in her mid-twenties, she was a completely different girl: kind, thoughtful, considerate, a joy, in fact. And she actually said to him, "You know Dad, when I look back and think what I was like as a teenager, I don't know how you and Mum put up with me." So when Bridget and I have an argument or I feel I can't do anything right as far as she's concerned, I just remind myself of what he said and tell myself that if I grit my teeth and hang on it'll all work out in the end.'

'You're right. I really do believe that.' Thanet yawned hugely. 'Sorry.'

'You're tired. You look tired, actually. Bad day?'

Bridget came in with two cups of coffee. 'I'm going to have a bath and wash my hair.'

'All right, love. Thanks.' He waited until she had gone, then said, 'Not bad, no. But you know how it is at the beginning of a case. And the Super hasn't helped.'

'Oh, why?'

'ODD.' Which reminded him, he really must take a look at the information sheet Draco had handed out.

"What is?'

'His new campaign. I told you one was brewing. Well, that's it. ODD. O-D-D. Standing for Organisation, Delegation and Documentation. Stop grinning like that. The acronym, I might add, was deliberate. He thought it might afford the men some light relief! Oh, he's cunning all right. Knows how to sweeten the pill. Though in fact—and you may not believe this—he actually apologised to me this afternoon!'

'He did *what*?'

'It's true.'

Joan wriggled into a more comfortable position, tucking her stockinged feet up beneath her. 'Tell me!'

She was always a gratifying audience. As he talked Thanet thought how much it meant to him to have her there, to be able to share these rare, quiet evenings at home together. He felt sorry for Martindale, who had apparently never known the pleasures of domesticity. No one seemed to mourn his passing—quite the reverse, in fact. A number of people must secretly be relieved or even pleased that he was dead. Thanet wondered what influences had worked upon Martindale to make him the man he was, a man apparently incapable of making lasting relationships or even, indeed, of needing them. Though he did seem to have remained attached to his last, French mistress. Or perhaps it was simply that he had found a comfortable billet and made sure he didn't lose it. Knowing Martindale, that was much more likely. Thanet said so, to Joan.

'Mm.' She was thoughtful. 'He certainly doesn't sound the most sensitive of souls. Practically everyone he met seems to have had a row with him.'

'Quite. At first I thought it strange that people would dive straight into resurrecting old grudges as though they had happened only yesterday, but when Mrs Byfleet told me how he had tried to pump her, quite unashamedly, it does seem that although he could presumably turn on the charm when he wanted to, if it didn't suit him to do so he really couldn't have cared less if he upset people or not.'

'Yes, but we're not exactly talking about trivial matters, are we? Crippling that poor boy for life and destroying his mother's marriage, causing the death of Mr Tiller's prize bull after all those years of effort, making a pass at a married woman whose husband has a reputation for jealousy . . .'

'He might not have known Fever was the jealous type.'

'Even so . . .'

'Then there's Jack Talion, the farm manager. We still

don't know what he had against Martindale.' Thanet sighed. 'Anyway, as I was saying to Mike, I'm beginning to wonder if we're going to get anywhere on this one.'

'Oh come on, darling! You've only been working on it for forty-eight hours. And if you gave me a pound for every time I'd heard you say that . . . Nearly every time, at some point in a case, you start having doubts about whether you'll be able to solve it.'

'I suppose that's true.' Joan was right, he had to admit it. 'But the problem is that this time, even if I do find out who killed him—assuming it wasn't a straightforward accident, that is—I don't see any prospect of proving it.'

'And I've heard that before, too! You'll get there in the end, I know you will. You're just tired, that's all. We'll have an early night and you'll feel quite different in the morning, you'll see.'

Thanet hoped she was right.

17

As usual, Joan was right. Although Thanet had lain awake for some time while the crowded impressions of the day jostled through his mind, in the end he did manage a good seven hours' sleep and by next morning his pessimistic mood had vanished. After all, he reminded himself as he squinted into the shaving mirror, he was far from at a dead end. Reports should now be in on a number of enquiries that had been set in motion, including the interview with the farmhand Jack Talion had sacked. Thanet was hoping that this was a local man who would be able to shed some light on the reason for Talion's animosity towards Martindale. Also, the forensic evidence on the van and the results of the postmortem should be in today.

Outside, Thanet's spirits rose further. The sun was shining, the sky was clear and it was several degrees warmer. The last of the snow had gone and they would be able to discard the Land Rover in favour of a car. Lineham would be pleased.

Whistling, Thanet set off for work. But his buoyant mood was soon to be severely tested. In good time when he left home, he was only halfway when there was a squeal of brakes ahead of him and the cars in front braked sharply. Thanet sucked in his breath as there was a dull ominous crunch and his car lurched. The driver behind had reacted too slowly and failed to pull up in time. There followed a time-consuming exchange of names, telephone numbers and details of insurance companies, as a result of which Thanet finally arrived at work only a matter of minutes before he was due at the morning meeting. It was unfortunate that as he hurried in Draco happened to be talking to the Station Officer in the Reception area. The Superintendent's hairy eyebrows elevated themselves in pained surprise, and he glanced pointedly at the clock.

To compound his problem the sight of Draco reminded him that he'd completely forgotten after all, last night, to read through Draco's information sheet on ODD. He wasn't exactly going to be top of the Superintendent's popularity poll this morning.

Muttering under his breath Thanet raced upstairs to his office, removing his coat as he went. Lineham glanced up, startled, as he burst in.

Thanet tossed the coat on to a chair. 'No time to stop,' he panted. 'Minor accident on the way. No, it's all right, I'm fine. Anything it's absolutely essential for me to know before the meeting?'

Lineham glanced at the papers littering his desk. 'Interesting but not essential.'

'Fine. See you shortly.'

Down the stairs again with seconds to spare. Outside Draco's door Thanet pulled up and paused long enough to take a couple of deep breaths before going in. Once again he was last.

Draco shot him a sideways glance but made no comment. He waited until Thanet was seated then said, 'Right, well now that you've had twenty four hours to think over my suggestions, perhaps we could begin by having your thoughts on ODD.'

Thanet slid down an inch or two in his chair, unconsciously betraying his desire to become invisible. Draco noticed and gave him a sharp glance. Thanet sat up again, straightening his shoulders. *Face it like a man,* he told himself with an inward grin, in a Midwestern drawl. And then, with a spurt of resentment, *I have had more important things on my mind.*

Tody and Boon had obviously done their homework. In turn they came up with constructive comments while Thanet continued inwardly to justify himself.

'Thanet?'

'Er . . .' Might as well come straight out with it. 'I'm

afraid I've been so busy with the Martindale case that I clean forgot you were expecting our comments today, sir.'

Draco's nostrils flared. 'I see.'

There was a brief, pregnant silence before the Superintendent went on, 'Well in that case perhaps you could tell us what you have been doing.'

Ignoring the emphasis on 'have' Thanet launched into an account of yesterday's activities. The others listened, asked pertinent questions and then Draco said, 'Anything interesting come in overnight?'

'I'm afraid there hasn't been time to check yet, sir.' Thanet was furious. Having seen him arrive only moments before Draco must have known he wouldn't have had time to read any reports. It had been a deliberate ploy to put him further in the wrong. Perhaps the Superintendent was paying him back for having wrong-footed him yesterday. 'I was involved in a minor accident on the way to work and there was some delay.'

'Not your fault I hope, Thanet.'

'No, sir.'

'Good. Don't like my officers to be seen to be infringing the law.'

The meeting broke up, but Draco called Thanet back. He clasped his hands behind his back and gave a little preparatory bounce, as if to lend more weight to his words. 'Look, Thanet, I do understand that you are very busy with this Martindale investigation, but it won't do to let other things slide, you know.'

'No, sir.'

Bounce. 'I don't think you quite appreciate the importance of this new initiative of mine. It doesn't do to let the grass grow under one's feet.'

'No, sir.'

Bounce. 'One has to keep a sense of balance, of proportion. It's so easy to become so obsessed with one aspect of one's work that one lets others slide. Not that I'm suggesting you do that, of course. It's just that one has to be on one's guard against it. . . . Perhaps by tomorrow you'll have had time to come up with some thoughts on ODD.'

'I'll try, sir. But . . .'

Bounce. 'I'll look forward to hearing them, then. Good. That's all.'

Thanet fumed silently all the way back upstairs and into his office.

Lineham took one look at his face and said, 'Been having fun?'

'Don't joke about it, Mike!' Thanet reached for his pipe and began filling it, stuffing the tobacco in with angry stabs.

'Bad as that, was it?'

'Let's just say it was an experience I shouldn't care to repeat too often.'

With an upsurge of the resentment common among smokers against a world which was making them feel more and more like social outcasts, Thanet lit up. Lineham could put up with it for once.

The door opened and Doc Mallard came in.

'Faugh!' he said, waving his hand to disperse the coils of smoke drifting towards him. 'At it again, Luke? How often do I have to tell you—?' He broke off. 'Do I detect a chill in the atmosphere?'

'He had a minor accident on the way to work,' said Lineham.

'Really?' Mallard advanced, concerned. 'You all right, Luke?'

'It's not that,' said Thanet irritably. 'That was nothing, I'm perfectly all right.'

'Sure? You don't want me to look you over?'

'No, no. If you must know, I've just been hauled over the carpet, that's all.'

'Oh dear. Our zealous Superintendent on the warpath again. What have you been up to this time?'

Thanet shook his head. 'It's not important. Any news for us, Doc?'

'Here's the PM report. I meant to give you a ring yesterday afternoon, but one or two things cropped up . . .'

'That's all right.' Thanet knew that if there had been something important to tell, Mallard wouldn't have forgotten. 'So there was nothing unexpected?'

'Not really. It's all there, but shall I give you a quick summary in layman's terms?'

'Please.'

'Well, as seemed likely from the tear in the overcoat and the head injury, the victim was struck in the back. My guess is that when the car hit him he was tossed upwards and backwards and struck the back of his head on the front offside corner of the roof.'

'That's right,' said Lineham. He glanced at Thanet. 'The forensic report on the van came in this morning.'

'Well, as I say,' said Mallard, 'the main impact was to the back left side. There was considerable muscle bruising, kidney damage and—this was the worst injury—partial dislocation of the spine. The scalp wound was relatively superficial, a glancing blow.'

'So he might have recovered consciousness?'

'He did.' Mallard hesitated. 'That's the unpleasant part.'

'What do you mean?'

'Work it out for yourself. Assuming that he was put into that ditch immediately after the accident . . .'

'Just a minute,' said Thanet. 'You said "put". The spinal injury meant that he wouldn't have been able to put himself in?'

'He certainly wouldn't have been able to walk. He could have dragged himself a short distance, but there were no cuts or abrasions on the palms of his hands. On the other hand, there were particles of dirt under some of his fingernails . . .'

Thanet stared at Mallard, appalled, his imagination at once conjuring up the scene: the injured man in the ditch, a thin mantle of snow covering his face, the gradual awakening, the increasingly despairing attempts to sit up, the dawning consciousness of his situation before the frantic scrabbling of fingernails against the frozen sides of the ditch and the final slide into numbing unconsciousness and death.

'If he'd been taken to hospital right away he'd be in pretty bad shape but at least he'd still be alive. Or if it had been summertime and the weather had been warmer . . . As it was, of course, he didn't have a chance and it's not surprising that he was dead by morning.'

Thanet shook his head to try and dispel the grim images lingering on the screen of his mind. 'I suppose you still can't be very precise about time of death, in the circumstances?'

'No. But from the rectal temperature and the tests on the eye fluid the findings are consistent with death occurring sometime in the early hours of the morning.'

Thanet was still feeling shaken. He took the report Mallard held out. 'Well, thanks for coming in, Doc.'

'You're sure you're all right, Luke, that you don't want me to take a look at you?'

'No, really. Some idiot behind me didn't brake quickly enough, that's all. The only damage was to the rear of my car.'

'It's the inconvenience of sorting it out that's the nuisance,' said Mallard sympathetically. 'Well, if there's nothing else . . . ?'

Thanet watched him go and then in contrition laid down his pipe. There was no reason why Lineham should suffer because of Draco's unreasonableness.

'Nasty,' said Lineham.

'Very. Hardly bears thinking about, does it?' Then, with an attempt at briskness, 'Right then, Mike. What have we got?'

'Various bits and pieces. As I said, forensic have confirmed that it was the van that knocked him down.'

'Good. Anything else there?'

'Hundreds of fingerprints, of course, all useless. So many people used it legitimately . . .'

'Quite. Never mind, at least we're now certain we're on the right track, and it wasn't just a passing motorist. And talking of passing motorists, anything come in as a result of the TVS appeal?'

'Nothing useful, sir. Of course, it was a bitterly cold night and I suppose most people were at home by the fire, watching television. And it's not exactly a major road, it's mostly local traffic along there.'

'Pity. We could just do with an independent witness.'

'Doesn't look as though we're going to get one. It's been two days now . . .'

'Don't rub it in, Mike. Anything else?'

'Several things, actually.'

'So? Come on, man, we haven't got all day.'

'There's an interesting report on an interview with the parlourmaid who served dinner to the Hamiltons and Martindale the night he died. She says she definitely heard him tell them that he was going to be staying on at the Hall and—get this—that he would be establishing his right to sole ownership.'

'Really? How did she hear all this? They wouldn't have talked about it openly in front of her, surely?'

'I don't know, sir. I have the impression that people like that think servants are pretty well invisible. But no, they didn't discuss it openly. It's just that she could tell there was a bit of an atmosphere and sensing that there might be some interesting gossip, she eavesdropped.'

'I see. Who interviewed her?'

'Swift, sir. I had a word with him and I gather it took a little while to winkle all this out of her.'

'Turned on the boyish charm, I suppose. She was young, I imagine?'

Lineham grinned. 'Yes. And pretty.'

'Why didn't she come up with all this before?'

'She was off duty the day the body was discovered, so he didn't see her till yesterday.'

'So what else did she hear?'

Lineham sat back and grinned. 'Only that Martindale informed them that they were welcome to stay on and work for him, if they liked.'

'His sister to run the hotel and Hamilton the estate?'

Lineham nodded.

'So much for all that "I'm sure we could all have come to some amicable arrangement." And, "It's a good-sized cake, there was plenty for everybody."'

Lineham was still nodding. 'Quite. It's a classic motive, isn't it? Two thousand acres and Longford Hall.'

'It certainly is. I must admit I was a bit suspicious when Mrs Hamilton told us about Sam Tiller and his bull. Oh, I know she put up a good show of reluctance, but I'm pretty sure that she still wouldn't have given in if she hadn't had a good reason.'

'To deflect attention away from herself, you mean?'

'Yes. Did the girl say how they reacted to the good news?'

'Unfortunately she doesn't know. She had to go and fetch the next course. But she didn't think there'd been an open row about it, judging by their behaviour when she went back.'

'I imagine they'd have been too subtle for that, tried persuasion first, or sought legal advice.'

'Quite.'

'We'll have to talk to the Hamiltons again, obviously. If only we could find out what Martindale was up to after Mrs Byfleet left him at 7.15 ... Well anyway, was there anything else?'

'Swift is still trying to trace Martindale's former lady loves. The address book was pretty useless, most of the stuff was way out of date. He thinks it might well take several more days yet. Some of the names were non-starters, of course. Just a postcard, with no address. Some of them were guests at the hotels Martindale stayed in, often some time ago, so it's a long job. Records have been lost or destroyed or the hotel's changed hands, or the women have moved ...'

'Yes yes, I get the picture. Has he managed to get any positive results yet?'

'Well, some of them were manageresses or even the owners of the hotels, so they're still around. Not surprising, really. Martindale was only fifty and he would have gone for middle-aged widows mostly, I should think. And if they owned hotels they wouldn't be likely to have retired yet. But some of them are now married, so it's proving a bit tricky. Swift's made a list.' Lineham shuffled through the papers on his desk and picked out a sheet of paper. 'Here we are.' He handed it over.

'Mm.' Thanet read out the names. 'Mrs Mary Wix in Norwich, Mrs Elizabeth Johnson in Broadway, Mrs Jeannette Martin in Eastbourne, Mrs Brenda Taylor in Worthing, Mrs Caroline Dempster in Folkestone, Mrs Kathleen Jackson in Bournemouth.' None of them rang a bell. But then, why should they, and what possible relevance could they have? Perhaps Swift was wasting his time. Thanet said so. 'What d'you think, Mike?'

'Well I agree, it does seem an awful lot of time spent to

little purpose. I'm not quite sure why you thought it important.'

'Not important, just a loose end to be followed up. But if it's going to be as time-consuming as that I'm not sure it's justified.' Thanet tapped the report. 'Did he actually learn anything useful from any of them?'

'Not really. Reactions varied, apparently. One or two refused to talk. As soon as they heard Martindale's name they slammed the phone down. One—Mrs Dempster, in Folkestone—was rather pathetic apparently, eager for news and pretty upset to hear he was dead. A couple more said they didn't want to talk about it, they were now happily married . . . No, I agree. I don't think there's much point in wasting any more time on it.'

'Pull him off it, then. That the lot?'

'Not quite.'

There was a glint in Lineham's eye which Thanet had seen before. It looked as though the sergeant had saved the most interesting item till last. 'What have you got up your sleeve, Mike? Ah, don't tell me. That sacked farmhand . . .'

'Right!' Lineham selected another report, opened it. But he didn't hand it over. Obviously he wanted to tell Thanet himself, watch his reaction.

Thanet decided to indulge him. 'Well?'

Lineham leaned forward. 'Talion's daughter Rose committed suicide when Martindale ditched her.'

18

Thanet remembered the satisfaction in Talion's eyes when Martindale's death was mentioned, the man's bitter hostility when questioned, the bleakness of the atmosphere in Home Farm, the frailty of Talion's wife, his protectiveness towards her. Had Rose been their only child, he wondered? And had her suicide cast over her home and family a blight from which they had never recovered?

'When was this?'

'Nineteen sixty-four. She was seventeen.'

Bridget's age. How would he feel about a man who drove her to suicide? Thanet shivered.

'Explains why Talion was so hostile, doesn't it, sir? Especially when we told him it was the hotel van that ran Martindale down and he knew he'd used it himself that night. No wonder he didn't want to tell us what he had against him. He must have known we'd consider it a strong motive.'

'True. All the same, it doesn't necessarily mean he did it. He might quite simply not have wanted to have what must have been a very painful business resurrected.' Thanet sighed. 'I must say, Martindale didn't do things by halves, did he? He seems to have left a trail of shattered lives behind him. Sam Tiller, Mrs Rankle, now Talion . . .'

'We'll have to go and see Talion again.'

'Obviously.' Thanet grimaced. 'He'll probably set the dog on us. But I want to see the Hamiltons first.'

'Shall I fix up appointments?'

'No. We'll take pot luck. It doesn't really matter which

161

order we see them in. If we can't find one we'll try another.'

It was a real pleasure to drive out to Sutton-in-the-Weald this morning. The countryside basked in the sunshine and it was possible to believe that spring really was just around the corner. Soon now the sheep grazing in the fields would be surrounded by lambs, the woods and hedges misted over with the tender green of young foliage. Thanet loved to watch the progress of the seasons and pitied city dwellers who depended on parks and gardens for visible evidence of nature's annual rhythms.

Longford Hall was at its best today, its rosy brick mellow in its serene setting of park and woodland. Far away over to the right tiny figures toiled on the Sisyphean task of clearing up the storm damage. Thanet wondered aloud if Hamilton were among them.

'Doesn't matter if he is. We can see Mrs Hamilton first.'

'If she's there.'

She wasn't, but was due back shortly, apparently. Thanet had noticed Toby Fever's car outside and thought that while they were waiting they might take the opportunity to clear up one or two minor points with him and Tessa.

The receptionist frowned. 'I'm not sure where they are. I think they said they were going up to see Nanny.'

Nanny! Thanet's ears pricked up. He wondered if, by any stroke of luck, she had also been Delia and Leo's nanny. Sometimes, in families like this one, the nanny became so much part of the household that she stayed on when her charges were grown up and then looked after their children. Such elderly retainers were a dying breed, of course. Today's nannies rarely stayed more than a few years at most, then moved on to fresher and perhaps more lucrative pastures. But in a house like this . . . 'Where would we find her?'

'I'm not sure that . . . Oh, I don't suppose she'd mind.' The girl laughed. 'In fact, come to think of it, she'd probably enjoy it! She's pretty lively still, it's only her arthritis that keeps her confined to her rooms. She's in the day nursery. I'll get someone to show you.'

A trim housemaid led the way up seemingly endless flights of stairs and along interminable corridors to a bright, sunny room on the south-east side of the house. At this hour in February the sun was streaming in and Thanet blinked, momentarily dazzled. The room seemed full of people but when his vision cleared he saw that there were only four: Adam, Tessa, Toby and an elderly woman in an orthopaedic wing chair near the fire. The room was comfortably but plainly furnished with sturdy central table and chairs and a number of sagging armchairs with worn loose covers. Adam and Tessa were seated in two of them and Toby was sprawled on the hearthrug in front of the fire, which burned brightly in a black Victorian cast-iron grate surrounded by glazed green tiles with animal motifs. A tall brass fireguard stood in front of it, relic of the days when the room really was a nursery and now presumably retained as a safeguard against the nanny's disability.

They were all clearly enjoying this cosy relaxed domestic interlude. They had been sharing a joke and the faces they turned towards the two policemen were still smiling.

'Inspector!' Adam jumped up. 'Allow me to introduce you to the love of my life, Nanny Foster. Nanny, this is Inspector Thanet, that I was telling you about, and his faithful sidekick, Sergeant Lineham!'

Gone were the dandy and the waif. Today Adam was very much the son of the house in cavalry twill trousers, tattersall shirt, old school tie and tweed sports jacket. Which persona would eventually emerge? Thanet wondered. Tessa, too, looked different today. The stiff spikes of hair were now horizontal instead of vertical, sticking out above her ears on either side, as if a mysterious force had visited her in the night, altering their disposition. If anything her mini was even more minimal; the expanse of inner thigh seemed to go on for ever leaving little to the imagination.

'That's enough, Adam,' said the woman, smiling. 'The Inspector will think I never taught you any manners.'

She was alarmingly frail, her thin body bent and twisted by the disabling disease, her hands as gnarled and misshapen as old tree roots. But there was plenty of evidence that she was well looked after. She was neat and clean, her sparse white hair neatly combed back into a bun. Beside her chair was an adjustable spotlight on a stand and a three-tiered trolley laden with books, magazines, radio, photograph albums, and all the cluttered pill and potion paraphernalia of an invalid's day. Nearby stood a hospital-type table which would swivel across her knees. On it was a half-completed jigsaw.

They all settled down, Thanet and Lineham on upright chairs at the table.

'I hope you don't mind us intruding, Miss Foster, but there are one or two minor details we wanted to check,' said Thanet. But his mind was only partly on what he was saying. When he'd come in just then and glimpsed Toby from that unfamiliar angle he had once again experienced that curious shock of recognition. He *had* seen the young man before, he was certain of it. But where? Toby was still on the floor but was now sitting up, elbows hooked over knees, leaning back against Tessa's armchair. Thanet glanced at him again and suddenly it came to him. Of course!

'Not at all. The children have told me about you and it's nice to meet you in the flesh, though I could wish it was for a happier reason.' Her face was sombre.

'You've been here a long time?' The question was mechanical. Thanet was still preoccupied with his revelation. He realised that Lineham, always sensitive to the nuances of his behaviour, had noticed and given him a questioning glance.

'Forty-six years. I came when Leo was four.' Briefly her face contorted and her lower lip trembled.

With an effort Thanet focused his mind on the conversation. He would think about the implications of his discovery later. Registering her distress he guessed that she was remembering those early, presumably happy days and wondered if this was, after all, a good idea. It was in any case difficult to talk to her as he would wish, with the young people present.

'He had wings and a halo then, didn't he, Nanny?' This was Tessa.

Adam laughed. 'Used to bore the pants off us with stories of Ma and Uncle Leo, didn't you, Nanny?'

'All very well for you to laugh, you two, but they were happy days. Right up until your grandmother died.'

'Ta-ra-ra, ra-ra ra ra.' Adam scraped away at an imaginary violin.

'Adam!' she said sharply and for once he actually looked a little shamefaced.

'You ought to be ashamed of yourself,' she snapped. 'It's all very well for you, brought up with the security of your mother and father behind you. Your Uncle Leo wasn't so lucky.'

Tessa sighed. This was obviously an old theme, retold so often that for them it had lost its impact. 'Nanny's trying to say that after Grandmother died Uncle Leo became a Deprived Child.'

'He did!' said the old lady. She put her hands on the arms of the chair and shifted herself into an almost imperceptibly different position.

Thanet recognised the signs. She was settling herself into a narrative mood. He hoped none of the young people would sabotage it.

Tessa and Adam exchanged glances. *Shall we go?*

Thanet willed them to leave but to his disappointment they stayed, through sheer inertia he imagined. It was comfortable in here and any entertainment was better than none. Tessa presumably didn't have a job, but what about Toby?

As if he had tuned in to Thanet's question Toby uncurled himself and stood up. 'I'd better be off. I'm supposed to be halfway to Maidstone by now and I'll have Dad on my tail. No,' to Tessa, 'don't bother to come down. I'll see you tonight. About half seven?'

She nodded. 'Fine.'

Thanet glanced at Lineham and gave an almost imperceptible nod at the door. *Go and ask him.*

Unobtrusively Lineham followed Toby out. Thanet saw that Tessa was frowning. The little exchange had not escaped her.

'Sorry, Miss Foster,' he said. 'You were saying, about Mr Martindale . . . ?'

'He was unlucky, that's all. As so often happens, the father favoured the daughter and the mother the son. Leo was the apple of Mrs Martindale's eye and I'm afraid she spoiled him rather. Over-indulged him. I don't blame her, mind, it was always very hard to say no to Leo. He was such a handsome lad, he could have charmed the birds out of the trees if he'd set his mind to it. But I'm afraid it set his father against him. It was the old story, really, I've seen it so often, the father jealous of the son . . . So when Mrs Martindale died, when Leo was twelve, he had a rough time.'

'In what way?'

'He was shoved off to boarding school for a start,' said Adam. 'Like poor little me.'

'You hadn't just lost your mother,' said Miss Foster reprovingly. 'And you'd boarded at your prep school, too. Leo had been a day boy until then.' She shook her head. 'Of course, he hated it, just went haywire. Personally, I think his behaviour was so impossible because he was hoping they'd throw him out and he could live at home again. He loved it here. But his father wasn't having that. Every time Leo was expelled he was just sent off to another school."

Lineham came back in and sat down again.

"Every time?' said Thanet.

'Well, it sounds worse than it actually was. He was expelled from three. After that I think it dawned on him that there really wasn't much point, he might as well settle down. But he was never happy. Did as little work as possible and then went to Cirencester, where he started the Estate Management course. Threw it in at the end of the first year and came home, lazed around doing nothing very much. His mother had left him enough for him not to have to work.'

"Sounds great!' said Adam. 'Wish somebody'd leave me enough to doss around and do nothing.'

'You'd be bored out of your tiny mind by the end of the first week,' said Tessa. 'I know. I've tried it. I'm off to Art College in September,' she said to Thanet, her eyes alight with the first sign of enthusiasm she had shown.

'Good!' he said. 'Where?'

'St Martin's School of Art.' There was pride in her voice now.

Obviously he had done her an injustice and he was careful not to sound condescending as he said, 'You must be good. It's very difficult to get in, I believe. Fashion?'

'Textile design.'

'It's all very well for you,' said Adam sulkily. 'You've always known what you wanted to do. There's nothing that really grabs me like that.'

'Give it time,' said Miss Foster, smiling. 'Just keep on doing as well as you are at school and who knows, you could end up Prime Minister!'

'Heaven forbid!' said Tessa. 'The imagination boggles!'

'I don't suppose,' said Thanet, anxious to lead the conversation back to Martindale, 'that Mr Martindale senior was too pleased, when his son dropped out of college.'

'He was furious. Barely spoke to him for weeks. There was always a clash of personalities between them but after that things were worse than ever. Mr Martindale was a good employer and I don't really like saying this, but he seemed to have this blind spot as far as Leo was concerned; couldn't see anything good in him at all. And that just made Leo behave more badly.' She shook her head sadly. 'It was a vicious circle, really.'

'And once he'd set his foot on the slippery slope . . .' said Adam. He made a sliding motion with his hand. 'Oops, it was downhill all the way.'

'I've never discovered why he finally went away for good,' said Thanet. He'd be interested to hear Miss Foster's version of the rift between father and son.

Miss Foster pursed her lips and shook her head.

'Simple,' drawled Tessa. 'Oh do stop looking so disapproving, Nanny. If we don't tell the Inspector someone else will. Can't you see, he's not the type to give up? It happened really because he ran out of money. Grandmother Martindale had apparently been rather unwise and instead of setting up a trust fund from which he had the income until he reached the age of wisdom—though from what we know of Uncle Leo I don't suppose he ever would have—she left him a capital sum outright. He had a whale of a time: wine, women, song, fast cars, expensive clothes, the lot. Grandfather kept on baling him out of debt but when he started betting on the gee-gees it was the last straw. I believe he gave him one more chance and when he finally blew it, to the tune of several thousand pounds— and that was an awful lot of money in those days—that was it. Grandfather did the "Never darken my doors again" act, and Uncle Leo never did.' She shrugged. 'We always felt deprived about that, didn't we, Adam, thought our lives had lacked a certain spice.'

Adam nodded. 'That was why I was so disappointed not to have seen him when he came back. Ah well, that's life, I suppose. Incidentally, Tess, you forgot to put the finishing touch to the scenario. When he went, he took half the family silver with him.'

'All right, that's enough!' said Miss Foster. 'I let you run on, Tessa, because I could see you were right and Inspector Thanet would have gone on asking until someone had given him the information. But I won't sit here and listen to you running poor Leo down any longer. I know he was bad in many ways but it wasn't his fault. Children aren't born spoiled, you know, it's adults that make them so. And in your uncle's case . . . to be so over-indulged and then suddenly to find himself out in the cold for good . . . I'm not a bit surprised he went off the rails, even if I couldn't approve of some of the things he did. No, I felt sorry for him, still do. He missed so much in life, through no fault of his own. And if you're not careful, Adam, you'll go the same way, with all this smart-Alec nonsense.'

Adam jumped up and went to lay his cheek against her hair. 'Not true, Nanny! You know that at heart I'm pure gold, right through.'

'That's a matter of opinion.' But the smile she gave him showed that she agreed, really.

Thanet decided to change the subject. 'Tell me, Tessa, when you drove home that night, did you happen to notice anything out of the ordinary on the way?'

'Such as a body lying at the side of the road, you mean! Honestly, Inspector, you can't really believe I wouldn't have got Dad to stop if I had!' Tessa was scornful and Thanet felt that her opinion of him had just taken a nose-dive. He didn't care, it had just been a way of leading into his next question.

'Of course, your father was with you . . . The Range Rover had broken down, I believe.'

'Yes. Infuriating. It was nothing serious, only a loose sparking plug apparently, but I'm not mechanically minded, I'm afraid. So I rang Dad and asked him to come and fetch me. I knew he'd still be up, he never goes to bed very early. Anyway, he managed to fix it.'

Thanet was certain that she was telling the truth. He had never really believed that Hamilton would stoop so low as to get his daughter to lie for him in case someone had seen him driving the van that night. And Mrs Byfleet had heard both cars return.

'What time did you get back?'

She shrugged. 'Soon after twelve, I think. I rather lost track of time, hanging around waiting for Dad.'

'Was it snowing when you got home?'

'Yes. It had just started.'

On the way back downstairs Lineham said, 'We still can't rule Mr Hamilton out, though, can we? He'd have had plenty of opportunity earlier on.'

Thanet sighed. 'What did Toby say?'

Lineham waited while a chambermaid went by. 'He confirms what Mrs Rankle told us. He did borrow his mother's car that night, to go to Canterbury on business for his father to discuss a haulage job with a chap who was unavailable during the day. His father was supposed to go, apparently, but then they had that phone call to say Mrs Fever's mother had been taken ill and he asked Toby to go instead. Toby couldn't use his own car because he was working on it and it was jacked up.'

'Cars, cars . . . They seem to crop up everywhere in this case. Should be just up your street, Mike.'

They had reached the head of the staircase and Thanet paused, glancing around to make sure no one was in earshot. Downstairs in the hall the receptionist was at her desk and a group of guests was seated around the fire, a tray of coffee on the table between them.

Thanet lowered his voice. 'By the way, I wanted to ask you . . . Did I mention to you that I thought Toby looked familiar, that I had a feeling I might have come across him before somewhere?'

'No, why? Have you?'

'No. But just think, Mike. Doesn't he remind you of someone else in this case? Not all the time, but just in fleeting moments?'

Lineham frowned. 'I don't think so. Who?'

'It didn't dawn on me till just now. And then . . . Well, first of all, when we went in, he was lying down, and then he sat up. Both positions were the same, you see, that was what made me realise . . .

Lineham was still puzzled. 'Sorry, I just don't see what you're getting at.'

'The first time we saw Martindale, lying in the snow . . . And then that photograph we saw in his room, the one of him and his sister, sitting on the steps . . .'

Lineham's eyes widened. 'You mean . . . ?'

Thanet nodded. 'I think Toby might be his son.'

19

Lineham was still looking stunned. 'But...'

Thanet knew how he felt. The implications were so complicated and far-reaching that it was difficult to take them all in at once. 'I'd like to discuss this with you before seeing Mrs Hamilton. Also, there's a check I'd like to run... Let's go outside.'

Delia Hamilton was back, apparently. Thanet asked the receptionist to tell her that he had an urgent call to make before seeing her, then he and Lineham went out to the car. There he put in a request for two pieces of information—Toby's date of birth, and the date of his parents' marriage. 'As fast as you can, please.'

'Will do.'

Lineham waited until he had finished before saying, 'If you're right, sir, do you think any of them realises?'

'Ah, now that's the million-dollar question. I haven't had time to think about it properly yet, but I doubt that the Hamiltons know. Otherwise they wouldn't be too keen on Tessa going out with him.'

'You mean, because they're first cousins... Sir!' Lineham's eyes widened in shock.

'What?'

'Do you realise what this could mean? No, perhaps it wouldn't. I don't know...'

'You're being incoherent, Mike. Start again.'

'Can illegitimate children inherit?' said Lineham.

Thanet could see why the sergeant had looked so thunderstruck. This had not yet occurred to him. If Martindale had been the owner of Longford Hall, and Toby was his son . . .

'I believe they can. Wasn't there an Act, to make it legal?'

'I remember something about it . . . In that case, perhaps the Hamiltons do know,' said Lineham. 'I should think they're pretty snobbish and I always did wonder if they approved of Tessa going out with Toby. But now . . . Perhaps they actually encouraged it, knowing that it was just possible that one day Toby could be heir to the whole estate.'

'Let's not speculate on that one until we're sure of our ground. We might well find that the fact that his mother and Martindale never married would rule him out.'

'All the same, I find it difficult to believe that Mrs Hamilton wouldn't have spotted the resemblance between Toby and her brother before now, if you cottoned on to it as quickly as you did.'

'I don't know. For one thing you and I are trained to look for connections, to be actively on the alert for them. And the fact that we are strangers means that we look at everyone with a fresh eye. The Hamiltons will have watched Toby grow up as just another village boy, remember, and probably always accepted him on face value as the Fevers' son. It isn't as if the resemblance is striking—and let's face it, I could be wrong.'

But he wasn't—or at least, it didn't look as though he was. A few minutes later the information came through: Toby's date of birth was 9 January 1966, that of his parents' marriage 4 August 1965.

After their initial elation that it seemed Thanet's hunch was correct, Lineham sobered. 'Doesn't necessarily mean he's Martindale's son, of course. He could still be Fever's— or anybody else's, for that matter . . .'

Thanet shook his head. Logically Lineham could be right, but Thanet knew in his bones that he wasn't.

Lineham grinned. 'OK, I give in. I've never known you wrong about something like this. So let's see . . . Martindale left in 1965. Right? And if Toby was born in January 1966 he would have been conceived in April 1965. I wonder in which month Martindale left.'

'We'll ask his sister.'

'In the summer, probably, if the Fevers were married in August. The sequence of events probably went: in April Yvonne becomes pregnant and in June she tells Martindale. That same month Martindale is thrown out of the ancestral home because of his debts—perhaps he was only too glad to get away, in the circumstances!—but Yvonne thinks he's gone away because of the baby, so she marries Fever who is waiting in the wings.'

'She might not have discovered she was pregnant until after Martindale had gone,' said Thanet. 'In which case he might never have known about the baby.'

'The question is, did he?'

'And if so, when did he find out? Before he left, while he was away, or after he came back?'

'It's all so complicated,' said Lineham with relish.

'I know. It's just occurred to me . . . perhaps you're right, and he did know about the baby before he left. Let's just accept, for the moment, that he did. You remember what the receptionist told us, about Martindale asking who Toby was, when Toby was talking to Mrs Byfleet? Perhaps there was something about the boy that reminded him of himself as a young man, and made him wonder . . .'

'I don't know.' Lineham was doubtful. 'Isn't it usually considered rather difficult to recognise a resemblance to yourself?'

'Possibly. But if Martindale knew he had a child, and was on the lookout for him . . .'

'Or her . . .'

'All right Mike, or her, but anyway, on the lookout; then when he saw this young man of the right age, he could have thought, I wonder . . .'

'It's possible. And then, of course, when the receptionist told him who Toby was, he'd have known this was his son—no, hang on, sir, he wouldn't, would he? Not unless he knew Yvonne had married Fever. And even then he couldn't have been sure—for all he knew, the Fevers could have had several children.'

'I think, for the purpose of this argument, we will assume that he did know she'd married Fever and that they'd had no other children. After all, Mike, if he knew

she was expecting his baby, he might well have made it his
business to keep an eye on her from afar, so to speak, find
out what happened to her and the child. If he didn't know,
this whole scenario collapses anyway. Still, we might as
well follow it through for the moment. So, you were
saying . . .'

'Well if he did find out who Toby was, by asking the
receptionist, I was just thinking it might have whetted his
appetite to get to know him. So I was wondering if, when
he ran into Mrs Fever in the village next day, he could
have told her he'd seen Toby and wanted to meet him,
make himself known to him, as his real father. Mrs Victor
said it looked as though he was trying to persuade Mrs
Fever to do something she didn't want to do.'

'The mechanic said that was because she was refusing to
go and have tea with Martindale, Mike.'

'But the mechanic wasn't present during the whole
conversation, was he? He had to go into the office to get
change. After all, it's not the sort of thing Martindale
would have been likely to discuss with anyone within
earshot, is it? He might just have pretended to have been
asking her to go and have tea with him, to fool the
mechanic when he came back.'

'Mm. Could be, I suppose. All right, let's accept that
Martindale was saying that he intended to tell Toby he was
his father. . . . Let's think. According to the mechanic, it
was after he teased Fever about Martindale's encounter
with Mrs Fever that Fever went rushing off—as we know,
up to the Hall, to tell Martindale to keep away from her in
future. Say Fever then went home and had a row with his
wife about it . . .'

'Fever must have known Toby wasn't his son, if his wife
was four months pregnant when he married her, mustn't
he, sir? If he's as jealous as people say, I expect he would
have gone on and on at her until she told him who the real
father was, and she may well have thought it was safe to
tell him as Martindale had gone away, apparently for
good. And if Fever did know Martindale was Toby's
father, it would explain why he reacted so strongly when
he heard Martindale was back and had been chatting
Mrs Fever up. And then, when Fever went home after-

wards and started going on at his wife about her talking to Martindale, in order to distract him she could have told him that Martindale had suggested making himself known to Toby . . .'

'Yes. I always think it must be pretty devastating when someone turns up on the doorstep claiming to be a long-lost son or daughter, father or mother. It must put all the family relationships in a turmoil, especially if the one who is being claimed had been kept in ignorance.'

'Of course, in all this we're assuming Toby has no idea who his real father was.'

Thanet frowned, thinking. 'I don't think he does. After all, if he had known Martindale was his father you'd have expected him to try to make contact with him when he came home, or at least to be affected to some extent by his death, but he seems completely unconcerned by it all. Anyway, assuming Martindale did suggest telling him the truth and Mrs Fever then told her husband, Fever could have been fuming about it all evening. And then, on his way back from Ashford in the van, if he saw Martindale ahead of him on the road . . .'

They looked at each other in silence.

'It's convincing,' said Thanet at last. 'But let's remember that at the moment it is still pure speculation and far from the only possibility. But it will be interesting to see what Mrs Hamilton has to say about it.'

They were shown into her office again. Her desk was littered with papers and she wasn't too pleased at the prospect of having to spend more time answering questions. 'I hope this isn't going to take long, Inspector. I really have a great deal to do today.'

It looked as though she had just been to the hairdresser's. Her hair was loose for once, framing her face and falling to her shoulders in carefully casual waves. It made her look younger and more vulnerable. She was wearing a finely pleated skirt in red wool and a long matching cashmere cardigan over a silky cream blouse with a finely scribbled abstract pattern in red and black.

'No longer than I can help,' said Thanet politely. 'May we sit down?'

She gestured impatiently. *If you must.*

No point in beating about the bush. 'It must have been a shock to you, to learn that your brother intended staying on and taking over his inheritance.'

A flash of anger, quickly suppressed. 'You've been listening to gossip again, Inspector. Do you enjoy scrabbling around in the refuse of people's lives?'

This accusation had been leveled at Thanet too often for him to be moved by it. 'Not at all, Mrs Hamilton. I'm only too well aware of the fact that after a sudden death, and especially a violent death, people close to the victim are often in a state of shock. To be honest, there are times when I find my work very distasteful.'

Recognising his sincerity Delia Hamilton had the grace to look discomforted, but she quickly recovered. 'It wasn't that much of a shock, to learn he intended staying on. My husband and I always knew that it could happen. We would have worked something out.'

'My information is that Mr Martindale suggested that you should continue to run the hotel and your husband the estate as his employees, and that you quarrelled about it.'

Again that flash of anger before she said coolly, 'Then your information is wrong, Inspector, or at least misleading.'

'You deny that there was an argument?'

'No. There was an argument, yes, I admit it. But arguments need not end in disharmony. On this occasion I think we managed to get my brother to see that in view of all the hard work Giles and I have put in, it would be a little unfair for us not to benefit by it, at least to some extent.'

'You're saying that you reached an agreement?'

'Let's say we were well on the way to it.'

'Despite the limitations imposed by the Trust?'

'Despite the limitations imposed by the Trust,' she echoed firmly.

No doubt Hamilton would back her up, but Thanet was certain that she was lying.

'Would you mind telling us the terms of that agreement?' He didn't think for a moment that she would, but there was no harm in asking.

'That's out of the question! It was an entirely private matter, and I . . .'

The phone rang and, with a muttered 'Excuse me', she picked it up and held a brief conversation about proposed repairs to the roof. After a moment she began shifting papers about on her desk and peering underneath. Then suddenly she tutted as if she had just remembered something, and stopped looking. A minute or two later she put down the receiver and said, 'While I think about it, Inspector, I've been meaning to ring up and ask . . . Did your men find a pocket calculator in the van? It's about so big,' and she made a window about three inches by two and a half with her fingers. 'My name and address are tucked into the inside flap.'

'I don't think so, no.' Thanet raised his eyebrows at Lineham, who shook his head. 'We'll ask, if you like, when we get back.'

'I'd be grateful. I really must buy another, it's just a question of remembering, when I'm in town . . .'

'You think you dropped it in the van when you went to fetch Adam?'

She shrugged. 'Well, it's several days now and it hasn't turned up anywhere else. I'm lost without it, it's just the right size to carry in my pocket. I've thought and thought and I know I had it just before dinner on Tuesday and that it was missing later on that evening.'

'Before your early dinner, you mean?'

'Yes. Anyway, if you'd just check . . .'

'Of course.' Thanet caught Lineham's eye. They had already arranged that the sergeant should question her about the two periods when the van had stood idle in the yard.

'You may be interested to know, Mrs Hamilton, that it has now been confirmed that it was your van that ran your brother down. We don't yet know whether this was deliberate or an accident, but in any case, as we explained before, it does seem from the position of the body in the ditch that whoever was driving must have moved it afterwards and can't claim ignorance of the accident. So we are questioning again everyone who had access to the van.'

He paused.

Delia Hamilton's lips had tightened, but she said nothing.

'We have therefore been trying to draw up a timetable of the van's movements on Tuesday evening. And there are two gaps unaccounted for, when the van was standing outside in the stable yard, unattended. So naturally we are now concentrating on those gaps.' He made a pretence of consulting his notebook. 'The first is between 8.10 and 8.30 that evening, the second between 10.30 and 11.15. Now, when we first talked to you, you told us that you got back from meeting Adam's train at twenty to eight, but unfortunately Adam and Tessa interrupted us before you could tell us what you did after that. We know, from what you told us subsequently, that you joined your guests for drinks, so if you could give us a summary of your movements from, say, eight o'clock onwards...'

'I see. So this is the inquisition, is it?'

'I wouldn't put it quite like that, ma'am.'

She stood up abruptly, folding her arms as if to protect herself. 'This is preposterous. I refuse to answer any more questions without my solicitor present.'

'It's up to you, Mrs Hamilton. You have every right to do that, if you wish, but...' Lineham glanced at Thanet.

Thanet intervened. He knew that the sergeant was asking his senior officer to use his authority to back him up on this.

'Mrs Hamilton, Sergeant Lineham is simply trying to say that although the choice is yours, there really is no need for you to take this attitude. These are routine questions, which we are asking of everyone who had keys to the van.'

'I'm not stupid, Inspector! I appreciate that, but at the same time it does seem to me sensible to protect my own interests.'

'Not if you have nothing to hide,' said Thanet.

There was a brief silence.

'Very clever, Inspector. By implication, if I still refuse, then I do have something to hide.' She sat down in her chair again, an angry, petulant movement, and tapped the polished wood of the desk with one crescent-shaped fingernail. The tiny, repetitive clicking was like the ticking of an alarm clock—or perhaps a bomb, thought Thanet. He watched her with interest. Would she explode?

Suddenly she folded her arms with that same defensive, self-protective movement he had noticed before. 'Oh very well. It irritates me to play your game, but when all's said and done, you're right. If I have nothing to hide there's nothing to be afraid of. And as I don't have anything to hide . . . From eight o'clock onwards, you say? Let me see. I know it's only a few days ago, but in a place like this our routine is such that one evening tends to merge into another . . .'

But it didn't take her long to work it out. After the guests went into dinner she had gone along to the kitchen to check that everything was running smoothly. At around five past eight she had gone up to have a brief word with Adam and make sure he had everything he needed before she retired to her room for half an hour. This was her usual practice, apparently, one of the rare periods of the day when she had time to herself, to relax.

'That would have been from, say, ten past eight until around twenty to nine?'

She pulled a face, aware that this covered the first period in question. 'Yes.'

After that she had gone down to the dining-room to check that all was running smoothly, then watched television with Adam and her husband until ten o'clock. After another trip downstairs she had retired to her room to take a leisurely bath before an early night. She had, she claimed, been in bed by around ten to eleven. She gave a wry little laugh and said, 'Hence my irritation just now, Inspector. I suspected that I might be unlucky and have no one to confirm my movements during the two periods in question.'

Thanet made no comment. Delia Hamilton qualified as a suspect in any case, having driven the van during the crucial period. Finding out what she had been doing during those two blank periods was at this stage not as important as it could have been. On the other hand it could prove vital later, if for example a witness was found who claimed to have seen Martindale leaving the house during one of them. 'What about your husband?'

She shrugged. 'I've no idea. This is a big house, we don't exactly live in each other's pockets. He has a bed in his dressing room and if he's late coming to bed for any reason he sleeps there, so as not to disturb me. He did that night, after going to fetch Tessa.'

'So you don't know what he was doing, during either the earlier or the later period in question?'

She shook her head. 'You'll have to ask him.' She reached for a sheaf of papers, pulled them towards her. 'And now, if you don't mind . . .'

'I'm sorry,' said Thanet, 'we're not quite finished yet.'

She gave an exasperated sigh. 'For heaven's sake . . . I'm never going to catch up on my work at this rate.'

'One or two more questions about Mr Martindale. He left the area in 1965, didn't he? Could you tell me exactly when? Which month, I mean.'

She frowned. 'What on earth d'you want to know that for?'

'Please . . .'

'It was the end of June.'

'Can you remember who his girlfriend was, at the time?' The frown was deeper now.

'The last time we talked to you we asked if Yvonne Fever had been your brother's girlfriend, before he went away . . . We have reason to believe that you were less than frank with us.'

'Really, Inspector, what can it possibly matter? We are talking about twenty-four years ago . . .'

'Let me put it this way. Mr Martindale left in June 1965. The Fevers were married in August. Toby Fever was born in January 1966.'

He let her work it out for herself. Delia Hamilton was no fool and he was rewarded by seeing the colour seep out of her face, leaving it chalk white. He saw her throat move as she swallowed.

'You're not suggesting . . .' It was scarcely more than a whisper.

Thanet said nothing. He had his answer. He stood up.

She put out a hand. 'No, wait . . . You've . . . Have you . . . Does anyone else know about this?'

'That,' said Thanet, 'is what we would like to know.'

He and Lineham turned to leave but she rose, pulled by invisible strings. 'Will you tell them?'

'That depends, I'm afraid.'

'On what?'

'On whether it becomes necessary.'

She sank back into her seat and he left her sitting at her desk, motionless as a statue.

20

By comparison with the last time they'd been in, the Drovers seemed positively crowded. There were eight other customers, five of them a group of young men in near-uniform of formal suit, white shirt and sober tie. Salesmen attending a conference nearby?

Sam Tiller was also there, enjoying a lunchtime pint with a couple of cronies. He gave the two policemen a hostile glance before firmly turning his back on them.

Thanet and Lineham waited until they had collected their beer and sandwiches before continuing their discussion. Delia Hamilton's reaction had convinced Thanet that the idea of Toby being Leo's son was entirely new to her, but Lineham was sticking to his guns.

'I think she'll tell whatever lies are necessary to get her off the hook.'

'Telling lies is one thing. Changing colour like that is another. I'd say it was virtually impossible to do it at will.'

'I don't know. Actors and actresses cry real tears.'

'Maybe. But they have years of practice, of thinking themselves into other people's skins, other people's moods. I imagine even the most experienced actor would need at least a few seconds to produce real tears, longer, probably. And she reacted just like that.' Thanet snapped his fingers in the air. 'One second she was her normal colour, the next she was white as a sheet.'

'I suppose so.' Lineham was still grudging, reluctant to relinquish his conception of Delia as a devious, scheming woman.

Thanet was shaking his head. 'Come on, Mike, you can't tell me she could have faked that.'

Lineham took a huge mouthful of sandwich and began to chew thoughtfully. A moment later he made an inarticulate sound.

'What?' said Thanet.

The sergeant's eyes were bulging with frustration as he tried to reduce the quantity of food in his mouth to manageable proportions.

'Serves you right,' said Thanet with a grin. 'I bet you tell the children never to bite off more than they can comfortably chew.'

Lineham swallowed, chewed, swallowed again. 'It's just that it occurred to me... The fact that Mrs Hamilton doesn't know Toby is her nephew doesn't mean that Mr Hamilton doesn't.'

Presumably the three negatives made a positive. 'You mean, perhaps he does know?'

'Yes. Leo Martindale could have told him.'

'And Hamilton didn't tell his wife? I doubt it, Mike. They seem pretty much in cahoots, those two.' Thanet took a thoughtful swig of beer. 'Besides, come to think of it, I'm not sure why it's especially important anyway for us to decide whether they knew or not. It's interesting, I grant you, but is it relevant to the case? If we're right about this and Toby really is Martindale's son, it could certainly matter whether Martindale himself knew, and also whether Fever knew. But the Hamiltons? I'm not so sure.' He paused. 'In fact, it could even be a point in their favour. Surely, if there was even the slightest chance of Toby inheriting the Hall the last thing they'd want to do is to get rid of Leo. At least with him in charge they'd be able to stay on, carry on their lives much as before, but with Toby installed there they would presumably have had to get out... We really must check whether or not he could inherit.'

'So are we going to see Mr Hamilton now?'

Thanet chewed the last mouthful of his sandwich—ham and pickle, this time—while he considered. 'No. I don't think we're going to get anything new out of him at the moment, I think he'll stick to whatever story he and his wife have prepared. If you're feeling brave enough to face the dog, I think we'll go and see Jack Talion next.'

'Are you, sir? Feeling brave enough, I mean?'

Thanet laughed. 'I'm counting on you to protect me, Mike. What else are sergeants for?'

Privately, Thanet wasn't looking forward to this interview. If Talion's daughter really had committed suicide because of Leo Martindale, it wasn't surprising that Talion had been dead against the idea of Martindale settling down in Sutton again. But that didn't necessarily mean he had killed him and, if not, Thanet hated the idea of reopening old wounds best left undisturbed. On the other hand, if Talion were guilty . . . Thanet sighed. He had meant it when he told Delia Hamilton that he sometimes found his job distasteful.

It took them some time to track Talion down. The farmyard at Home Farm was deserted and when they went up to the house there was no answer to their knock. Thanet shivered while they waited. During the morning the sky had clouded over again, the sunshine become fitful and now, suddenly, a chill wind began to blow.

Thanet turned up his collar. 'We'll have to come back later, Mike. Let's see if we can find Fever instead.'

They were heading back to the village when Lineham spotted a tractor coming towards them. 'Wonder if this chap works for Talion. If so, he might know where he is.' He flashed his lights, sounded his horn and pulled up. The tractor stopped and Lineham got out of the car.

'Have you any idea where we can find Mr Talion?'

Talion, it seemed, was repairing fences and after following the tractor driver's directions they donned their boots and had to plod across two huge fields of winter wheat. It was hard going. The soil, sodden and sticky in the aftermath of the snow, adhered to their boots in heavy lumps and after a few hundred yards it began to feel as though their feet were weighted down with blocks of concrete.

'Should be at the far side of the next field,' panted Lineham.

'Mm.'

The interlude had given Thanet time to think and he was beginning to wonder if this was a good idea. It was all very well to joke about the dog, but it was distinctly inhibiting to have to watch every word he said in case he provoked a hostile reaction from its master.

'There they are.'

They had reached another five-barred gate set into a thick hedge backed by post and wire-mesh fencing. On the far side of the next field were a tractor and trailer and a group of three men working on the boundary fence nearby.

The words were no sooner out of Lineham's mouth when a furious barking confirmed his guess and Talion's Alsatian jumped out of the trailer and began to streak towards them. The two policemen faltered. Would Talion call the dog back?

Talion allowed the dog to get halfway across the field before shouting a command. 'Rhett! Stay!'

To Thanet's relief the dog skidded to a halt.

'Rhett! Here!'

Reluctantly, it seemed, the animal turned back and trotted towards its master. Thanet and Lineham exchanged relieved glances before continuing on their way. After a word to the other two men Talion advanced to meet them with the measured stride of a countryman, the dog beside him.

'Sorry to interrupt your work, Mr Talion,' said Thanet when they were within speaking distance.

'Sit!' said Talion as they came up to him, and the Alsatian obeyed, ears pricked.

Thanet gave the animal a wary glance. This was definitely a bad idea. It was virtually impossible to concentrate out here in the open with the rising wind whistling about his ears and the dog alert to every move. It would have been more sensible to ask Talion to come into headquarters to make a statement. Here, on his own ground, legs planted firmly apart, Talion looked as sturdy and unlikely to bend as one of his own oak trees.

'Well?' said Talion, shoving his hands deep into the pockets of his windproof jacket. His eyes were wary, hostile.

'There are one or two more questions...'

Talion said nothing, merely raised his eyebrows a fraction.

'We're still checking on the movements of everyone who has a key to the van.'

Still no reaction.

'Could you give us an account of your movements after you returned to the Hall that night.'

'Why?'

'A man is dead, Mr Talion. It has been confirmed that he was knocked down by the van. We now also know, from the post-mortem, that it was not the impact which actually killed Mr Martindale. After the incident his body was moved into the ditch where he was found, and where he later died from exposure. This is therefore now definitely a murder investigation, and the movements of every person with access to the van naturally have to come under close scrutiny. So if you would just give us the information we need . . .'

Talion shrugged. 'I don't see that it'll help you much, but for what it's worth I went straight home, and spent the rest of the evening there.'

'You walked?'

'Yes.'

'Which way?'

'Along the footpath which links Home Farm with the Hall.'

'Is there anyone who can confirm that you were at home all evening—apart from your wife, that is?'

Talion's expression hardened. 'No. And I don't want you bothering my wife, either. I told you, she's not well. You'll just have to take my word for it.'

'It would only be to . . .'

'No!'

The dog's hackles were up and it again gave that alarming deep-throated growl. Thanet could see the muscles in its front legs bunch as it tensed, ready to spring on command. Time for a strategic withdrawal, he decided. The death of Talion's daughter would, understandably, be a very touchy subject indeed, and even to mention that they now knew Talion had good reason for hating Martindale and therefore a possible motive for leaving him to die would provoke the man even further. Thanet had no intention of putting either Lineham or himself at risk.

From now on, if they wanted to talk to Talion it would be on Thanet's terms.

He shrugged. 'We'll have to leave it there for the moment, then.'

Moving with unprovocative care he and Lineham turned away. They had gone only a few paces when Talion shouted after them. 'Remember what I said. Just keep away from her!'

Thanet raised a hand in acknowledgement but did not look back until he and Lineham were safely in the next field. Talion and the dog had almost reached the tractor and as they watched the animal leaped up to its former position. Thanet could see the silhouette of its head and shoulders above the boarded side of the trailer. It seemed to be watching them.

Lineham grinned with relief. 'I was beginning to work out when I'd had my last tetanus jab.'

'Yes. Not very clever of me, was it, to interview him on his own ground again. Talk about inhibiting! If there has to be a next time, it'll be safely back at headquarters, minus that dog.'

They began to plod back across the fields, collecting more mud on their boots on the way.

'D'you think there will have to be a next time, sir?'

Thanet shrugged. 'Difficult to tell. We haven't exactly made much progress with him, have we? But he's got as good a motive as anyone.'

'Will we talk to his wife?'

'Not at this stage. No point in provoking him unnecessarily.'

'Beats me why people keep animals like that,' said Lineham as they struggled on. 'I wouldn't trust that dog within a mile of my kids.'

'Ditto.'

'Let's hope Mr Fever is feeling a bit more cooperative.'

'It would make a change!'

Back at the car they changed into their shoes, banging their boots on a fence post to remove the worst of the mud then wiping them roughly on the grass.

'Give me a nice warm office every time,' said Lineham as he slammed the car boot.

It was a relief to get into the car, out of the wind.

Thanet glanced at his watch. Half-past one. Unless Fever's lunch hour was from one to two, he should be back at work by now. Anyway, if not, the house was only a stone's throw away. 'We'll try the yard first.'

Most of the farm buildings from which Fever ran his haulage business looked on the verge of collapse. The old Kent peg tiles had been stripped off and replaced with corrugated iron—a common sight since the hurricane, when the value of the old tiles had tripled overnight—and there were ragged gaps in the traditional weatherboarding. Lineham swung in between the open double metal gates which fronted the yard and parked alongside a small brick twin-kilned oast house marked OFFICE, the only building in reasonably good repair. As they got out of the car they became aware of raised voices within. The door was slightly ajar and as they drew closer Thanet put a warning finger to his lips.

'Honest, Mr Fever, I swear I never—'

'Don't give me that guff! Think I was born yesterday? I been over and over those records and there's no way I can come up with any other answer. If you think I'm going to sweat my guts out supplying easy money for toe-rags like you, you've got another think coming!'

'But—'

'But nothing! I've said all I'm going to say. That's it. Finish. There's your card, there's your money up to date. Now get out!'

Silence, then the sound of a door closing and footsteps approaching. A typewriter started clattering. Fever's secretary starting work after listening to the row?

Thanet and Lineham stepped back as a man emerged. He was grossly overweight, his belly hanging over the waistband of his low-slung trousers, his round moon-face wearing a hangdog expression. After a flicker of surprise at the sight of the two policemen he slunk past them and walked away through the gates, hands in pockets, shoulders slumped.

Thanet knocked at the door and they went in.

They were in a short, uncarpeted corridor floored with scuffed, grubby vinyl tiles. To their left was a closed door, to their right a notice saying ENQUIRIES stuck on to a glass partition through which they could see a girl typing on an antiquated machine. It was increasingly obvious that however freely Fever lavished money upon his private life, he didn't believe in spending it on his working environment. Presumably most of his business was conducted by telephone and as there was no one to impress he didn't think it worth the expenditure.

Lineham tapped on the glass and the girl looked up, then came to slide a section of the partition open.

'Yes?'

She was young and plain, shoddily dressed in a short, tight black skirt and striped acrylic jumper.

'We'd like a word with Mr Fever.'

Her eyes darted anxiously to the door across the corridor. 'I'll see if he's free. Who shall I say?'

'Detective Inspector Thanet and Detective Sergeant Lineham, Sturrenden CID.'

She looked alarmed. 'Yes,' she said. 'Right. I'll ... er ... I'll just go and see.'

She came out into the corridor and crossed to knock at the door on their left.

'Come in.'

With a nervous glance over her shoulder at the two policemen she opened the door just wide enough to sidle in, closing it behind her. After a brief murmur of voices she came out again, holding it wide open this time. 'Mr Fever can see you now.'

Fever was seated at a paper-strewn desk. He cast up his eyes. 'This is all I need.'

'Trouble?' said Thanet benignly. 'I'm afraid we couldn't help overhearing. The door was open.'

'Nothing I can't handle.' He waved a hand at a spindly metal stacking chair with a plastic seat. 'I'm afraid there's only one chair.'

Personal appearance mattered to him. His clothes, by contrast with the tattiness of his surroundings, were again sleek and expensive: creamy silk polo shirt and soft beige suede jacket. His rather sparse brown hair was well-cut, if rather long for Thanet's taste, and a faint aroma of aftershave hung in the air.

'Not to worry.'

Thanet sat down and Lineham moved across to lean against the windowsill, taking out his notebook.

'Right, Mr Fever, now perhaps we can start again.'

Fever's eyes narrowed with suspicion. 'What d'you mean?'

'Some rather interesting information has come to light since we saw you last.'

'Oh?' said Fever, warily.

'Yes. First, it has been confirmed that Mr Martindale was knocked down by the Ford van from Longford Hall Hotel.'

'So?'

'The one used principally by Sam Tiller.'

Something flickered in Fever's eyes. Dismay? Guilt? Fear? Impossible to tell. His facial expression did not alter. He had himself well under control. He raised his eyebrows in polite enquiry. *What has this got to do with me?*

'Secondly, we have also learned, from the post-mortem, that Mr Martindale did not die as a result of the collision. After the "accident" '—Thanet's voice implied quotation marks around the word—'his body was placed in the ditch where it was found next morning. He died from exposure, Mr Fever.'

'Too bad. But . . .'

The man's indifference infuriated Thanet and, longing to puncture it, he cut in. 'We understand that at some point he must have recovered consciousness and tried to get out. Unfortunately his spine was broken and he couldn't.' Fever, he was glad to see, was looking shaken. 'A very unpleasant death, as I'm sure you'll agree.'

'Poor bastard . . . But I still don't see what all this has to do with me.'

'Well, as I was explaining, you must see that this is therefore now a murder investigation.' Thanet paused, sat back and folded his arms. 'We were interested to learn that you drove the van that night, Mr Fever.'

The implication was too obvious to ignore. Fever sat up with a jerk, looking suitably outraged. 'Now look here . . .'

'No, you look here, Mr Fever. You admit, do you, that you drove the van that evening?'

'Well yes. But I had a perfectly good reason . . .'

'So I believe. But that is beside the point. The point is that you did drive it. I think you'll have to admit, it doesn't look good for you. First of all you have a blazing row with Mr Martindale, telling him to keep away from your wife . . .'

'Why shouldn't I—?'

'Then,' Thanet raised his voice, cutting Fever off, 'only a few hours later, Martindale is knocked down by a van which you admit to driving that same evening.'

Fever's face had become suffused with colour and his eyes bulged slightly as he said through his teeth, 'I refuse to put up with this.' His hand went out to the telephone. 'I'm going to call my solicitor.'

Thanet sat back, folding his arms. 'Do, by all means. But it might be a good idea to hear the rest of what I have to say, first.'

Fever's hand hovered above the instrument then fell back. 'Spit it out, then, why don't you?'

'It's obvious, surely. Means, motive, opportunity.' Thanet ticked them off on his fingers. 'I think you'll agree, you had them all.'

'Agree! Like hell I will.' He gave a cynical bark of laughter. 'Motive, indeed. What motive? Just because I told him to keep away from my wife?'

'Partly, perhaps. But I think we both know it goes a lot deeper than that.'

Fever was suddenly motionless, his eyes gleaming. 'What the hell,' he said softly, 'do you mean by that?'

'You had good reason to be jealous of Martindale, didn't you, Mr Fever?'

'What's that supposed to mean?'

'Oh come on, let's not play games. We both know what I'm talking about.'

'Do we?'

About to deliver a mortal blow to Fever's pride, Thanet steeled himself. Aggression did not come easily to him and it was only the knowledge that with this particular man he couldn't afford to let up for a moment that enabled him to sustain the attack. And if Fever was guilty, if he had indeed dragged an injured man into a ditch and left him to die, then he deserved all he was getting. But if not, if he was innocent . . . Thanet was well aware that Fever's hostility might well be a defence mechanism to cover up his vulnerability, that the man could have been more sinned against than sinning.

'I must admit that I was a little surprised that a few minutes' conversation in public between your wife and Martindale was enough to send you rushing off to have a row with him . . .'

Fever was very still, waiting.

'And then this morning, of course, I realised why you had reacted so strongly.'

The tension in the air was almost tangible.

'What did Martindale say to your wife that afternoon, Mr Fever, to make you so angry?' Thanet paused before playing his trump card. 'Did he threaten to tell Toby that he was his father?'

'No!' With the explosive monosyllable Fever was on his feet, hands gripping the edge of his desk. 'Who the hell . . .' he shouted and then, remembering his secretary's proximity, 'who the hell,' he hissed, 'do you think you are, coming here like this, poking your nose into my private life, making irresponsible accusations right left and centre . . . ?' His eyes were wild and flecks of spittle flew in Thanet's direction.

Thanet didn't flinch. 'Irresponsible, Mr Fever?' he said softly. But, although he didn't show it, for a moment he wavered. What if he were wrong?

'Yes!'

'You deny, then, that Toby was Martindale's son?' Thanet held up a hand. 'And, before you say "yes", I must warn you that this is not just idle speculation. We have been in touch with the General Register Office to check dates and so on.'

Fever stared at him, the anger gradually dying out of his eyes, to be replaced with despair. Then he slowly subsided into his chair and putting his elbows on the desk buried his head in his hands.

The silence was sufficient answer. Thanet was relieved. At least he hadn't been wrong in this. He glanced at Lineham who gave a satisfied nod.

Thanet waited a moment or two longer and then said,

'Look, Mr Fever, whether you believe it or not, I'm not enjoying this. I don't get a kick out of other people's misery and I'm not here either to make judgements or to broadcast people's secrets unless it is absolutely necessary. I am merely trying to discover the facts but you must see that until I do I can't even begin to decide whether this matter is relevant or not.'

Fever was listening, he could tell. Encouraged, he went on. 'I've had to be rather hard on you because, as I'm sure you'll admit, you weren't exactly in a cooperative mood. But if we could now have a sensible and rational discussion . . .'

Fever raised his head and looked at Thanet, a long, assessing look. *Can I believe what you're saying?*

Thanet waited, meeting Fever's gaze squarely and hoping that his expression was suitably frank and open.

After a moment or two Fever sat back, lifting his hands a little way off the desk and dropping them again in a gesture of surrender. He shrugged. 'OK. What do you want to know?'

21

As the tension in the room began to ebb away Lineham shifted his stance and cleared his throat, unconsciously signalling the fact that one phase of the interview had just ended and another was about to begin. Briefly Thanet wondered if highly charged emotion actually generated its own—what?—static electricity? Magnetic field? He didn't know. He felt depleted, suddenly aware of an ache in the small of his back, always his weak spot. He longed to get up and ease it, to walk about, light his pipe, relax, but he couldn't afford to do any of these things. It was important not to lose the impetus he had won.

Fever, by contrast, had now given up. Slumped in his chair, he was waiting for Thanet to begin, eyes dull, hands clasped loosely across his stomach.

'I'll be as brief as I can. Toby is Martindale's son?'

A tightening of the lips, a nod.

'And you've known this right from the beginning.'

Another nod.

'Does Toby know?'

This brought a reaction. Fever straightened up. 'No! And I—we, don't want him to know.'

'You've brought him up as your own son?'

'Yeah.' A wry attempt at a smile. 'We always thought if he took it into his head to count up on his fingers, he'd simply work out we'd enjoyed a bit of hanky-panky before we walked up the aisle.'

'You had no other children?'

Fever shook his head. 'No such luck. So it was all the more important that Toby never suspected . . .'

'Yes, I can see that. All the same, a bit risky, wasn't it?'

Fever shrugged. 'Even if he'd been adopted we wouldn't have told him till he was at least four. By then Leo'd been gone nearly five years and as time went on it seemed less and less likely he'd ever come back.'

An uncomfortable thought struck Thanet. 'Does anybody else know, or suspect?'

Fever was shaking his head again. 'Not that I know of. It's never even been hinted at. There was a bit of ribbing, of course, when Toby was born only six months after the wedding, but we just let everybody think we'd been at it before we should've.'

Oh God, thought Thanet. And I've told Delia Hamilton. What would she do, if anything? He shook his head, to clear it. He'd have to think about that later. Ought he to mention it to Fever? No, not now, when the man was being cooperative at last.

'I'm not sure of the legal position of an illegitimate child, but did you ever think that you could be depriving Toby of a fine inheritance?'

'Well yeah, that did worry us, I must admit, but we took legal advice, confidential-like, when old Martindale died, just for our own peace of mind. Anyway, we discovered Toby didn't have no claim at all, in law. According to the solicitor, illegitimate kids can now inherit, but only if the parents are together. To be honest, we was relieved. Having kept it from him all that time . . . And the last thing we wanted was a legal battle on our hands, that sort of thing can drag on for years. Besides, Toby's happy as he is. He's got everything he wants or needs. He's a good lad, we get on well together, he enjoys working in the business with me . . . Nah, we decided ignorance was bliss and to leave well alone.'

'You implied just now that one of the reasons why you'd never told Toby was because you thought Martindale would never come back.' Now for the important question. 'Does this mean that Martindale knew your wife was pregnant by him, before he went away?'

It was clear that the thought of Martindale impregnating

his wife was even now, after all these years, painful to
Fever. He compressed his lips and shook his head.

'You're sure?'

'Of course I'm sure! We just thought that if Leo did
come back he might work it out for himself.'

'And did he?'

'No!'

Thanet didn't think he was lying. But what if, knowing
her husband's jealous nature, Yvonne had told Martindale
before he went away, but had never had the nerve to
admit it to Fever? Remembering Martindale's questioning
of the hotel receptionist in regard to Toby's identity,
Thanet considered this possible.

Thanet tried to work it out. If Fever truly believed that
Martindale had never known and had therefore never
been in the position to threaten to tell Toby, the case
against him was strongly undermined. Though there still
remained his jealousy. Would that have been enough to
drive him, on impulse, to murder? Remembering Fever's
reaction just now Thanet thought that it might. For Fever
to have stepped in and married Yvonne the moment it
became obvious that Martindale had abandoned her, it
was more than likely that Fever had been in love with her
for some time, that he had had to stand back and watch
helplessly while she was swept off her feet by the son of
the big house. Jealousy was a cruel emotion, a classic
cause of murder. In the case of a man like Fever, whose
reputation was such that his wife scarcely dared even
speak to another man in his presence for fear of provoking
an outburst, the reappearance of Martindale, who had
once actually possessed Fever's wife, perhaps stolen her
from under his very nose while he looked impotently on,
could well have reactivated all his original resentment and
hatred of the man. Jealousy had certainly driven him to an
immediate confrontation with Martindale. Thanet wondered
exactly what had been said during that row, how Martindale
had reacted to Fever's warning. Could he have laughed at
him, thus provoking him even further and sending him
away in an even greater rage? If so, and if, later, on his
way back from taking his wife to her mother's house in the
van, Fever had been presented with the spectacle of

Martindale walking along the road ahead of him, alone . . .
Yes, it was still possible that Fever was their man.

Thanet became aware that both Lineham and Fever
were watching him, intrigued by his long silence. He
stood up. 'Right, thank you.'

Fever came to his feet. 'That's it?'

'For the moment, yes.'

They left him staring after them with a puzzled frown.

'No point in asking him if he'd seen Martindale later,
when he borrowed the van. He'd only have denied it,' said
Thanet as they got into the car. He wound down the
window and took out his pipe, began to fill it.

Lineham was nodding agreement. 'He could be our
man, though.' He smacked his clenched fist into the palm
of the other hand. 'If only we had some hard evidence
against one of them. Just one tiny scrap!'

'I know.' Briefly, at the very back of Thanet's mind
something flickered. What was it? He struggled to grasp
it, drag it out in order to examine it but already it was
gone. Had he imagined it?

Lineham was watching him. 'What?'

Thanet shook his head. 'It's gone.' He struck a match, lit
his pipe.

'Where now, sir? Hamilton?'

Thanet shook his head. 'Not much point. You realise
I've put my foot in it there, Mike?'

'By telling Mrs Hamilton about Toby? I can't see that
you've done much harm.'

'In any case, it's done now. There's no point in worrying
about it, I suppose.'

'It'll give them a few uncomfortable moments, I dare
say. But I can't say I feel much sympathy for them. They
haven't done too badly, have they?'

'I wasn't thinking of them, I was thinking of Toby.'

'I shouldn't lose any sleep over it. The Hamiltons aren't
exactly about to shout it from the roof-tops, are they?'

'No. All the same, for Toby's sake I think I'll have to
have a word with Mrs Hamilton.'

Lineham's expression indicated that he thought Thanet
overscrupulous on this point, but he merely said, 'So what
now?'

Thanet glanced at his watch. Two-thirty. 'Might as well go back to headquarters, have a session going over the papers. There could be something we've missed. And I really ought to glance at the Super's directive on ODD. He'll go through the roof tomorrow morning if I still haven't got around to it.'

It was a silent journey back, each of them preoccupied with his own thoughts. Back at the office they wrote their reports on the morning's interviews, then settled down to work systematically through the considerable stack of papers which had accumulated since the case began. They were methodical, both going through each report in turn, in case one of them spotted something the other had missed. In this particular case, when suspects were many and hard evidence against any one of them sadly lacking, it might well happen that some tiny detail which at the time had seemed of no importance could prove to be of crucial significance. The atmosphere in the room was heavy with concentration, the silence broken only occasionally by a murmured comment or enquiry. From time to time Thanet stood up and walked about, conscious that the dull ache in the small of his back was intensifying. He longed to stretch out on the floor, relieve tense muscles of the downward tug of gravity. Instead, he would sit down, pick up the next sheaf of paper and carry on the task.

By twenty to five he had to admit defeat. Nothing of any importance had emerged. Both he and Lineham were bleary-eyed, their thought processes clogged with the mass of information through which they had sifted. He put down his pen, rubbed his eyes, sat back and stretched. Time to glance at Draco's notes on ODD before going down to report to the Superintendent at five. 'See if you can rustle up some tea, Mike, while I look at this.'

When Lineham got back Thanet was looking much more animated. 'Something occurred to you, sir?'

'Not to do with the case.' Thanet tapped the ODD directive. 'Did you have any thoughts on this, Mike?' He took the cup Lineham was offering him. 'Thanks.'

Lineham sat down. 'Not really. Why, have you?'

'Possibly. Organisation, Delegation and Documentation. Now, the whole point of this campaign is to improve efficiency. Which one of those three would you say is the most time-consuming?'

'Documentation, I suppose.'

'Exactly!' Thanet leaned forward across his desk. 'Now tell me this. How much time is wasted in the front office looking through the files for, say, a key-holder's card for shop or office alarms that has been put back in the wrong place by some officer in a hurry?'

'Quite a bit, I'd say.' Everyone in the situation had ground his teeth over this particular bit of inefficiency, at one time or another.

'Well, why don't I suggest that all that information is put on the computer, instead? It's being done more and more—Maidstone introduced it a couple of years ago, for example. And not only key-holders' lists, but names and updated addresses of station staff, charge cards, details of emergency action plans...'

'But if all that information was stored on the computer what happens if you need it in a hurry when the computer operator is away at lunch or, even worse, off sick?'

'Obviously it would mean that everyone in the station would have to be trained to use the computer.'

Lineham groaned. He wasn't into computers. 'Oh, no!'

'Come on, Mike, don't be faint-hearted. It would all be in a good cause and besides, it wouldn't be too difficult. Not if we got hold of a simple, user-friendly system. Just think how much time it would save in the long run!'

'Well ...'

'I think I'll suggest it. If Draco doesn't like the idea, then too bad, but at least I'll have come up with a positive suggestion.' Thanet glanced at his watch. Two minutes to five. 'I'd better go down to give my report.'

At the door he turned. 'Oh, by the way, while I'm away, give Mrs Hamilton a ring, tell her her calculator wasn't in the van.' This was clear from the report on the van's contents. Thanet had checked. 'She must have dropped it somewhere else.'

On the way downstairs he was again conscious of that strange, almost physical sensation at the back of his mind. He had felt it before, many times, and it meant that his subconscious had registered something which his con-

scious mind had not, and the information was trying to get
through. Experience had taught him that it was pointless
to try and work out what it was. Sooner or later it would
surface in its own good time and the best way to speed up
the process was to think of something else.

Outside Draco's office Thanet paused, braced himself.
What sort of a mood would the Super be in this afternoon?
A better one than this morning, he hoped. He knocked.

'Come in.'

Draco was sitting in front of an immaculately tidy desk,
pens and pencils neatly aligned, in-tray empty, out-tray
full, empty blotter before him. He looked relaxed, com-
posed, positively benign. 'Ah, Thanet. How's it going?'

Thanet gave a succinct summary of the day's findings,
Draco nodding from time to time, putting in a question
here and there. It looked as though the session was going
to go off without incident and, encouraged, Thanet decided
to float his new idea.

'By the way—'

'Just a minute . . .' Draco held up a hand. He was
peering out of the window, which overlooked the main
entrance to the building and enabled the Superintendent
to keep a watchful eye on comings and goings. If anyone
sneezed in this building, Draco liked to know about it.
'Sorry to interrupt, Thanet, but who's that?'

Thanet rose and crossed to the window. Walking towards them were two men deep in conversation, one in
uniform, the other in civilian clothes. He assumed Draco
wasn't referring to Inspector Storey, an old friend of
Thanet's now working in Maidstone, and he'd never seen
the civilian before. 'Sorry, I don't know. Some member of
the public coming to—'

'No, no,' said Draco testily. 'That's Councillor Watford,
I know him. The other man, in uniform.'

'Inspector Storey. He's one of the instructors at the
Police Training School in Maidstone.' The words came out
mechanically. Thanet was barely aware that he had spok-
en. He was staring at the two men, dumbfounded.

Of course! Why hadn't he seen it before?

'Wonder what they're doing here,' muttered Draco,
heading for the door. 'Was that the lot, Thanet?'

'What? Oh, sorry, sir. Yes.' His suggestion could wait until the morning meeting tomorrow. Besides, he couldn't wait to tell Lineham . . .

He followed Draco out of the office and took the stairs two at a time.

Lineham glanced up, startled, as Thanet burst into the office.

'Mike! Listen to this!'

Thanet watched the light dawn in Lineham's face as he talked.

'I see! Brilliant, sir! So what do we do now?'

Thanet told him.

22

'Let's hope they haven't gone to bed.'

'Shouldn't think so, Mike, it's only ten o'clock.'

It was five exhausting hours later. After making the necessary appointment, clearing it with the Sussex police and ringing Joan and Louise to tell them they'd be late home, Thanet and Lineham had set off on the longish drive to Worthing. The interview there had verified Thanet's hunch and presented them with a clear motive where none had apparently existed before. Now they were about to put his theory to the test.

Thanet shifted in his seat in an attempt to ease his back and rubbed his eyes, which were beginning to feel gritty with fatigue. He was glad he wasn't driving. He glanced across at Lineham who still looked relatively fresh.

'I gather you got the problem with your brother-in-law sorted out?'

'Yes. Or at least, he did. Went back to his wife this morning.'

'Good.'

Lineham leaned forward to wipe the windscreen, which kept on misting up. Since darkness fell the temperature had plummeted rapidly and along the sides of the lane the grass and clumps of tangled undergrowth were encrusted with frost.

The sergeant was driving carefully, leaning forward slightly to peer at the road ahead. 'Lucky we haven't had any rain today, or it'd be like a skating rink.'

'Mm.' Thanet was preoccupied with the interview to come.

'Of course, it still doesn't necessarily mean one of them did it,' said Lineham, for the third time.

Thanet realised that the sergeant was merely armouring himself against disappointment. 'I'm aware of that, Mike,' he said patiently. 'But it's a powerful motive, you must admit. And I've just got this feeling...'

The gateposts at the entrance to Longford Hall loomed up ahead and Lineham put his indicator on. 'Even if you're right, I still don't see how we're going to prove it.'

Ay, there was the rub indeed. 'I know.'

'I mean, we've no more evidence against them than against any of the others.'

Yet again Thanet experienced that flicker at the back of his mind. What was it that he was trying to remember? Was it possible that there was something he had missed, some minute scrap of evidence that could turn the tide in his favour? Not that, if his theory proved correct, an arrest would give him much satisfaction. After the initial excitement over that flash of inspiration he had felt progressively more and more depressed and now he felt only a dragging weariness at the prospect of the interview ahead. He braced himself as Lineham drove into the stable yard and parked. Whether he liked it or not, he had to go through with it. Murder had been done and if one of these two were guilty it was his clear duty to bring the perpetrator to justice, whatever his personal feelings in the matter.

They walked across the cobbles to the stable block, climbed the indoor staircase and knocked at the door at the top.

It was a few minutes before it was opened by Desmond Byfleet, peering out into the semi-darkness. 'Oh, it's you, Inspector.'

'May we come in?'

Byfleet stood back to let them pass, closing the door behind them. 'We were just about to go to bed.' He was in his shirtsleeves, tieless, carpet slippers on bare feet. Without a jacket he looked thinner than ever and more vulnerable, as if with the outer layer of cloth he had peeled off his defences.

'I'm sorry to trouble you so late, but we'd like a word with you both.'

'Do you have to see my wife? She's very tired.'

Thanet shook his head. 'I'm sorry,' he repeated. He meant it. 'I'll have to talk to her sooner or later. Better to get it over with.'

Byfleet hesitated a moment or two longer, apparently trying to make up his mind whether to refuse pointblank, the muscles in his cheeks moving as he clenched his teeth. Then he turned away and flung open the sitting-room door, switching on a light inside. 'I'll go and see.'

The sight of the cosy, welcoming room reinforced Thanet's distaste for the coming interview. He strolled restlessly about, his gaze wandering abstractedly over the attractive soft furnishings, the books, plants, records, chess-game, bowl of odds and ends on the coffee table. He sat down heavily, his back protesting at the softness of the cushions. 'I'm not looking forward to this, Mike.' What if he were wrong? He could see the headlines. WOMAN MISCARRIES AFTER POLICE HARASSMENT. He rubbed his eyes, shook his head in an attempt to clear it. It had been a long day.

Lineham had chosen an upright chair which stood in front of a small writing desk. He picked up one of the ornaments on it, a glass paperweight, and peered into it as if it were a crystal ball. 'Fascinating things, these.' He put it down hastily and stood up as Byfleet entered the room, followed by his wife.

Thanet rose too. 'I apologise for disturbing you at this hour, ma'am.'

She attempted a smile but said nothing, walking past him to sit on the settee. She was wearing a man's woollen dressing gown, her husband's presumably, loosely tied across her protruding belly. The shade, a drab fawn, did not become her, leaching any colour from her sallow skin and from the lank, lifeless brown hair.

She looked as tired as he felt, thought Thanet. Scarcely surprising, really. If he was right, she couldn't have had much sleep over the last few days.

Byfleet sat down beside his wife and covered her hand with his.

Thanet glanced at Lineham to check that he was ready and the sergeant nodded. *Go ahead*.

'There's no point in beating about the bush, so perhaps it would be best to begin by telling you that we have just come back from Worthing, where we have seen your mother, Mrs Byfleet.'

Mona Byfleet blinked and blindly put out her other hand to her husband who took and clasped it. Neither of them said a word, just stared at him, awaiting the next blow.

'She was naturally very distressed when she heard what had happened. She realises that you and your husband had no idea, when you married . . . It must have been an awful shock for you.'

Thanet paused expectantly. He didn't want to spell it out if he didn't have to.

Desmond Byfleet cleared his throat. 'We don't know what you're talking about, Inspector.'

Thanet shook his head wearily. 'It's no good taking that line, Mr Byfleet. We know, you see.'

'Know . . . what?' Mona Byfleet spoke for the first time, in a near-whisper.

'That your mother told Mr Martindale and that he must have told you, Mrs Byfleet, when he called you into his room, the night he died.'

'We still haven't the faintest idea what you're on about, Inspector.' Byfleet's voice was stronger now. He had obviously decided on the line he was going to take and was sticking to it.

His wife was less certain. She shot him an agonised glance and said, 'Des . . .'

Byfleet gave no overt sign of having realised that she was on the point of capitulation. There was no frown, no shake of the head, just a brief exchange of glances. But the message still came over loud and clear. *Stand firm*.

She glanced back at Thanet. *Don't say it*, her eyes pleaded. *Please, don't say it*.

But he had to, somehow, Thanet realised, or they would get nowhere. He sighed. 'Perhaps it will help if I tell you a story.'

Byfleet clicked his tongue impatiently but his wife,

recognising perhaps that Thanet was proposing an oblique approach to the subject in order to cushion the blow, laid a restraining hand on his arm.

'Once upon a time,' said Thanet, 'there was born in London's East End a girl called Brenda. She had eight brothers and sisters and her father was a drunkard who couldn't keep any job down for more than a few weeks at a time. Needless to say she couldn't wait to get away from home and in 1949, at the ripe old age of seventeen, she married the first man who asked her and moved to the Midlands.

'Unfortunately it wasn't long before she discovered that she had jumped out of the frying pan into the fire. Her new husband was a bully and a brute and not long afterwards, when she was seven months pregnant, he beat her up so badly that the baby was born prematurely.'

He had their attention now. They were gazing at him as if mesmerised.

'This was the last straw as far as she was concerned. In hospital she refused to see her husband again and on the day she was due to be discharged she left earlier than the time arranged and, having borrowed the train fare from one of the other women in the ward, came straight to London, leaving her baby boy behind. Being premature, of course, he would in any case have had to remain in hospital for some time but this was, she felt, the only way she could get away from her husband and be certain that the baby would be well looked after. She had had this plan in mind right from the moment of that last, brutal beating and although the baby seemed healthy enough she insisted on his being christened immediately after the birth. In fact, the husband refused to have anything to do with the child, who was brought up first in a children's home then in various foster homes.

'Meanwhile, Brenda changed her surname and, despite the nationwide appeal for her to come forward, disappeared into the lowest stratum of London's catering trade where employers didn't bother about National Insurance cards and were only too glad to get cheap labour. For some time she washed dishes, waited at tables in the smallest and meanest cafés and then, when she felt it was safe, reverted to her married name, legitimately got hold of a National Insurance card, and began to work in earnest towards furthering the career she had meanwhile decided to pursue. Shrewdly, considering her lack of qualifications, she chose the hotel business. I won't go into the details. It's enough to say that beginning on the bottom rung and by working twice as hard as anyone else, in five years she managed to work her way up to Housekeeper in a smallish hotel. During this period she also divorced her husband. Then, late in 1954, she managed at last to get the kind of job she'd always been aiming for, a post as Housekeeper in a hotel out of London, on the South Coast. At this time she was still barely twenty-three and perhaps it's not surprising that now, for the first time, romance entered her life. It was a small, family-run hotel, and the Assistant Manager was the son of the owners. In due course Brenda and he were married and the following year they had a daughter.' Thanet paused. 'In a minor way a fairy-tale ending, as I think you'll agree. Unfortunately, the story doesn't end there.

'In due course first the owner and his wife were killed in a holiday air crash and then Brenda's second husband died, so the ownership of the hotel passed to her. Her daughter grew up and when she left school worked in the hotel with her mother. Although she wasn't exactly antisocial she was never the type of girl to have lots of boyfriends and it wasn't until she was in her late twenties that at last she met a man she liked. He had recently moved down to the South from Birmingham. For some reason—shyness, perhaps?—she kept their association a secret. Finally, when they began to talk of marriage, she broke the news to her mother and asked her to meet him. She was taken aback by her reaction. From the outset, before she had even met him, Brenda seemed prejudiced against him. The girl put it down to overprotectiveness of an only chick and told herself that when her mother met the young man and saw how respectable and hardworking he was she would become reconciled to the idea. Instead, the meeting merely served to harden her mother's attitude. The young man, she insisted, was unsuitable, completely wrong for the girl.

'Naturally, the daughter thought that her mother was being totally unreasonable. But in fact, she was misjudging her. Brenda was against the marriage for quite another reason.

'As soon as she heard the man's name—a fairly unusual one—she had realised to her horror that he could be the son she had abandoned long ago and there was a real possibility that brother and sister were planning to marry.'

23

With an abrupt, desperate movement Mona turned her head and buried her face in Desmond's sleeve as if ashamed to look Thanet in the eye any longer. Desmond shot Thanet a furious, resentful glance and put his arm around her.

Thanet took a deep breath and attempting to ignore the pity that was churning his stomach said softly, 'It would perhaps be more accurate to say, "half-brother", and it is clear that the young people were entirely the innocent victims of tragic circumstance. Although Brenda had confided the details of that early, disastrous marriage to her husband, she had never told her daughter about it. All that, she had thought, was behind her, best forgotten. Now . . . Well at first, of course, she couldn't be sure that her suspicions were justified. So she agreed to meet the young man and when she did knew at once that he was her son. He was the spitting image of his father. That, together with his name . . . She may have abandoned him, you see, but she'd never forgotten him, and ironically her daughter's name had even been chosen in a rather subtle way to complement his.'

Desmond and Mona glanced at each other as they worked out what he meant and the name shivered unspoken in the air between them. *Desdemona*.

'A few questions about his background convinced Brenda that she was right. Now she was in a real dilemma. If she told her daughter the truth, the girl would never forgive her for not having been frank with her from the beginning.

If she didn't, her daughter would think that she was against the marriage for far more trivial reasons. Either way she ran the risk of losing the only person she really loved. It wasn't surprising that that night she tried to drown her sorrows in drink, but it was unfortunate that she did so in the company of one of the guests in the hotel, a man by the name of Leo Martindale. He was a confidence trickster who made a habit of preying on lonely middle-aged women and she was his favourite type, the hotel owner who was reasonably well off and might be sweet-talked into parting with some money if he played his cards right.

'In Brenda's case he had got as far as hinting at marriage and had managed to worm his way into her bed. On this particular evening, more than a little drunk and desperate to share her problem with someone, she confided in him and asked his advice. He did in fact tell her that he thought it would be best to tell the girl the truth but when it came down to it Brenda couldn't bring herself to do it. Finally, just when she had screwed up sufficient courage to do so, she found it was too late. Furious at her mother's opposition to the marriage, the daughter had decided to elope. The young people were both over age and there appeared to be nothing to prevent them marrying. For marriage in a registry office couples do not have to produce birth certificates unless they are under twenty-three years of age, so in all innocence they went through the ceremony and as far as the mother was concerned, just disappeared. Eventually they found work as a husband-and-wife team here, at Longford Hall.'

For the first time Thanet addressed the Byfleets directly. 'Ironic, wasn't it, that you chose this particular hotel, Martindale's family home. The owner's name, of course, was different, Hamilton, so you had no reason to connect your new employer with the man your mother hoped to marry, and it must have been a shock when he turned up as Mrs Hamilton's brother . . . And even more of a shock when he told you what he had learned from your mother, Mrs Byfleet.'

Mona was staring miserably down at her lap now, twisting the cord of the dressing gown round and round one finger, releasing it, twisting it again. Still she did not speak and, meeting Byfleet's stony stare, Thanet realised with something like despair that if they chose to remain silent there was absolutely nothing he could do about it. So where did he go from here? He had no stomach for browbeating these people into a confession, they were suffering enough as it was. And, too, there was the possibility that he was wrong and they had had nothing to do with Martindale's death.

Lineham was watching him, aware no doubt of Thanet's predicament. The silence in the room stretched out uncomfortably.

He had miscalculated, Thanet realised. He had thought that informing the Byfleets that he knew their unhappy secret would be such a shock to them that they would break down and confess, especially if he could do so in such a way as to convince them that he was sympathetic to their predicament. To this end he had put all his ingenuity into devising a way of breaking the news gently—too gently, perhaps. Compassion may have made his efforts self-defeating. In any case, he had not thought beyond that point.

Well, they had reached it and it had got him nowhere.

If only, he thought desperately, he could remember whatever it was that had been eluding him. It was, he was sure, highly relevant. He could feel the knowledge struggling to surface, lacking that final impetus which would bring him enlightenment. He glanced around the room seeking inspiration but seeing only an Eden that was for the Byfleets perhaps forever lost.

It was pointless to prolong the interview. He was about to rise, had actually put his hand on the arm of his chair preparatory to levering himself up when his gaze fell upon the blue-and-white ceramic bowl of odds and ends and, at last, he spotted it.

Of course! That was what his subconscious had registered, the last time he was here!

Despite the pity he felt for the couple still clinging on to the shreds of their dignity, for the second time that day he experienced the unique explosion of triumph which invari-

ably accompanies such rare flashes of understanding—
followed at once by doubt.

What if he were wrong?

He longed to put out his hand and pick the object up,
his fingers actually ached with the need to do so, to open
it, examine it, verify that it really was what he thought it
was.

Lineham was now watching Thanet intently. After years
of working together he was attuned to even the slightest
shift in Thanet's mood and he knew that something of
significance had just occurred to him.

Thanet glanced at the Byfleets. They too were watching
him, still warily but with the beginning of hope that the
worst was over. What should he do? Should he risk making
a monumental fool of himself?

His heartbeat accelerated as alternative ways of approaching the subject flashed through his mind.

He took a deep calming breath and exhaled slowly.
Then he said, 'The last time I was here I asked if either of
you had driven the van the night Mr Martindale died.
Now I'd like to ask you again. Did you?'

They did not look at each other but he sensed the
unspoken communication which flashed between them
before they shook their heads. Thanet waited a moment
and then, with a complete change of tone, leaned forward
and pointed. 'Is that yours, Mr Byfleet?'

'No. It's my wife's.'

Mona twisted to look up at him. She frowned. 'No it's
not, Des. Mine's back at the hotel, in my office. I was
using it this evening and that one's been there for a couple
of days. I thought it was yours.'

Now it was Byfleet's turn to look puzzled. He leaned
forward and reached out to pick the object up, but Thanet
put out a hand to prevent him from touching it. Their eyes
locked and for a moment there was an unspoken battle of
wills between them, Byfleet's hand hovering uncertainly
over the coffee table. Then he capitulated, leaning over
and pulling towards him the jacket which was lying across
the arm of the settee. He patted one of the pockets, put
his hand in and took out a virtually identical small black
object. Then he looked back at the one in the bowl. *So*

whose is that? His wife was looking at it too, but Thanet guessed that she at least now knew the answer and that the question in her eyes was, *How did it get there?*

Now for the moment of truth. Taking a polythene bag from his pocket Thanet slipped it over his hand and then, with care, picked up what he had first thought was a diary, flipped it open. Relief that he had been proved right mingled with regret as he saw the slip of paper tucked into the flap. Even before he carefully extracted it with a pair of tweezers he knew what would be written on it.

Delia Hamilton's pocket calculator had turned up.

Briefly he held out the paper for the Byfleets to read the name and address on it. Their bewilderment was now mixed with apprehension. They couldn't understand why the calculator was important but Thanet's behaviour showed them that it was.

'Where did you get this?' Thanet tossed the question at them both.

They looked at each other. 'I really have no idea,' said Mona Byfleet. But Thanet could tell that in her husband's mind a memory was beginning to stir.

So Byfleet was their man.

Thanet breathed a silent prayer of thankfulness that at least he would not have to charge a pregnant woman with murder. If she were completely innocent and knew nothing of what her husband had done that night this was going to be a terrible shock to her, potentially disastrous as far as the baby was concerned, and it would be better if she were to leave them now. Perhaps he should insist that she do so. But it was still possible that she was an accessory after the fact. Byfleet was not the sort of man to commit a murder and return home with no sign of distress, and given the closeness of their relationship Thanet thought it highly unlikely that Byfleet would have been able to hold back from telling her what had happened. No, she would have to stay for at least a little while longer.

'Perhaps it would be best if I spell this out. I can see, Mr Byfleet, that you now remember just how Mrs Hamilton's calculator got here. On the night Mr Martindale died she distinctly remembers using it just before she drove to the station to pick up her son. Later, after hunting for it everywhere—as I'm sure you know, Mrs Byfleet, she realised that she must have dropped it in the van. Mr Talion didn't notice it when he used the van a little later but you, Mr Byfleet, I'd guess that after you put Mr Martindale in the ditch you quickly checked to see if you'd dropped anything and seeing this familiar object on the floor picked it up and put it in your pocket. I also think that you were so shaken by what had happened and in such a hurry to get back to the stable yard before anyone realised that you'd used the van that you scarcely realised what you were doing and later, when you found two calculators in your pockets, simply thought that you must have picked your wife's up by mistake. So you put it in the bowl there and she, of course, thought it was yours, and left it there.'

During this brief speech the expression on Mona's face had gradually changed from puzzlement to horrified realisation. Now she looked up at her husband who was staring down at his lap, chewing the inside of his lip. He shook his head in defeat and after a moment Thanet nodded at Lineham, who came forward and delivered the caution.

Mona Byfleet burst into tears.

Her husband put both arms around her and drew her close to him, smoothing her hair. 'It's all right, love. Hush. It's going to be all right.'

Thanet and Lineham exchanged uncomfortable glances. Thanet longed to get up and walk out, leave the whole miserable situation behind, but duty kept him pinned to his seat. Whatever he did now, sooner or later Mona was going to have to face the consequences of what had happened that night. It wasn't surprising that she had been looking so ill. Ever since she had learned the appalling truth from Martindale she must have been in a state of turmoil, worried sick about the health of a child born of an incestuous union and terrified of the effect of this new knowledge upon their future. And then, on top of that, to know that her husband had committed a murder . . . The last few days must have been a torment for her. What would become of her, he wondered—and of the child?

The ragged sobbing was beginning to abate. Byfleet was still trying to soothe her and now he took a handkerchief from his pocket, moved slightly away from her and began to mop the tears gently from her face. Finally she took the handkerchief herself, blew her nose and looked at Thanet. 'You . . . You don't understand. It wasn't the way you think. It . . . It was an accident, wasn't it, Des?' And she gave her husband such a look of love and faith that Thanet could hardly bear to see it.

'It was because I was so upset, you see.' She blew her nose again, wiped her eyes and sat up straighter. 'He . . . Mr Martindale . . . was so foul to me.'

'When he called you into his room, you mean?' Thanet attempted to make his tone both matter-of-fact and sympathetic. It was important to try to lower the emotional temperature.

She nodded. 'It was an awful shock when he turned up at the hotel. I never liked him and he didn't like me—I think he knew I saw through his smarmy ways.' She shuddered and made a little moue of distaste. 'I knew he'd recognised me, of course, in the foyer.' Her voice was getting stronger now as she regained control. It was clear that she wanted to set the record straight, to state the facts in such a way as to present her husband's behaviour in as good a light as possible.

'At first I thought Mum had found out where we were, and had sent him to check up on me. When I left home he seemed to be pretty well dug in there and I'd often wondered if they'd got married. Then when he turned up here and someone told me he was Mrs Hamilton's brother, I didn't know what to think . . . In any case, I wasn't too surprised when he called me into his room. I was glad of a private word, really. I wanted to find out what the situation was, and if he and Mum weren't together I wanted to make sure he didn't tell her where we were . . .

'At first it was all right. We just chatted, and I was relieved to find he had been living in France and had lost touch with my mother soon after I left. Then it was just like I told you before, he started asking questions about the hotel and when he got on to things that I didn't feel I ought to tell him, I said I couldn't answer any more questions, if he wanted to know he'd have to ask Mrs Hamilton, she was the boss, after all. He just laughed.

* * *

'That's what you think, Mona. Things are going to change around here from now on. My dear little sister isn't going to play at God any more.'

'What do you mean?'

'Simply that I've come home to stay. And to claim, somewhat belatedly, my inheritance. So you see, I'm going to be in charge here from now on and I have every right to ask you whatever questions I choose.'

'I'm sorry, I'm afraid I shall still have to talk to Mrs Hamilton first.'

'Think I'm lying, do you? Well I'm not, as you'll soon find out, perhaps to your cost.'

'What do you mean?'

'Simply that I could find your excessive devotion to my sister rather tiresome. And if you should find it impossible to transfer your loyalty to me, it might be necessary for me to look around for another housekeeper. You're not exactly the ideal candidate anyway, are you?'

'Because of the baby, you mean? I've never let my work suffer because I'm pregnant. Ask Mrs Hamilton.'

'I wasn't talking about the baby, not exactly, anyway.'

'What do you mean, not exactly? What were you talking about, then?'

'I was thinking more on the lines of bad moral influence.'

'Bad moral influence?'

'Yes. My God, you still don't know, do you?'

'Don't know what?'

'Why your mother was dead against you marrying Byfleet.'

'And then he . . . he told me . . .' Even now, when it was out in the open, Mona couldn't bring herself to say it. She was shaking as she relived what must have been the worst moment of her life. 'It . . . Oh, it was horrible.'

'I don't believe you.'

'Ah, but it's true, my dear. Ask your mother. She'll give you chapter and verse all right. So unless you want the whole world to know the truth about you and your so-called husband, I suggest you remember to toe the line, as far as I'm concerned. Both of you.'

* * *

Mona was twisting and tugging at Desmond's handkerchief and now there was a small tearing sound as the material ripped. Engrossed in her story, she didn't even notice.

'I ran away, then. I couldn't bear to stay there a moment longer, to see that... triumphant look on his face. I came back here and waited for my husband.' She looked up at Desmond. 'It seemed such a long time before you got here, but I suppose it wasn't, really.' She turned back to Thanet. 'He could see at once I was in a state and then... when I told him... He was so upset... and angry because Mr Martindale had been so foul to me... And then, when I told him what Mr Martindale had said, about the whole world knowing the truth... Suddenly he just took off...'

'It was all such a shock,' Byfleet broke in. 'I hardly knew what I was doing. I couldn't keep still, I was walking about, and while my... wife was talking I'd happened to glance out of the window and see Mr Martindale crossing the stable yard, heading towards the drive. I stood there, watching him and listening to what she was saying and, a few minutes later, when she told me what he'd said about telling everyone...'

Byfleet's voice broke and he dropped his head in his hands. Now it was Mona's turn to give comfort and she stroked his back, gently, as if soothing a frightened animal.

How was he going to make this arrest with equanimity? Thanet wondered.

Byfleet straightened up again. 'In all my life this is the first place I've really felt I could call home. We've been so happy here. Haven't we, love?'

Mona nodded, biting her lip.

'The thought that it was all going to end, that he had ruined it all... And my wife was in such a state... I'm not trying to excuse myself, but it's true, it really was an accident.'

'What actually happened?'

Byfleet was shaking his head. 'I don't know what came over me... I suppose I just felt I had to do something, anything... So when Mona said that, about him threatening to tell the whole world... I just rushed out. I wanted to have it out with him at once, then and there. When I got down in the yard he was out of sight and the van was just standing there so I jumped in. I always carry the keys in my pocket. Then the damn thing wouldn't start. It was so cold, that night... Anyway, it fired in the end and I went after him. When I was nearing the end of the drive I could see him ahead and I slammed on the brakes. I suppose I left it too late and had to brake too hard... Anyway, the van skidded and went out of control. He'd glanced around when he first heard me coming, and moved right in to walk at the side of the road, but there was nothing I could do to prevent myself hitting him.' Byfleet closed his eyes as if to block out the memory.

Mona Byfleet pressed her husband's arm.

Thanet waited.

'It was like a bad dream. It all happened so fast... It was over in a flash, in a matter of seconds...' Byfleet put up his hands and massaged his temples as if to erase the shock and bewilderment he still felt. 'I got out of the car. He was lying at the side of the road. I tried to find a pulse and couldn't... I realised he was dead, that I'd killed him...' Byfleet shook his head in despair. 'I'm afraid I just panicked. I knew that at any second someone could come along and... We were near the gates and I thought, the roads are so icy, if I put him in the ditch just outside the gates, it would look as though anyone could have done it... So... So that's what I did.'

'You see, Inspector. It *was* an accident.' Mona Byfleet was still holding on to her husband's arm, as if clinging to the wreckage of their life. 'The roads were icy and Desmond wasn't drunk...'

'It's all true, Inspector. It happened exactly as I've told you, I swear it.'

'Maybe so, but I'm afraid it's not quite as simple as that,' said Thanet, bracing himself to deliver the blow.

'What... What do you mean?' said Mona.

They stared at him with identical expressions on their faces. The likeness between them had never been more apparent.

'If it happened just as your husband told us...'

'It did!' broke in Byfleet.

'I believe you,' said Thanet. 'And if you had immediately gone for help...'

'But he was dead!' Byfleet was leaning forward now in his eagerness to convince Thanet of the innocence of his intentions. Then he sat back. 'Oh hell, why not admit it, you're right, I know you are. Even though there was nothing to be done for him...'

'Unfortunately, that's where you're wrong.'

Again that identical expression, an unspoken question in both their eyes. Perhaps they dared not ask it. Suddenly the tension was back in the room, the air was thick with their fear.

Thanet steeled himself. There was no way to soften the impact of what he was about to say and in any case it was true that it was Byfleet's action that had cost Martindale his life. 'I'm afraid Mr Martindale wasn't killed by the collision with the van,' he said, 'When you put him in the ditch he was still alive, but then it snowed, of course...'

He hesitated. Should he tell them that Martindale's spine had been injured, that he had recovered consciousness and been unable to get out of the ditch? No, at this point he couldn't bring himself to do it. They would learn, soon enough.

'So after lying outside all night in those conditions it's not surprising that he was dead by morning,' he concluded.

Mona fainted.

24

Noon next day, Saturday.

Thanet laid down his pen, sat back, stretched, then reached for the telephone.

'Joan? It's me.'

'Hullo. How's it going?'

'Just finished. I was thinking ... Fancy an afternoon out?'

'Lovely! Where?'

'What about Rye?'

'Bit chilly, d'you think?'

'Nice and quiet, though. No tourists.'

'True.'

'If there's anywhere you'd prefer ... ?'

'No. I like Rye, as you know.'

'Yes. That's why I thought ...'

'Good. That's settled, then.'

'What about the children?'

'Ben's going ice-skating in Gillingham, remember?'

'Ah yes, of course. And Bridget? Think she'd like to come?' Much as he loved his daughter, Thanet hoped she wouldn't. There was so rarely time these days for him and Joan to talk, just to enjoy being alone together.

'She's going shopping with Mandy this afternoon.'

'Fine.'

'What time will you be home, then?'

'Soon as I can. Twenty minutes?'

Outside on the steps Thanet stopped to inhale appreciatively. It was a perfect winter day: crisp cold air, blue sky decorated with puffs of cotton-wool cloud, and a sun which was doing its best to make you forget that it was February.

By 1.30 they were on their way, with a delicious feeling of escape. Across the Weald the landscapes immortalised by Rowland Hilder basked in the unaccustomed warmth, the bare trees casting long shadows across furrowed fields and empty roads.

For a while they drove in a contented silence, relishing the sense of freedom, and then Joan stirred.

'Feel like telling me how you worked it out?'

Thanet would have preferred to forget about work this afternoon but it was part of the pattern of their lives to have a 'post-mortem' at the end of every case and Joan, he knew, would be disappointed if he demurred. 'If you like.'

He paused, ordering his thoughts. 'Actually, believe it or not, it was the Super who finally put me on the right track.'

'Really? How?'

'Oh, I don't mean he did it consciously. No, it was just that while I was talking to him, yesterday afternoon, we saw two visitors coming in—his window overlooks the forecourt, as you know. And as you also know, he likes to know every last thing about what is going on in the division. So I wasn't in the least surprised when he said, "Who's that?" and because I didn't know one of the men I assumed he was referring to him. Then I discovered he was referring to the other chap.'

'I don't get it. How did that help?'

'Well, when Leo Martindale arrived at Longford Hall on Monday evening he saw Mona Byfleet, the housekeeper, talking to Toby Fever in the entrance hall, and he asked the receptionist the same question: "Who's that?" Mona was wearing her housekeeper's dress and the receptionist therefore took it for granted that Martindale would realise who she was and that he must be referring to Toby. So she told him it was Miss Hamilton's boyfriend. Then she said, "He was just going to say something else when Mrs Hamilton arrived."'

'And you think the "something else" would have been, "No, I don't mean him, I mean the woman with him."'

'Exactly. In other words, it was Mona Byfleet who

interested him, not Toby, and when I realised that I naturally asked myself why? If she'd been an attractive woman, the sort that Martindale was always on the lookout for, it would have been a different matter, but she's fairly plain and heavily pregnant. So it seemed to me that the most likely answer was that she interested him because he had recognised her and wondered what she was doing there. Until then, you see, I had assumed that the Byfleets couldn't possibly have had any motive for wanting him dead because they didn't appear to have any connection with him, past or present.'

'So then you asked yourself what that connection could possibly be?'

'Yes. We knew that Martindale had been abroad for several years but before that, when he was in this country, he tended to move from hotel to hotel, living on any pickings he could glean from women he met, mostly wealthy widows or middle-aged spinsters. They're always the most vulnerable, the most susceptible. Well, Mona didn't really fit that pattern but it did occur to me that her mother might. I knew that Mona had been to school in Brighton and that her maiden name was Taylor—I saw it in the fly-leaf of one of her old books—and then I remembered that one of Martindale's former women friends had been called Taylor and ran a hotel in Worthing, which is near Brighton.'

'So you thought, Aha, I wonder if she was Mona's mother and that was where Mona and Martindale met?'

'Precisely.'

'But even so, what possible relevance did you think it could have?'

'I didn't know. But if the connection had been entirely innocent I didn't see why Mona shouldn't have owned up to it.'

'Not necessarily, surely. If I became innocently entangled in a murder investigation I'm not sure that I'd be particularly anxious to volunteer information that could connect me with the victim, would you?'

That was a tricky one. 'I don't know. It would depend on the circumstances, I suppose. But in this case I just felt that this particular connection could be important.'

'Your intuition again.'

'Probably.'

'I once read that a policeman should never underestimate the value of intuition.'

'I think I'd agree with that. Though I know a lot who wouldn't, who are distinctly suspicious of it.'

'Why is that, d'you think?'

'Probably because nobody quite understands how it works.'

'I suspect,' said Joan slowly, thinking aloud, 'that although it sounds very vague it's really a perfectly logical process. Without our even being conscious that it's happening, the brain takes note of facts, impressions, expressions, reactions and then assesses them all and comes up with a conclusion.'

'I think that just about sums it up. An article I was reading the other day claimed that the brain is infinitely more powerful than the computer and that we only ever use a minute fraction of its potential.'

'I'm sure that's true. So anyway, your intuition told you you were on to something...'

'Yes. I'd put DC Swift on to checking back on Martindale's women friends and Mrs Taylor was one of the ones he'd managed to track down, so we rang her up, made an appointment, and went to see her.'

They had reached Appledore and Thanet stopped talking while they drove through the picturesque village, pausing to admire a pretty Georgian house built of rose-red brick with a FOR SALE notice outside.

'My ideal house!' sighed Joan.

'Mm.' It was Thanet's too, but a policeman's pay was unlikely ever to stretch to their buying anything like it.

As they turned into the Military Road to Iden Lock and drove along parallel to the Royal Military Canal, Thanet told Joan the sad tale of Brenda Taylor's two marriages and the disastrous meeting of the son she had been forced to abandon and the daughter ignorant of her mother's past.

'Bit of a coincidence, wasn't it? That they should meet at all?'

Thanet shrugged. 'Coincidences do happen. And I've often thought that the danger of this sort of thing, the innocent coupling of close relations, is going to become more and more frequent as time goes on. With divorce and remarriage becoming more common, artificial insemination by donor and surrogate motherhood . . . It would be a miracle if half-brothers and -sisters didn't occasionally meet.'

'And become attracted to each other for that matter. With all those genes in common . . .'

'Yes. I noticed the resemblance between the Byfleets the first time I met them, you know, but I didn't realise its significance. Just thought how interesting it was that some husbands and wives do grow to resemble each other.'

Joan grinned. 'D'you think we have?'

He smiled back. 'Don't know. I suppose we'd be the last to see it even if we had.'

'So, all right, you'd discovered that the Byfleets had a possible motive for the murder. You assumed that Leo Martindale had recognised Mona Byfleet, and had told her the truth about Desmond being her half-brother. Presumably you also thought he must have threatened to blackmail them in some way with this knowledge?'

'I didn't know. I just felt that it was a potentially explosive situation.'

'But how did you guess which of them had run him down? Or did you think they'd acted together?'

Thanet shrugged. 'Again, I didn't know. At that stage neither of them was even admitting to having driven the van that night and at one point in the interview, I really thought I wasn't going to get anywhere. All along, you see, Mike and I had been saying that even if we did find out who'd actually killed Martindale, there'd be no means of proving it. All the other suspects had admitted driving the van but even so there was no specific evidence, or so it seemed, to link any of them with the crime.'

'"Or so it seemed . . ." There was something, then?'

'Yes. And I knew it. But I simply couldn't put my finger on it. It was just nagging away at the back of my mind . . . Infuriating.'

'So put me out of my suspense. What was it?'

Thanet told her about Delia's pocket calculator, picked up in the van by Desmond and mistaken by Thanet for a diary when he first saw it in the Byfleets' sitting-room. 'A diary and a calculator can look extraordinarily alike.'

'True.'

'Though when I looked more closely at it, of course, even without picking it up I could see that it wasn't a diary.'

'Bit of a gamble, though, wasn't it? You were only guessing that it was Mrs Hamilton's.'

'I know. I had a few nasty moments there, I must admit. But as soon as I started questioning them about it, it became obvious at once that each thought it belonged to the other and that it therefore belonged to neither. I knew then that I was probably home and dry.'

'Because you could then definitely prove that they were lying and that one of them must have driven the van that night—no, wait a minute. Not necessarily, surely. Desmond could still have claimed that he'd picked the calculator up somewhere else, and you'd never have been able to prove it.'

'Not really. Because then he'd have *known* it wasn't Mona's. And as I said, they'd both already revealed that each thought it belonged to the other and the only way that could have happened was if one of them had acquired it unconsciously, when they were too agitated to know what they were doing.'

'It could still have been Mona, though.'

'Less likely, I thought, because Delia had told her the calculator was missing and she was on the lookout for it. But the last place she'd have expected to find it would be in her own sitting-room, obviously.'

'So when you'd proved that they'd lied about having been in the van that night, Desmond confessed?'

'Well it was his wife, really. She just broke down. The past few days had been a terrible strain. I honestly don't think she could have gone on indefinitely, living with the knowledge that Desmond had killed someone. It was only her genuine belief that it had been an accident that had enabled her to keep quiet as long as she did.'

'I should have thought that would be the very reason for getting him to own up! After all, no one knew about the connection between her and Martindale.'

'I don't think she was thinking straight at the time. Not surprising, really, after what she'd just learned. Her whole future had just collapsed around her ears and I suppose she must have thought, illogically, that if Desmond did own up the truth would come out. But I agree, if he'd only called an ambulance and said it was a straightforward accident, a skid on icy roads, then that would probably have been the end of it.'

'I notice you're saying "she" all the time. Are you implying what I think you're implying? That Desmond either ran Martindale down deliberately or at least knew that he was still alive when he put him in the ditch?'

'Well, I must admit I can't help wondering if he did genuinely believe Martindale to be dead. After all, Martindale alive was an unexploded bomb as far as he and Mona were concerned, whereas Martindale conveniently dead would enable them to decide in their own time and on their own terms what would be their best course of action in the light of what they had just learned. If Martindale were unconscious but still breathing there must have been considerable temptation simply to leave him out in the cold and let nature take its course. And Desmond did move him, remember, put him in the ditch, where he was less likely to be found before morning. And that's what is going to put him in the dock. If only he hadn't moved him, if Martindale had simply died in hospital as a result of the accident, Desmond would probably have got away with it. As it is, because Martindale wasn't dead when he was moved to the ditch we've been able to charge Desmond with manslaughter, on the basis of recklessness in regard to his post-accident conduct.'

'You're still on tricky ground there, though, surely. Doesn't it depend whether or not Martindale would have died anyway from his injuries?'

'Doc Mallard says he wouldn't.'

'Maybe, but will he be prepared to stand up and say so in the witness box? You know how reluctant expert witnesses are to commit themselves on matters of opinion in Court. And the Defence might well be able to dig up someone to disagree with him. I can imagine a good Counsel having a field day over this.'

'The Prosecution too, for that matter. I can imagine them pulling out all the stops, playing on the jury's emotions by painting a horrendous picture of Martindale struggling to get out of that ditch with an injured spine... It's something that's going to haunt me for a long time yet.'

Joan shivered. 'I know. But if Desmond continues to swear that he thought Martindale was already dead when he put him in the ditch... Surely, if he can convince the jury of that it would make a considerable difference to his sentence?'

'Yes. If he could pull that off and if there was some doubt as to whether or not the injuries would have been fatal anyway... I suppose he could get as little as two years suspended... Otherwise he'd get between three and seven, don't you think?'

'Between three and four, I'd say.' Joan sighed. 'Poor things. What will become of them, d'you think? How is Mona?'

'Still in hospital, under observation.'

'They're still afraid of a miscarriage?'

'Yes.'

'What will she do? What will they do, even if he does get off?'

'I know.'

'What is the legal position of a couple in a prohibited relationship innocently marrying?'

'The marriage is null and void from the beginning, I gather. And in this case there's obviously no question of prosecution because both parties were ignorant of the connection between them.'

But in any case, the future for the Byfleets looked pretty bleak. Thanet thought of their pretty, comfortable sitting-room with its evidence of a rich, satisfying life and mourned the bitter blow which fate had inflicted on them. He would never know for sure whether or not Desmond had dumped Martindale in that ditch knowing that he was still alive, but in any case they were to a large extent the innocent victims of a past tragedy not their own and he couldn't help feeling sorry for them.

They were coming into the outskirts of Rye now and with an effort he shut his mind to repercussions of the case. This was a rare treat and he was going to make sure they enjoyed every moment of it.

In summer Rye is always a magnet for tourists but at this time of year it was blissfully empty and they spent the remainder of the short winter afternoon wandering through the steep cobbled streets, gazing in shop windows, browsing in the second-hand bookshops. Before setting off for home they indulged in a cream tea.

In the car Joan settled back into her seat with a smile. 'I did enjoy that.'

He leaned across and kissed her. 'We ought to do it more often.'

As they drove through the darkening countryside; ahead of them like a welcoming beacon shone the thought of home, of the pleasure of a leisurely evening together, of drawn curtains, lamplight, a blazing log fire.

Thanet could think of no better way of spending the evening. He glanced across at Joan's serene profile and gave a sigh of pure contentment. With the case behind him he would be able to relax at last.

He felt at peace with the world.

ABOUT THE AUTHOR

DOROTHY SIMPSON is a former French teacher who lives in Kent, England, with her husband. Their three children are now all married. This is her ninth Luke Thanet novel. Her fifth, *Last Seen Alive*, won the 1985 British Crime Writers' Association Silver Dagger award. Her other books are *Suspicious Death, Element of Doubt, Dead on Arrival, Close Her Eyes, Puppet for a Corpse, Six Feet Under,* and *The Night She Died.*

BANTAM MYSTERY COLLECTION

- ☐ 28479 **THE ART OF SURVIVAL** Maxwell $4.50
- ☐ 18507 **DEATH IN FASHION** Babson $2.25
- ☐ 27000 **DEAD ON ARRIVAL** Simpson $3.50
- ☐ 28175 **ELEMENT OF DOUBT** Simpson $3.50
- ☐ 28073 **JEMIMA SHORE'S FIRST CASE** Fraser $3.95
- ☐ 27773 **LAST SEEN ALIVE** Simpson $3.50
- ☐ 27723 **MURDER MYSTERY TOUR** Babson $3.50
- ☐ 27470 **MURDER, MURDER, LITTLE STAR** Babson .. $3.50
- ☐ 28096 **MURDER SAILS AT MIDNIGHT** Babson $3.50
- ☐ 27772 **NIGHT SHE DIED** Simpson $3.50
- ☐ 28070 **OXFORD BLOOD** Fraser $3.95
- ☐ 27774 **PUPPET FOR A CORPSE** Simpson $3.50
- ☐ 27663 **THE RAIN** Peterson $3.95
- ☐ 27361 **REEL MURDER** Babson $3.50
- ☐ 28297 **ROUGH JUSTICE** Peterson $3.95
- ☐ 28019 **YOUR ROYAL HOSTAGE** Fraser $3.95
- ☐ 18506 **SIX FEET UNDER** Simpson $2.25
- ☐ 28450 **SUSPICIOUS DEATH** Simpson $3.95

Bantam Books, Dept. MC, 414 East Golf Road, Des Plaines, IL 60016

Please send me the items I have checked above. I am enclosing $_____
(please add $2.00 to cover postage and handling). Send check or money
order, no cash or C.O.D.s please.

Mr/Ms _____

Address _____

City/State _____ Zip _____

MC–9/90

Please allow four to six weeks for delivery.
Prices and availability subject to change without notice.

DOROTHY SIMPSON
is a former French teacher who lives in Kent,
England, with her husband. Their three
children are now all married. This is
her ninth Thanet novel. Her fifth, *Last Seen
Alive*, won the 1985 British Crime
Writers' Association Silver Dagger award.
Her other books include *Suspicious
Death*, *Dead on Arrival*, *Close Her Eyes*,
Puppet for a Corpse, *Six Feet Under*,
Element of Doubt, and *The Night She Died*.

A FROZEN STIFF

In life he was Leo Martindale, the dissolute son of one of rustic Sutton-in-the-Weald's most genteel first families. Now he is a snow-covered corpse lying outside the seventeenth-century ancestral home he'd fled nearly twenty-five years before. It looks like Leo was the victim of a hit and run. But was it accidental or was this particular black sheep deliberately slaughtered?

DETECTIVE INSPECTOR LUKE THANET

Inspector Luke Thanet has a sneaking suspicion that it was the latter. For Leo's sudden homecoming seems to have been an unpleasant shock to too many people—including the victim's own sister, who doesn't relish sharing the wealth. But what had Martindale done to provoke the wrath of the entire town? Thanet is stunned to discover that nearly everyone in Leo's boyhood village had a long-standing grudge against him—and ample opportunity to commit the crime. As the inspector probes deeper into the secret life of the dead man, he comes up against a chilling conspiracy of silence. Just who are the locals protecting...and why?

DEAD BY MORNING

"Simpson can disinter the past with the best of them."
—THE TIMES, LONDON

"Simpson's mysteries are beautifully crafted and turn on character and psychological insight." —THE WASHINGTON POST BOOK WORLD

28606

0 76783 00395 8

N 0-553-28606-4>>395